His Lord

Colm Luibhéid

His Lordship

A novel

ARLEN
HOUSE

ISBN 1-903631-33-5 *paperback*

First published by Arlen House in June 2004

Arlen House
PO Box 222
Galway
Ireland

42 Grange Abbey Road
Baldoyle
Dublin 13

arlenhouse@ireland.com

The author and publisher wish to thank Susan Bennett
for her diligent and enthusiastic editing, and Mike
McCormack for his support of the project.

Typesetting: Arlen House
Printed by: ColourBooks, Baldoyle, Dublin 13

For Josephine

His Lordship

I

Should I start with the murder of Tim McDermott? Or is there some better way, such as to introduce myself? I could begin by saying that I am sixty, that I am tall, thin and with a full head of grey hair. But if I go down that route I can foresee no end to the details which may in the end provide no real sense of the type of person I am. Actually I occasionally feel I am like something made out of pieces of lego, straight bits here, knobs there, circles formed onto squares, a purple, red, blue and yellow shape constructed by a complicated past and by an emerging present. I have been stuck together. Therefore I am.

But since I no longer hold office as bishop of Dysart, the question of who I am now lifts itself over the horizon like an Atlantic squall. So perhaps I should turn aside to focus on the murder. Here the essentials are clear, and the media spliced them into a play. At least for several days. After all, he was a major politician, currently minister for finance, much sought after by journalists, a continuously interesting face on the television set even with the volume turned down. His house was next to mine but one had to go up a long avenue to see it. And his official car, a blue Mercedes, had just emerged on the main road one morning when a hooded man carrying a gun jumped out of hiding and, like some demented riveter, battered the doors and the windscreen. The car twisted sideways into a ditch. The killer jumped onto a motor bike hidden behind some bushes and rushed away. The minister and his driver were dead. The sun lit up the new daffodils beside the road.

I was at home and my first news of the murder came when the postman drove up to my front door and pounded continuously on it. When I let him in he was very breathless. 'It's the minister. He's been shot. Oh God he's been shot'.

Some expression on my face must have disturbed him, because he grabbed my arm. 'Really. It's true. I've seen them, it. O Lord God, what a sight! What a thing to happen'.

'But when?'

'On the roadway! Just outside his gates. He's still in the car. So is the driver. The squad cars are already there. They're sealing off the place. Two sergeants have just pulled a tarpaulin over the Merc'.

'I'd better go down', I said

'What for? They're dead. You should see their faces. The hole in his forehead. It's too late for prayers. There's nothing you can do. I'm telling you! You'd be as well to pray here. If that's what you're thinking'.

Suddenly he ran over to the lawn and vomited.

The phone on the hall table started to ring.

'Yes?'

'Have you heard?' It was my secretary, calling from the cathedral.

'I've just been told'.

'They've found the motorbike already. Or what's left of it. The roadblocks are up. But it looks as if the killers have made it out of the area. At least that's what the word is here. My God!'

'Does his wife know?'

'She must have heard by now. In fact, yes. One of the detectives, Jim Morris, was sent up to the house. The poor woman'.

Although we had been neighbours for several years we rarely met. She said to me she was a bit of a recluse. I have no memory of having seen photographs of her on official occasions when her husband was in the company of dignitaries of one kind or another.

'I'd better call to the house to offer my sympathy and to see if I can be of any help to her. What a pity she has no children'.

'Well, if you go, you'd better bring your mobile phone, because I'm sure there will be people looking for you'.

'Alright Tom. Keep in touch'.

I decided to walk over to the McDermott house. I was not ready to face the crowd which would have gathered near the car and the dead man. So I headed across a field behind my own bungalow. The grass and the many trees had the sheen of early spring. A few bloated clouds moved their white intensity across a blue sky. Birds were calling. And when I reached the stream which formed the border of the McDermott property I stopped and looked for a while at the rush of clear water over multi-coloured stones.

What could I say to this woman? How could I escape from the way in which words would surely fade into banality in the courtyard of death? I could imagine her wishing to bay uselessly at an empty sky. Anything I said might well be an irritation, a mouthing of lifeless platitudes. But of course job description implied that a priest, a bishop, would bring comfort. That was supposed to be part of my expertise. I knew better. Each time I was face to face with distress I recognised my inadequacy, even with those who had decided in advance to be helped by me. When I mentioned this to a fellow bishop on one occasion he looked at me with the annoyance of a man with undisturbed certainties.

I thought of this when I crossed the wooden bridge over the stream and followed a path through the trees as far as the house. I became aware of voices. There were cars in the driveway. Detectives had gathered beside one of them. They all turned when I emerged from the woods. But I was quickly recognised and ceased to be of interest. A bishop, I suppose, was an unlikely suspect.

The house amazed me. I had never had a proper look at it, and I could only marvel at its assertive dourness. There were two floors and there were barred windows on a basement below the level of the driveway. The only colour seemed to be a dirtied grey, until I saw the red door at the head of the granite steps. But it was the massive presence of the whole building which filled my mind. It seemed to be posing some brutal threat, as it stood in the clearance amid the pines and birches. I knew it had not been the ancestral home of Tim McDermott. He had owned it for fifteen years, having bought it from an old woman, the last of three eccentric, wealthy sisters, who for years had survived on crusts of bread and the eggs laid by the hens in the kitchen. It had come cheap, this house, but why he would have wanted it at all was something which baffled me as I gazed up at its menacing proportions.

I knocked at the door. It was opened almost immediately by Mrs McDermott. She looked at me. Her eyes were dry, her face pale.

'Ah', she said, at last. 'Come in. Of course. Won't you come in?'

I followed her across the maple floor of an extensive hall, past a marble fireplace and an ornate stairway and into a living room. For an instant I had the sense of being in familiar surroundings. I was reminded of seminaries and convent halls and I could only wonder all the more at the fact that Tim McDermott had chosen to buy the place. Perhaps he had been taken by the contrast between the solid exterior and the elegance within the walls.

'Won't you sit down?' she pointed to a winged chair beside a bay window. I glanced around. The room was sumptuous.

'My husband considered himself to be a man of taste', she said, drawing a straight-backed chair over to a point where she could sit opposite me.

'I only heard the news a little while ago. I can't tell you how shocked I am. This is all so horrible. I just wanted to tell you how sorry I am. And if there is anything I can do for you. I presume members of the family are on their way here to be with you. But, still, I'd like to help if I can. Have you anyone here?'

'No. The house is empty. I expect my husband's two brothers will arrive before the end of the day'.

'Am I right in thinking you had no children?'

'We had no children'.

'But is there anybody to be here with you now?'

'You've come'.

'I mean someone who is close to you'. A discomfort was beginning to spread within me. Her face was pale. Her dark eyes were gazing at me in a calm manner, which made me uneasy. One hand rested undemonstratively on the other. She was eerily quiet, and not because she was in shock or denial. It was almost as if the murder did not concern her at all.

'Of course the detectives have been in and out. They wanted to know if there had been any phone calls or if anything unusual had happened before my husband drove off. I don't think I was any help to them. But of course they'll be back'.

'I imagine they will. And that doesn't make things any easier for you. I'm really sorry you are alone at this time. I hope your brothers-in-law will arrive here soon'.

'Did you know Maurice Townley?'

'No, I don't think so', I answered, noticing the change of subject.

'He was my husband's driver. He lived about fifteen miles from here. I suppose Maisie - his wife - has been told. God. The poor woman'.

It was the first sign of emotion since I had come into the room.

'I really should go over to her', she continued. 'It's the least I could do. After all she's a widow now just because Maurice was working for my husband. It's so unfair. I feel really guilty about her'.

'Oh no! Surely not. Anyway you have more than enough of a burden yourself now, and I really wonder if there is anything I can do to be of help'.

She smiled.

'Thank you. This is very kind, and I appreciate it more than I can say. But I'll be all right. I'll manage'.

'And then there's the funeral. You've going to have to start thinking about it, and that's awful. Oh, I hope your family hurries here to take some of this off your shoulders'.

'My brothers-in-law are very efficient men', she said.

A phone rang.

'Excuse me', she said, getting up from her chair. She went out into the hall. There was the silence of someone who is listening and then her voice sounded briefly before she reappeared in the room.

'That was my brother-in-law. He says he will be here by six'.

'It's a pity you have to be on your own'.

'That's alright. Anyway I'll go over to see Maisie Townley. It's the least I can do'.

She led the way to the front door and I returned across the fields to my own house. I was puzzling over my encounter with her. But the first of many calls arrived on my mobile phone, and I had other matters to think about now.

'Shocking news. Quite awful'. It was an advisor to the government and he was calling me from Dublin. 'There has just been an emergency cabinet meeting. It's been decided that he is to be given a state funeral'.

'Of course you have consulted Mrs McDermott about this?'

'Sorry?' he seemed astonished by my question.

'The dead have no interest in funerals. The last ceremonies are for the sake of the living, don't you think?'

'Oh, quite. But it is obviously important to make a gesture'.

'A gesture to whom?'

'To the world. To society. To the terrorist who killed him'.

'Ah'. I resisted the temptation to irony. 'But, to repeat, you have consulted Mrs McDermott, haven't you?'

'We have not yet had the opportunity to do so, my Lord'.

The use of my title was clearly meant to placate me.

'Don't you think you should do so?'

'Of course. Of course. But in anticipation of her co-operation with us the government would like to know if your cathedral may be of use for the occasion. The local parish church is probably too small, and there is sure to be a great crowd for the occasion'.

'No doubt. And naturally I agree to the use of the cathedral. But I must make my agreement conditional upon the willingness of Mrs McDermott to have the matter proceed in this way'.

'I understand. We will contact her immediately and get back to you'.

He sounded displeased. Not indeed that this bothered me. But I wondered if I should call Mrs McDermott to make clear to her that she need not feel under pressure to fall in with the plans of the cabinet, especially if what was envisaged was a political gesture instead of an act to express solidarity with her. Having thought about the question I decided to let her be, for I had a feeling that she would know how to declare her own wishes.

And indeed she did. By the end of the afternoon the main decisions had been taken. My secretary called to say that the government advisor had phoned to announce that the body would be brought to the cathedral on Wednesday and the funeral held on the following day. All this had been conveyed to Mrs McDermott who had agreed to the arrangements.

Phone calls continued throughout the afternoon. There were messages from the government, questions from the media, suggestions from colleagues and an inquiry from the archbishop of Dublin who wanted to know about my plans for the funeral. This last intrigued me, as did any of my contacts with him. I could never shake off a vague sense that his dealings with me were conducted from within the frontiers of what the Jesuits used to describe as mental reservations. In his deep voice he would speak slowly to me, as if he had some doubts about my capacity to understand him. The truth of his feelings seemed always to be masked. I never knew why, though I sometimes wondered if the reason lay in the report, current at the time of my appointment as bishop, that I was being groomed to succeed him in Dublin.

When I told him that I had not yet had the opportunity to think in detail about the programme for the funeral he paused, as though I had confirmed his own suspicion regarding me. Then, softly, he asked to be kept informed of whatever I decided. Of course he knew that no protocol compelled me to announce my plans to him. But he also understood the manipulative effects of the obligation of a bishop to charity and collegiality, and so he could confidently look to me to get in touch with him as soon as I had made a final decision on arrangements. When he hung up, therefore, it was with expectation left to dangle in the air between us.

'If you want to see the news it's time', Mrs Maloney, the cleaning lady, was looking into my study. She had stayed much later than usual.

'Come in', I said, reckoning that she too wanted to see what the television had to offer. We watched the extended news bulletin, and at various intervals Mrs Maloney, like a well trained member of a chorus, broke in with a compassionate 'O God help us', whenever the film clips showed Tim McDermott. He was a tall man, self-consciously handsome and with a very refined sense of how to present himself to the television camera. He managed even to project his receding hairline as a mark of distinction. He spoke in the lower registers of a cultivated baritone, the right hand gesturing slowly but insistently. And when an extract of a recent interview about his budget speech was shown, my mind wandered back to the day when I had met him for the first time. I had just arrived at the bungalow which, in the survival of old terminology, was referred to locally as 'the bishop's palace'. I was unpacking when I heard the doorbell.

'We're neighbours', Tim McDermott said. 'I wanted to welcome you'.

The ministerial car had stopped at a discreet distance from the house as if to give us both a chance to talk freely.

'That's very nice of you', I said. 'Please come in, and my apologies for the disorder. My secretary was supposed to be here to help me unpack, but he has just called to tell me he's been delayed. But I'm sure we can find a couple of chairs in my study'.

'Don't worry about it. In any case I can't stay. I have to head for Dublin. A meeting of European Finance ministers is starting this evening and I'm supposed to make suitably welcoming noises at the opening session'.

'A few spontaneous remarks, of which advance copies will be supplied to the media?'

'Oh no!' he grinned. 'You see, I need something from them, so you can count on it that I'll be speaking from the heart'.

'Touché, minister! Won't you sit down for a moment at least? Can I make you a cup of tea or pour you a drink?'

'Ah no. We're both busy. I just wanted to take the opportunity to tell you that I live nearby and that I'll be glad to help if you need me. These must be hectic days for you, being made a bishop and all that'.

'A bit hectic, yes. And I certainly never expected to be made a bishop. But I suppose I'll grow into it. At least I hope so'.

'I knew your predecessor, Dr McHale. An interesting man', McDermott said.

I looked at him carefully, knowing that he and the bishop had briefly shared media space a few years ago. Dr McHale had been a prominent member of the hierarchy for over two decades. He had what were referred to as strong views, meaning that he could be described as very opinionated. My own feelings about him were such as to compel me to reflect seriously and self critically on my obligations of Christian charity. For it was plain that he suffered little from doubt, and, unlike most of his colleagues who had adopted a policy of running for cover on difficult public issues, he had chosen to blare his uncomplicated point of view on every available occasion. He had particularly robust views on matters of sex. Unaware of or indifferent to how much times had changed he took it upon himself one day to denounce the minister for education as looking like a merchant of immorality. This followed a declaration by the minister that a properly formed curriculum of sex education was required in the schools. Dr McHale bluntly asserted that only the church and really suitable expert figures such as himself had the competence or the right to lay down the necessary guidelines in such matters. It was a foolish thing to say, and when Tim McDermott was asked about it during some press conference his reply was that he found it hard to believe that the deliberately celibate would wish to supervise the bedrooms of the nation. It was an adroit remark because McDermott, with his unfailing sense of current moods, knew that, while twenty per cent of the public might be outraged by this declaration, the remainder would either agree wholeheartedly or else would chuckle at the cunningly evoked image of an elderly bishop stalking the sexual activities of the homes of Ireland.

'Of course the two of you jousted in the past', I said, pulling out a chair for him. 'I used to read about it in the papers in the days when I had no idea I would be a bishop myself'.

'Does that make you wary of me?' He was smiling again, and I realised I was being tested.

'Oh I'm sure I have nothing to fear from an eminent minister for finance. Unless of course you are planning to impose a special levy on bishops'. He gazed around my study.

'This must be quite a change for you. I mean the move from academic life to being a bishop'. He had an aura of unlimited assurance. The elegant clothes, his faintly slouched pose, the hands seeming undramatically to draw ideas from the fertile air, all this conveyed an image of insouciance and I wondered how much of it was contrived. But he looked like a man for whom the thick skin often ascribed to politicians was much too vulgar a garment. He was or at least he was determined to be impressive.

'When you say quite a change I presume you are hinting at a move from the theoretical to the practical', I said.

'Oh I don't know about that. After all you have been a professor of history and what could be a better preparation for your job? Your books on the early days of Christianity and, especially on how the bishops of Rome learned to claim power, must have taught you a lot about the staking out of positions in the streets of the world'.

'I'm impressed that you should know about my books', I commented, adding 'Or could it be that you've had your secretary check up on me?'

'Well said!' he laughed. 'But it may surprise you to know that in fact I read your most recent book. I do a lot of reading at night. I'm an insomniac. Have been since I was in my twenties. But I take your point about checking up. In my job I have to know by the hour what I'm dealing with. It's urgent in a way that it might not be for a bishop'.

'Why so?'

'Because if I don't think of this afternoon and to-night and tomorrow I may be out of a job. There are lots of people who would like to see the back of me. And I'm not just talking about the opposition. Anyhow it's their business to get rid of me, and, to tell the truth, I don't think that between them all they amount to much. No, it's my own colleagues, the people who are supposed to be on my side – these are the ones to watch. You must know about that!'

I looked at him in astonishment. His sudden vehemence had really taken me by surprise.

'What are you saying?'

'Oh, come now!' The tone had reverted almost to a purr. 'You're a historian, and you're also an experienced man. Next to the membership of professional organisations for welfare there's no more vicious infighting to be found than among those who see themselves as God-fearing missionaries of truth'.

'That's a bit extreme, isn't it?'

'You think so? Well I hope you never find yourself seriously out of line with the ecclesiastical bureaucracy to which you belong. Because if you do, then you'll really learn about high-class lynching for which holy men have a special talent'.

'I'm amazed at your cynicism, minister!'

'Ah well', he was laughing again. 'Your future is probably more secure than mine. Obviously the institution has decided it can trust you. So you're in for life. Neither stupidity nor senility will be a disqualification from doing your thing'.

'You're beginning to sound positively envious!'

'I might have to confess to that', he replied banteringly. 'And you look like someone who might even forgive me'.

'Do I detect a bit of ministerial flattery here?'

'Why not? Anyhow we have a lot in common. Especially since we are in the same business'.

'Are we, indeed?'

'But of course. Each of us has to put on a good show. And if we do I'll get re-elected and you might even be called a saint'.

He said it so charmingly that I could only laugh, and I felt glad at the prospect of having him as a pleasant and amusing neighbour whom I might get to know well. But in fact it was not to happen that way. We met occasionally at a few receptions, and when I was on a delegation of bishops having talks with a team of government ministers he was on the other side of the table from me, elegant, affable and taking in the nuances of everything under discussion. The bishops were engaging in an effort to hold onto some of the powers they once had to influence seriously the programmes in the schools, and the administration had decided to concede nothing. Our meeting therefore resolved itself quickly into an exercise, which pushed each case as far as possible without having to spill into the messy uncertainties of public scrutiny. Neither side wanted to be put into the position of having to attack the other, and it was the amiable cunning of Tim McDermott which ensured that such a situation did not arise.

As I watched the television clips illustrating his career I remembered a moment during an especially ugly display when strikers had laid siege to the homes and offices of ministers. Police protection had to be laid on. There were scuffles and at least one charge. The most militant among the protestors were interviewed outside the Dublin apartment of Tim McDermott. Their leader, an immense man, was smiling. He and his colleagues had been invited in for tea and sandwiches. They were promised nothing. But when they emerged they proclaimed to the world that the minister was the only one who really understood their point of view and the needs of their families.

He was a man whose company I felt sure I would enjoy. But he maintained his distance. Even when I invited his wife and himself to dinner in my house to celebrate the publication of my last book he sent a bottle of expensive wine and a witty refusal. Sometimes I wondered why. Perhaps he had taken a dislike to me. Or, being a politician with very active antennae, perhaps he had simply decided to write me off. Who could tell? Especially now when he had been transformed into no more than an anthology of dated images and soundbites.

'Did you know him?' Mrs Mahony said, 'I did. He was a grand man. That's as sure as you're there'.

I was sitting at the kitchen table having a cup of tea. Mrs Mahony stood by the sink. It was Wednesday morning and she had arrived in case I needed help during the hours before the body of McDermott was brought to the cathedral. I was glad to have her there because sudden chores seemed to be appearing, the phone was ringing constantly, and in the midst of all the activity I had the uneasy feeling I had overlooked something important.

'He was a great one for giving the bit of help when it was needed'.

'What do you mean?' I asked.

'Oh if people fell on hard times he was always doing something for them. He got Mrs Quinn from down the road into the nursing home. She had Alzheimer's and Denis her husband was going demented trying to mind her. And when Mrs Crowley from the other end of the village got her son back from jail Mr McDermott bought him a suit and found him a job in the quarry. He was always doing for people. And it was the way he did it. He didn't send some snooty civil servant down to a house to tell them about a job or a welfare cheque, he'd come himself, and he could be so nice. Tommy Cloherty ... do you remember the time he was beaten up by the burglar? Well he told me he was lying in the bed and wishing he was dead and Mr McDermott called in to see him and they had a mighty chat and him a busy minister. And you can imagine the state of the house. Tommy lives alone and was never one to keep the place tidy'.

As similar stories came in during the day I began to realise how little I knew Tim McDermott. Indeed the thought came that even though I was the bishop in the area I might well be the least aware and the least informed of what was going on around me. I could imagine how the words 'man of God', would trip from the lips of that busy minister.

My picture of McDermott acquired new dimensions later that morning after I had a chat on the phone with one of the parish priests, Jack Hession. He called to inform me that he was planning to have a bonfire on Sunday after the eleven o'clock mass. He wished to get as many copies as possible of three tabloids and to burn them before the eyes of his congregation. This was to mark his displeasure at a series of articles and photographs which had highlighted a gay wedding presided over by a well-known priest.

'What are you hoping to gain from this demonstration, Father Hession?'

'Publicity, my Lord'. He was a stickler for titles.

'I'm not sure I understand you'.

'I want publicity', he repeated. 'Not for myself, of course, but for us'.

'Us?'

'Yes. For the church. For God's point of view. I want the readers of these Sunday papers to see that there is another way at looking at these things, the right way. I want it clear that there are people who won't give this priest and those two men a pat on the back. I want people who buy tabloids to see that there is another and better image to be accepted'.

'The image of you burning the paper?' I had no wish to sound flippant, and in any case I knew that Father Hession had no sense of humour.

'My Lord, if right thinking people do not take a stand who will?'

This is the kind of pious generalisation which induces a fog in my mind, and I moved rapidly to end this conversation.

'Thank you for telling me and of course ...' I was immediately interrupted.

'And there's something else, my Lord. I know that the cardinal and other members of the hierarchy are coming for the mass tomorrow morning. And, naturally, the priests of the Diocese will be there too. But I very much want to be on the altar to concelebrate the mass. You see, Mr McDermott sometimes came over to my house during the night. He couldn't sleep much. And when he came we used to talk for hours'.

I was astonished. If Tim McDermott found himself unable to sleep and had a wish to see Father Hession he would have had to travel nearly forty miles from home. But what did they have in common? This question intrigued me. What did a sophisticated politician have to say to a priest who was regarded by his colleagues and parishioners as not very attuned to the world around him? Some likened him to a free spirit, while others declared him to be mad. Certainly he was different. Two years before my own appointment as bishop he had been sent to be parish priest of a rural community, where farms were small and young people scarce. Within twenty-four hours of his arrival he was seen digging the grass near the main entrance to the church. For three days there was bemused speculation regarding what he might be doing, but by Sunday the nature of the project was clear, and in any case he spoke of it during his first sermon. It was his own grave. Drunks fell into it, as did plastic bags, old tins, newspapers and tissues. Complaints began to reach me and I was asked to intervene. I had no idea what to do. I had no wish to hurt the feelings of the priest, but in view of the increasingly litigious proclivities of the general public I had to intervene. I picked a convenient opportunity to talk to him and in the course of the conversation I referred to the grave, suggesting that if some kind of cover were not put over it the insurance policy on his church would likely be cancelled. I remarked that no parishioners who fell into it would think of suing him, but one never knew about tourists, especially those who came from the cities. I deliberately emphasised this last remark because I had been told that biblical denunciations of rampant evil were nothing in comparison with the opprobrium piled by Father Hession on the wickedness of everything beyond the horizons of green fields and rural solitude. So the grave was covered and Father Hession looked for other ways to emphasise human mortality.

And yet this was the man sought out by Tim McDermott.

'Well, of course, Father Hession, in view of what you say, I will naturally welcome you as a concelebrant'.

It was a solemn pageant, this state funeral where politicians and ambassadors, clergy and laity had come together. There were the uniformed and stylish and all joined to project images of contrived poise in the face of the crude pressure which is death. It would have been so if Tim McDermott had drawn his final breath in the quiet of his bedroom. But the coarse scythe of assassination gives an extra nuance of fright which the ceremonies of burial must seek to assuage, and I wondered how far we had managed to help or, indeed, to hinder the requirement of Helen McDermott to face all that had now been thrust upon her.

Certainly she had been calm on the evening when the coffin was brought to the cathedral, and she had remained so throughout the Thursday morning when every pew was filled and every corner taken by those who had arrived for the funeral. Sunlight tinged with blue and red and green cascaded through the stained-glass windows. There was the usual ebb and flow of coughs and shuffled feet. Faces seen regularly on television were counted and remarked upon. Political rivals exchanged polite handshakes. The President, accompanied by a bored aide-de-camp, looked duly representative of the nation. On the altar a dozen fellow bishops and Father Hession gathered around me to join in the prayer while the cardinal brought in his own splash of distinctive colour to the episcopal throne which was more usually occupied by myself.

But when I stood in the pulpit to address the congregation, as protocol required, I felt a surge of foreboding, a spasm not unlike stage fright, and for the merest instant I had a vibrant wish not to be here. I wanted to run away. I yearned to be plain Conor Mahon, better still, to be without a name in a packed soccer stadium or on a distant shore where no one would notice me or glance in my direction, where I could be seen but not be remarked upon.

In the days when I taught history I was always apprehensive at the start of a lecture, and the feeling had not left me after I became a bishop. But this flutter around the heart and stomach was different and I had no idea why it was so.

Of course I had to speak. So I talked of the need to close ranks, to draw together for the sake of the bereaved family and, indeed, for all of us. I pointed out that the murder was much more than the horrible destruction of a good man, that it was an attack on every one of us, on society and on the institutions which, for better or worse, were all we had. I asked everyone to pray that there would not be a slide into revenge, that what was best in us would remain intact and, especially now, that the widow of our massacred brother would find the strength to endure her terrible loss.

I looked at her. She had no children and she sat alone, beached. The brothers and sister of Tim McDermott were in the same pew. They were grim-faced and sad, their eyes straying occasionally to the coffin, which lay on a trolley. Behind them were the dignitaries, rank upon rank as far back as the double doors under the rose window. The side aisles were packed, and the lines and angles of the cathedral, its lights and its decorated walls, seemed to form a comforting fortress from which the harshness of the world could be repelled.

So I looked at Helen McDermott and I called upon the congregation to join in heartfelt prayer for her comfort, for divine help at this time of catastrophe.

Slowly she turned her gaze up at me in my pulpit. The dark eyes paused over mine, and I was almost swept out from under my own words by what I could see. I had expected her to be numb or distraught. But there was nothing here of a widow's grief. Instead, I witnessed a flicker, quickly withdrawn, of amusement, of some brief but potent urge, heartfelt and unmistakable, to break into a long laugh.

Luckily I had come to the end of what I had to say. I made a slight bow to her, descended from the pulpit and led the concluding moments of the ceremony. I had done what I could. But I was unable to shake off that glimpse of suppressed laughter, and my mind was full of it as we marched in slow procession ahead of the coffin and out of the cathedral to where the hearse and the military guard of honour were waiting.

There was a pause while wreaths were gathered by the undertaker and his assistant. A murmur of conversations slid along the people who had gathered in a semi-circle around the space where the hearse stood with its polished hatch-back door still open to receive the piled flowers. The officer in charge of the guard of honour looked serious while he inspected his men. The cardinal and the bishops stood together like birds of vivid plumage amid an assembly of sparrows, and I could only marvel at the way in which the need to cover nakedness had been turned into a claim for status and validation.

There was a signal and we began to move towards our cars. Soon we were on our way, and within ten minutes we had reached the cemetery. Then the leaders of the government and the opposition stood together beside the grave. They spoke briefly, taking care to be heard by television microphones. The coffin was lowered into the earth under a blue sky. I projected a final prayer over the crowd, and we all moved away.

At the cemetery I had been facing Helen McDermott. Her expression was a gentle mask during the final moments of the interment and it had continued to be so while a military trumpeter standing in the sunlit air played the last post, bringing the ceremonies to a discomfited close. Her two brothers-in-law hovered on either side of her. But no one took her arm or touched her in any way. She stood alone, while politicians and ambassadors took it in turns to sympathise with her. She smiled at them all. At last it was time to turn from the grave. She walked slowly to a nearby car, sat into the front passenger seat and waited to be driven away.

I had to remain. The president, members of the government and other prominent figures came in their turn to me to exchange a few words, to lament what had happened or else to thank me for the ceremonies in the cathedral. This went on for nearly three-quarters of an hour before I felt free at last to think of going home.

But while I was moving out of the cemetery I saw a man glance in my direction, turn from a small group near the main gate and head over towards me. He was big and broad-shouldered, the sort of figure I associated with a rugby scrum. But the expression on his face was like that of an ashamed schoolboy. I recognised him at once from a photograph in one of the morning papers. His name was Michael Fortune and he was the second of the official drivers assigned to Tim McDermott.

'You'll be at the funeral mass tomorrow for Maurice Townley?' It was more a challenge than a question.

'Of course I will. I've told them to expect me'.

'That's good', he said 'It's very important for Maisie Townley to have you there. The poor woman'. His face twisted into a grimace. 'She shouldn't have to go through that. I'm telling you she shouldn't. I'm the one who was supposed to bring the minister to Dublin on Tuesday morning. But I was doing a bit of painting at home and wanted to finish it and so I swapped hours with Jimmy. He was always like that. Always helpful. And now look where it's got him. A bullet in the head and Maisie and the boys left behind to miss him'.

'Had you swapped before?'

'Of course we had'.

'Well, then, you can't start blaming yourself for this. It's not your fault he's dead. The killer didn't decide to spare your wife the grief of not having to bury you. Please don't start tormenting yourself with a guilt which really is not yours at all. You must try to see that, even if it is all very hard'.

'I know, I know, I know. But he's dead and I'm not'.

We walked towards the gates of the cemetery, and for a while he was so upset that he remained silent.

'Do you know if any progress has been made in the search for the gunmen?' I asked, trying to distract him.

'There's not much yet'. He shook his head and then sighed. 'No it's too early. They found the motorbike and the men from forensics are trying to see if they can get anything from that. But I don't expect too much here. That ... that animal was a professional killer. He had all his plans worked out. And there must have been others involved. How could he have known when Mr McDermott was going to leave his house? And when he got rid of the motorbike how did he get away? It would have been too dangerous for him to hitchhike. Somebody with a car was probably waiting to pick him up. At least that's what it looks like now. But of course it's too early to tell. The bastard is probably sitting in a bar in Dublin with his pals and feeling all smart'.

We continued to walk together, and I could tell that he was not ready to let me go.

'If he was a professional killer who would have hired him?' I asked.

'Ah it's all too soon for that'.

'But you did say a gunman and not a paramilitary'.

'That's what the boys are inclined to think. But they're working on it and of course they've ruled nothing out'.

We had arrived at the gates and I could see my secretary waiting for me in his car. Michael Fortune recognised him, but he stayed with me and we walked along by the grass margin until we reached a stone bridge over a culvert.

'Did you notice his wife?' he asked suddenly.

'Mrs McDermott?'

'Yes'.

'Well naturally I saw her. Why do you ask?'

He paused.

'She didn't shed a tear did she? I watched her, and all that time her eyes were dry. You could tell she hadn't been crying and she sure wasn't on valium', he concluded violently.

'What are you implying?'

'Ah nothing', he answered in a disgusted tone. He lit a cigarette. 'Nothing. I suppose it's a rough time for her. It has to be. Unless she has a heart of pure granite'.

'Are you suggesting she's not affected by his murder?'

'I'm not. I'm not. It's just that ...'

'Yes?'

'I'm thinking about him. About him and her. They didn't get on and that's a fact'.

'I'd be sorry to think that was the case. You're sure of what you're saying?'

'It was something he said one night. We were coming from Dublin. He'd had a long day and you could tell he was glad to push back the passenger seat and stretch his legs. We got talking. He was great that way. When he didn't have to read his documents he chatted and that made a big difference when there was a lot of driving to be done. We got talking that night. About all sorts of things. And then he started asking about how things were with me. I noticed something about what he was saying. You know when you'd ask a man about his wife and family. But he didn't mention the family. Only the wife. He wasn't asking about her and me the way a reporter would. It was roundabout, but you could tell he was really interested. I mean, in how we were getting on together. The two of us like. And when he saw it was great with us you could tell he was glad for us. But the way he was glad made me realise he was comparing us with himself and his own missus. Can you see what I'm getting at?'

I nodded. But I was getting uncomfortable. There were things you would rather not know about others. But Michael Fortune needed to talk. He was trying to get away from his distress and from his feelings of guilt. So I did not interrupt him. He had thrown away his cigarette and was already fidgeting for another one.

'Don't get me wrong', he insisted, turning to face me. 'He wasn't bad mouthing his own wife. He was a gentleman. You could always tell that about him. And he wouldn't do that sort of thing. But it was the way he reacted about me and Joan. You couldn't make any mistake about it. He was a lovely man. It showed'.

'Did you ever meet Mrs McDermott?'

'Of course I did. She'd ride in the car sometimes. Or at least she used to. Actually, now that you mention it, she didn't go to these public functions when the minister had to appear. In fact she hardly ever went out with him'. He paused, as if a frown would extract another piece of information from inside his head. 'But she was always nice to me. Always. I'll have to give her that. She'd offer me a cup of tea if he was delayed on the phone. Or if we knew we had a long day ahead, and I'd have to hang around waiting for him, she'd make me a packet of sandwiches'. He stopped again. And then he added reluctantly. 'She could be good that way ... But I never saw her kiss him goodbye when he was leaving home. She wouldn't even come out on the steps of the house to see him off'. The way he said 'even' was unmissable.

We went slowly back towards the cemetery. It was obvious that the thought of Mrs McDermott had distracted him from the grief he felt for his dead co-driver. When we had reached my car he stopped as though to consider something very significant.

'She's one tough woman', he said finally, and turned away.

The words moved around within me as I was driven home and they came together with the remark about her untearful eyes, those eyes where I had seen that brief intimation of smothered laughter.

A week later I decided I should find out how Mrs McDermott was coping with her new situation. I phoned her, and she seemed surprised both to hear from me and to learn that I wished to call on her. But she agreed and promised to be at home throughout Thursday afternoon.

I decided to walk there, and set out on a shortcut through the nearby fields, over the wooden bridge across the river, along by a corner of the wood and, eventually I was out on the main road. I was less than a hundred yards from her driveway. In fact I was just at the spot where Tim McDermott was murdered. I had been listening to birds. I watched the patterns of light on grass and trees and paused when a line of white birches had stirred in the quiet air. But now I could see only that place beside the wall where the car had come to a halt and where two lives had been blown away. There was a sort of palpable absence here, vivid as the thrust of an intimation, and I recognised it of course for what it was, a childlike wish to contrive that nothing had really happened, that there had not been that cold-hearted instant of bloodletting.

Moving more slowly now, I came to the grey carved posts on which wrought-iron gates were hanging and I turned into the driveway. To one side of me were beech trees, old, tall, their leaves slurring, and on my left was a spread of fields. The gravel laid a powdery coating over my shoes and I walked slowly until I came to a curve from which I glimpsed the house. Somehow I could not co-relate the solid, almost brutish concrete coloured exterior with the elegant, fashion conscious Tim McDermott whom I had so rarely met but whose presence on television and in the newspapers had been part of our way of life. I thought of the studied chic of the man as I came, wonderingly, towards what looked to me uncommonly like a fortress, a grim bastion rather than a home. I realised that there was a quality of innate elegance about Mrs McDermott. I had noticed it at the funeral but even more so when she now opened the door to invite me into the house. She was wearing a simple black dress and had a silk scarf around her neck. However, it was the chosen colours and the pattern in the scarf, which gave a touch of class to her whole appearance.

'Will you join me in a glass of white wine?' she asked, after she had pointed me to a winged chair beside the fireplace in the living room.

'That sounds fine'.

'I have it in the kitchen. I'll be right back'. And indeed she quickly returned carrying a tray on which there was a bottle of Graves, two glasses and some crackers. There was also a corkscrew, and I stood up to help her with it, but she shook her head.

'No, that's quite alright, thank you. But I do have a problem'.

'Oh? And what's that?'

'I don't know what to call you. Should I address you as "My Lord" or "My Lord Bishop" or just "Bishop"?'

'You can call me whatever you like!'

'You shouldn't say that!' she remarked, handing me my glass of wine. 'Your colleague, the Archbishop of Tuam, seemed upset when at a reception last year in Dublin Castle, I didn't give him his full and correct title'.

'Oh. Well, then, let me confess that, like you, I also have a problem here, because so far you've given me no clue as to what you'd be comfortable with. For instance, one of my priests would be greatly scandalised if I were to suggest I be addressed in any way other than "My Lord". Another one, however, feels obliged to test my humility each time we meet, so he calls me Conor. And because I know he considers me to be dim-witted I am only surprised he doesn't call me "little Conor" or "Conorkins"'.

'My God!' she raised both hands upwards. 'I didn't realise it could be so complicated. So then, if I call you Conor you will not feel put down?'

'On the contrary, it will force me to call you Helen without seeming either to patronise you or to indulge in strident egalitarianism!'

We both laughed and I raised my glass.

'Cheers, Helen!'

'Cheers, Conor!'

In the moment which then passed I imagined I could feel the heavy silence of this crudely looming house. It was as if Helen McDermott and I were facing one another in some kind of clearing on the side of a forested mountain where even to relax was to abate only slightly the sense of some encompassing possibility of threat. Indeed her next words seemed to confirm this.

'If you don't mind my asking you, why did you decide to come here today?'

'After the horrible thing that happened, I wanted to find out if you needed anything'.

She thought about this.

'You mean this is what is called a pastoral visit? Or have I got that wrong? One of the corporal works of mercy, perhaps'. She looked unblinkingly at me.

'I try not to be impressed by such terms', I replied, as gently as I could. 'We are neighbours. Probably we have not met often enough. But when funerals are over and done with, those left behind often need some sort of help. I just wanted to find out if there is anything I can do to ease the journey which you have to make alone now'.

'Ah', she said, and smiled. 'I appreciate that'. She seemed to be reassured. At least for an instant. But something like the need to face down a possible foe came into her looks when, without meaning to be anything more than sociable, I moved my hand to point to all of the house and said, 'I suppose you have some help to manage this? It really is a big place, isn't it?'

'Yes, it is big, but I'm well used to taking care of it myself'.

'Alone?'

She smiled at my astonishment.

'Since I moved here', she added.

'But ...'

'But you assumed the wife of a government minister, living in a house of this size, would count on having some kind of domestic help with the place'.

'Well, yes', I said, a little confused. 'Something like that, I suppose'.

She raised her glass to her lips, then, without drinking, put it down again. 'If I were to say to you that my husband was a very miserly man who detested the thought of having to spend anything more than he absolutely had to, how would you react?'

'I'd be astonished'.

'Astonished that I said it? Or astonished if it happened to be true?'

I gestured vaguely. 'I had an image of him, and if indeed your husband was miserly, then, yes, I suppose I'd have to say this is a surprise'.

'Tell me about the image', she suggested, her voice soft.

This conversation was going in directions which I had certainly never anticipated. Indeed I felt a discomfort beginning to rise within me. Yet at the same time I could look at this woman only in rueful admiration. It was I who had chosen to come visit her. She had never summoned me, I had asked for the meeting, as I had done such things before, though always with an unacknowledged conviction that I could take control of whatever happened. But Helen McDermott was not going to be typecast, nor was she going to fall into some allotted stance.

'Yes, do tell me about that image', she repeated.

'He seemed so very astute, well informed, elegant. He had poise'.

I was not doing well, and we both recognised that fact.

'The truth is, of course, that I met him on only a few occasions. He came to visit me when I first moved into my house. I also met him when I was on a delegation of bishops to the government. Like everyone else, I read about him in the papers, and saw him on television. He seemed so controlled, relaxed, assured. Only a very self-confident man could have been so continuously witty and chic in public. Or so I thought. Certainly nothing about his looks or his behaviour would have suggested to me that he was a miser'.

I stopped, because in my mind now came the words he uttered to me about putting on a good show. He had laughed when he said it and I had assumed at the time he was thinking more of me than of himself. But now I wondered, and I felt an increasing discomfort as I looked silently into the eyes of Helen McDermott where there was a flicker of that amusement which I had glimpsed during my homily in the cathedral on the day of the funeral.

'That's known as taking the charitable view, isn't it?'

'No', I answered. 'I don't think so. You asked me a question, and I'm hoping to answer it. I'm trying to tell you what I saw'.

'But you put kindly labels on what you saw. You used words like "relaxed" and "assured" and there was no disapproval in your tone of voice'.

'Should there have been?'

'That's beside the point', she replied firmly. 'I'm just remarking that automatically – or charitably, perhaps – you presumed that what you saw must be described in a positive and not a negative way'.

'Actually, what I was trying to do was to deal with your question regarding the image I had of him'.

'Yes, but your very words make it clear that you were putting yourself, your kindliness, your assumption of the best into that image'.

'In that case it seems you have me at a disadvantage'.

'Not really', she returned, after a pause. 'Maybe I've just shown you up to be a kind-hearted man'.

Was she patronising me? I don't really think so. But I noticed one thing. I was blushing, and I could not remember having done that for many years.

'Which brings me to the things you said on the day of the funeral', she went on, as though to keep me from becoming comfortable.

'You mean during the funeral Mass'.

'Yes'. She rose from the chair, topped up my wine glass and then her own, moved over to the table and pulled out a local newspaper which had appeared on the day after the ceremonies in the cathedral. Standing there in the light of a bay window, she read the front page and seemed so completely caught up in the words that I had an almost schoolboy need to be still, to cause no distraction. Then she turned to me.

'Just listen to this', she commanded, and began to quote from my homily. It was an odd sensation, this playback of what I had said on that solemn occasion, and although I could find nothing wrong with what I had then uttered, I felt somewhere within me a stir of unease, faint but unmistakably there, as when one is about to succumb to a heavy cold.

'So?' I leaned forward when she had finished.

'It's so very much ... what you would expect, isn't it?'

'I don't think I follow you'.

'It's what any bishop in the whole world would say. "An attack on him is an attack on the institutions of the state and therefore on us all". Of course it all sounds well when pronounced solemnly'.

'But what did you want me to say?'

'Something from within yourself'.

'But that was from within myself'.

'No', she said. 'It was a party line, and a fairly trite one at that'.

'But I said what I believed to be true!'

'Fine! But why not put together the words of your own deeply felt truth?'

'Are you telling me I am a hypocrite?' Resentment was uncoiling inside me.

'No. But don't forget that the word "hypocrite" started off by meaning an actor, someone who puts on a show'.

I was startled, because I remembered the comment of Tim McDermott to me when he compared bishops and politicians. I had to smile. And when I did she laughed and at once, changed the subject and for the rest of my visit talked only of the house and the difficulty of planning what to do with it.

When at last I took my leave of her and headed back home, she had accepted the promise I had made to help her in any way I could. She had seemed grateful. What

she could not have known, however was that her words
to me about my homily had uncovered just a little more
of a nerve of whose existence I had only become aware in
the previous few months.

II

The document containing the agenda of the meeting had one striking feature. Or, to be more precise, it was the revised agenda which attracted my attention.

All the bishops met together at least four times a year, and about a fortnight before the gathering we would receive the list of items to be discussed, together with all the relevant documents. Usually it would take me a couple of days to digest the material which had been sent to me, and by the time we stood to join in the opening prayers for the guidance of the Holy Spirit we were ready and briefed for business. How long we worked together depended of course on what we had to deal with, and from the beginning of my time as bishop I used to keep my diary clear of engagements for at least three days.

We were to assemble on a Tuesday and the revised agenda came in Monday's post. There was no major change. In fact I had to go through the document twice before I realised what had happened. The third item on the original programme had been demoted to second last among thirty-five headings. It preceded Any Other Business, but its words were unchanged. 'Appointment of spokesman to the media'.

I had been long enough a historian to recognise that this was not something innocuous. Preparation of the agenda, like the writing of minutes, is one of the techniques by which to control the outcome of a meeting, and if this item had been moved at the last minute, then something interesting was afoot, interesting because it directly concerned myself. For I was the one who was to take over as spokesman to the media. I had agreed to do so in response to a request from the cardinal. The term of bishop Joseph McGrath was coming to an end, a replacement was needed and the cardinal said it would be a good and useful experience for me to deal with the media. We both knew what he meant. My appointment to the hierarchy had been intended by Rome as a preparation for the anticipated day when I would take over as archbishop of Dublin.

It was the secretary of the conference who normally drew up the agenda and who assembled the necessary documents. He was the man who I myself would naturally call if I wanted something discussed by colleagues, but I also knew that he never issued the final programme without previous consultation with the cardinal. Which meant that both were involved in transferring the item concerning the new appointment. But why?

The question intrigued me throughout Monday and I could think of no solution. Furthermore, as I prepared to go to bed I suddenly realised that there had been none of the usual pre-conference telephone calls from any of my fellow bishops, and I could not decide if this was merely coincidence or an extra indication that something odd was actually happening.

Even after I had put out the light and had settled down under the blankets my mind refused to let go, and I recognised here the working of an old habit, a consequence of my interest as a historian, a disposition to look for significance even when there is none, or at least none worth mentioning.

When I got into my car to drive to Maynooth early next morning the sight of an old newspaper in the back seat reminded me again of the mystery of the moved agenda item, but this time I was in much more relaxed form and indeed I quietly chuckled, for although Joseph McGrath was a delightful and good man, inclined to fits of shyness which he tried to conceal under a manner of noisy joviality, he was also prone to accidents. During a ceremony attended by government ministers and solemn ambassadors he turned after a sermon and began to descend from the high pulpit in the cathedral, subsided gracefully from the general view – his mitre like the tower of a submarine entering the depths – and then, three steps before reaching earth, he caught his heel in the richly embroidered hem of his long surplice and pitched headlong, like a swimmer diving into a pool. This, along with a trail of handkerchiefs, coins and keys from his pocket, which formed a predictable rite of passage during his many public appearances, had undoubtedly enhanced his reputation for unworldliness and, hence, for sanctity. There was also about him an aura of kindly helplessness which tended to evoke the good humour and the protective instincts in people, and this response to him had shaped the case for giving him a three-year term as spokesman for the bishops in their dealings with the media.

In an image-conscious world it would have been hard to make a more disastrous appointment. His new responsibilities seemed to uncover in him a vein of inspired fatuousness which soon had reporters hurrying to ensure a place at his all-too-many press conferences. And when at one of our own meetings of the hierarchy he cheerfully adverted to the unprecedented eagerness of the media to learn the views of the bishops on all contemporary issues there was a clear stillness in which one could sense a struggle to compel the requirement of Christian charity to suppress the collective urge to batter him.

For only two weeks before our meeting and on television he had let loose an eloquent discourse on the subject of condoms. Of course he was not the first bishop to do so, but the argument he used was uniquely his. In an effort to fashion a theologically based moral principle which would be readily intelligible to even the dimmest among the general public he declared expansively that if contraception had been part of the divine plan for the world then God undoubtedly would have created an anatomical shield just as he created other parts of the body.

'You mean like the manufacturer making the sheath for your umbrella', the interviewer asked with an apparent urge for clarification.

'Precisely so', answered Bishop McGrath with such a degree of satisfied firmness that, despite momentous events that day in Argentina and the Middle East, the interview was carried fully on all the television news bulletins. And, of course no cartoonist, no comic and no bar sage missed an opportunity in the ensuing days to conjure up images of stricken figures calling to lost property offices to ask for umbrellas and mislaid members.

Bishop McGrath was in the process of bringing his car to a halt when I reached Maynooth, and as I drove up to where he was I could see some border marigolds crushed under his front wheels. 'Conor!' He greeted me cheerfully and waited to accompany me to the building where we held our meetings. We were almost an hour early but this meant there would be time for coffee and chat before we settled down to business. And indeed we were among the last to arrive. Colleagues were standing in groups or else lounging in the big old armchairs scattered around the room. There was a smell of coffee. The maple floorboards were gleaming in the light which was spread by the high windows. Cups clattered against saucers, and there was the unique atmosphere of a very exclusive club.

I collected some coffee from a table and was turning around when the cardinal came over to me.

'Good morning, Conor'.

'Hello Jim. Nice to see you. How are you?'

'Oh, the old bones are not doing too badly, given their age and what they've been through'. He smiled. 'I'm glad to have the chance for a quick word with you. There's something I wanted to raise with you'.

'Oh, yes?'

'You know about this commission that the Holy Father has set up under Cardinal Goldoni to make recommendations on the future development of Catholic university education?'

'I can't say I have much information on it, but anyhow I see it's one of the items on our own agenda here'.

'Exactly, because we have to send a representative. It'll be a bit of a chore for whoever's appointed, because it'll mean having to make fairly regular trips to Rome over the next year and putting in a week or so there each time. But it's important work and I was wondering if you'd do it for us'.

I hesitated, not simply on account of the suddenness of the request but also because of what I anticipated to mean an uncongenial task. I had met Cardinal Goldoni. He was Archbishop of Ravenna, a man in his fifties, imperious as only Italian ecclesiastics can be and, I suspected, thoroughly vain. He carried his aquiline nose and greying hair like someone waiting for Michelangelo to immortalise him in rich marble. He was authoritarian and conservative, which, I imagine, was the reason for his appointment to Ravenna, and I had the feeling that the conclusions of any commission of which he was the president would be determined in advance of any apparent routines of dialogue.

'It's really important, Conor'.

'I realise that, Jim'.

'I think you're the one among us best able to make a contribution there'. The cardinal had taken hold of my elbow and I was surprised to note a hint of anxiety in his face. In all my dealings with him I had never seen him to be so insistent.

'Is there something happening that I should know about?'

'Conor', he said, drawing me with him into the movement of my colleagues towards the room for our meeting. 'Right now, I have a number of very troubling problems on my plate. There isn't time to go into them here, if you don't mind. But it would really help me if you would agree to have me nominate you as our representative on that Commission. I'll talk to you later on about it in detail'.

With the matter put in those terms only one answer was possible. 'Well, Jim, if that's what you really want, then of course I'll go along with it'.

'Thanks, Conor', he said, and slid away from me as though to ensure that we would have no further discussion.

We all stood for a moment to pray, and there was a gradual falling off in the sounds of adjusted chairs, unzipped cases and spread papers. Tables formed a rectangle and the cardinal sat under a photograph of the Pope. On his right was the archbishop of Dublin, and on his left those of Cashel and Tuam, and the rest of us settled down as the first item on the agenda was called.

Mostly, the topics were routine, and there were moments when my attention wandered so that, as had happened before, I gazed around the room and admired once again the details of the ceiling, of the walls, and of the windows. There was an intricate play of light on carved panels and on whorls and rosettes. The meander of natural pattern was restful and untroubled within the sweep of manmade lines. Nothing jutted or obtruded, and I could only marvel at the inwardness with wood which had enabled a master-carpenter to plan and to bring into being this partnership between the grain of many years and the enhancement of this particular room. He had the authority of someone in whom a profound love and understanding of trees had so flowered together that he could sense which corner of which branch had the potential to yield something beautiful. He humbled me and he was dead, gone a century and a half, and I thought of the authority which as bishop I was proclaimed to have and I compared it, in so far as I could, to the authority which had steadily come together in this carpenter whose name I had forgotten and whose grave had long grown cold. It made me uneasy.

I had been half listening to the proceedings around me but I became suddenly aware of a change of atmosphere as a familiar voice began to sound. Charles John O'Donnell, archbishop of Cashel, had taken over. White-haired, slightly hunched, he had a way of sitting which conjured up to me an image of what it must have been like in the early days of Christianity when a bishop, occupying the only chair in sight, would hold forth to a standing congregation on the subject of their misdemeanours. He did not discuss matters. He engaged in well-ordered harangues, and on my first day as a member of this assembled hierarchy I had been fascinated by the mixture of sullen resentment and wry amusement which he managed to evoke. He was the most senior among us, having been archbishop for thirty-one years, and he trailed an aura of high connections which, I suppose, derived in part from the fact that before his appointment to Cashel he had worked in the Vatican Curia and had been on friendly terms with many who were now cardinals and ecclesiastical potentates.

'I cannot understand it', he was saying, his hands resting on the arms of his chair, his right index finger ready to accompany an assertion. 'We commissioned the best and the most reliable people to prepare authoritative texts for all occasions, baptisms, funeral rites, the lot. The faithful have become used to them. And now there is all this talk about the need for change, for innovation, for new texts. And why?'

When he paused there was a sigh next to me. It came from Joseph Lee, bishop of Meath, a man who was humble and good and with an openly confessed hatred of being lectured. Fidgeting with his pen he had the air of someone who knew that a tirade of at least half an hour was about to be launched and he was too undiplomatic in temperament to be able to conceal his impatience. But he was well accustomed to the fact that archbishop O'Donnell was not easily halted, so, after shuffling around some more he began to read an article from a journal which he had brought with him to allay moments of boredom.

But after a few paragraphs he stopped. He turned towards the archbishop and listened carefully. So did we all. For Dr. O'Donnell was clearly exercised by something more than a proposal for an up-to-date format to our commonly used prayer. The finger was jabbing the air and his voice, usually suave and self-confident, was lined with anger.

'Our task is difficult enough as it is. We have to contend with the bombardments of media which are either left-wing or godless or both. We are surrounded by people wallowing more and more in materialism and bringing disturbance to the faithful. We have to fight to be listened to, and then in the midst of all this and from within our own ranks and when we least expect it, we find something rising which is uncommonly close to sabotage'.

I looked at the agenda, wondering for an instant if I could have made a mistake. We were supposed to be talking about some translations of Latin prayers, but the rage of the archbishop was out of proportion to the matter at hand. Michael Russell, my colleague of Clonfert, had been reporting on criticism from Rome of the effectiveness of some of the translations. The fact that there were objections was not in itself something unusual. Ecclesiastical bureaucrats, ensconced in the

Vatican, had the habit of implying that only they really knew how God liked to be addressed, and, in any case, they did not miss opportunities to show their own power. So it was not startling to hear that a document had come asking for revisions in what had been sent by Michael Russell on behalf of the Irish hierarchy.

'I do not wish to be misunderstood', the archbishop continued, 'Clonfert has done exactly what we asked him to do'.

This highbrow tendency of his to refer to a bishop not by his personal name but by his diocese was one to which I could never quite get accustomed. I had managed to sit through my first attendance at one of these meetings without realising that when Dr. O'Donnell mentioned Dysart he actually meant me. And he was now in the process of indicating that Michael Russell was neither the object nor the cause of the anger.

'Indeed I commend the business-like way in which Clonfert has dealt with the whole matter. The real issue here is something else entirely. There is an enemy within the gate, pushing change for the sake of change and doing untold damage in the process'. For over half an hour the archbishop lectured us on the threat posed by innovation and at last seemed to run out of breath. The cardinal who had been looking sad and depressed pushed his own paper to one side and called the lunch break twenty minutes before the scheduled time.

As we drifted out of the room, I found myself beside John Kelly, the bishop of Cork.

'What in the world brought that on?' I asked. 'Charles wasn't taking about translation'.

'Of course not'.

'He was turning the guns on somebody. But who?'

John Kelly looked at me in what I thought was an odd way. ''Twas you, boy', he answered. I was so astonished that words dried up in me. At the same instant John Kelly was summoned to an urgent phone call. My hope of catching up with him at lunch was frustrated and indeed it was evening before I had a chance to talk to him again. He joined me for a walk after dinner. Daylight was fading and there was an unhurried rustle along an avenue of nearby trees.

'John', I said, 'I want to get back to the remark you made to me this morning'.

'Oh, yes?'

'It's about my being the target for Charles' morning outburst. What did you mean?'

He stopped and gazed at me. 'I'm surprised to hear you ask that', he said. 'So far as I can see, everyone else understood what was in his mind'.

'Well I didn't! So please tell me, because I really am baffled'.

'It was what you said on that radio interview a week ago. Or was it two weeks? Anyhow, that's what set him off'.

We had resumed our walk.

'It was a half-hour programme', I remarked. 'So what was the part that bothered him?'

'Your answer to the questions about girls serving on the altar in the same way as boys. You remember what you said, don't you?'

I laughed. 'Of course I remember what I said. The interviewer asked me if I'd have altar girls in my diocese and I replied that until recently I would not. He asked me why, and I pointed out to him that there had been regulations governing such matters and that I had to abide by them. When he went on to question me about my attitude to this particular regulation, I told him that my attitude was irrelevant, that the rule had been there and that as bishop I had to see to it that it was observed in the diocese for which I was responsible. He then wanted to know if I myself had any difficulty with the fact that the regulation had been relaxed. I answered that

I had no difficulty at all and I added that a change of this kind made eminently good sense, given the times that are in it. And that was it, John. The interview moved to other topics'.

There was a distant sound of traffic but here, beneath the trees, a stillness prevailed, a layered hush. 'It was the phrase about the change making eminently good sense which got through to Charles', my companion murmured. 'And he has been on the rampage ever since'.

'Not to me'.

'No, I wouldn't have imagined so. Or at least not until the moment is right'.

'You mean, until he feels he can browbeat me?' I asked lightly. For I knew the archbishop to be a man who since the time of his appointment had created for himself an ambience in which he usually prevailed. If he spread the Gospel it was only to the compliant. He wasted no energy on those who were disinclined to be submissive. He kept away from any arena in which the expression of differing opinions was taken for granted, and in his many years as archbishop he had concentrated his talents on the priests and nuns, on the students and lay people who took him to be their natural guide and master. He had grown accustomed to power and even among many of my colleagues, his fellow bishops, he could create a kind of disquiet which was soon translated into support for his point of view on the things that mattered to him.

'No', I repeated. 'He said nothing to me. But tell me, if you can, what was the objection to my remark about making eminently good sense? What was it that so upset him about it?'

'You'll have to ask him, Conor'.

'Don't you know?'

He stopped again and looked at me with those placid grey eyes.

'What I do know', he said, 'Is that you have the cardinal, the other archbishops and the Papal Nuncio lined up against you, and, in my experience, that is a rare achievement'.

'What in the world are you talking about? Really, John, this all gets odder by the minute'.

He continued to gaze at me. 'You really are not in the picture', he finally remarked. 'I can see that now. In fact you must be the only one of us who hasn't heard of the doings of the past few days, and you needn't ask which doings because I've clearly lost you already'. He sighed. 'Conor, I hope you had not been looking forward too much to the job of spokesman for the hierarchy, because in fact you're not going to get it. Charles has seen to that. He's going to propose a second term for Joe McGrath. I know! You needn't tell me! We all know about Joe, but Charles' proposal will be accepted. Nothing unkind to you will be said. It will be smooth and brief and clean, and when it's over we'll be close to the moment of heading for the door like kids out of school'.

'Is that why the agenda was changed? To make the appointment virtually the last item of business?'

'Yes'

'I see. Or, rather, I don't see!'

I had a strange sensation, a consciousness on the one hand of being there, alive, walking, conversing with my companion, seeing the pebbles on which my shoes were about to descend, and yet it was somehow as if I were disconnected, though from what I couldn't tell. It was like having the horizons moved out of sight and no point of reference left to direct me.

And then came other thoughts.

'Did you know I was to be asked to represent the hierarchy in the Goldini Commission?'

'I did'.

'So that's why Jim was so anxious to get me to accept. One could then say that since I had this important assignment, I could hardly be asked to handle the other job also. Very considerate and very reasonable of course. Get me appointed tomorrow and then, on the following day, back off from the idea of having me as spokesman, and all out of concern for my workload. Is that how it is?'

'Something like that'.

'And you don't know why?'

'What I know is that Charles has been in full operation to block you, that the reason derives from what you said in the interview, that something more of that reason was hinted at in the morning's tirade, though if you didn't understand it then the hint was not really effective. I know that there have been rumours, though I have not been a party to them, and in any case I don't deal in rumours. Obviously he doesn't like you or approve of you, and that's another element in the scenario. But don't ask me to put it all together, because, Conor, I honestly don't know. I'm just sorry it's happening to you and if you want my help in any way, just say so and you'll have it. In any case, when I think of all that we really should be doing I don't have much patience with these hidden power plays. And if you want my advice I'd suggest you go and confront him, find out what's biting him and then get on with your life. That's my opinion anyway'.

'Thanks, John. I really appreciate that'.

And I did seek out the archbishop. I went to his room, knocked on the door and watched his look of surprise when he saw me. His expression showed a quick decision not to invite me in.

'Ah, Dysart', he said.

'Charles!' I responded, determined neither to address him as Cashel nor your grace. 'You are well, I hope'.

He nodded.

'There was just a quick question I wanted to put to you!' I went on, suppressing a sudden image of bishops listening at keyholes up and down the corridor where I was standing. 'I gather you have been actively assembling support for a decision to block my appointment as spokesman for the hierarchy. Not indeed that I covet the job, since it would demand a lot of extra work. And I am given to understand that this activity of yours, together with your words this morning, grew out of something I said in a recent interview on radio. So what's it all about, Charles? Do tell me'.

He frowned, and I knew immediately that my instinct to confront him had been the right one. He always liked to master events and for years he had developed the habit of maintaining a distance from any scene whose outcome he could not predict and which he might therefore not be able to control. This was why there were places to which he did not go and people to whom he would not talk, and in this way he had acquired an aura of power to which many in the church around him felt obliged to yield. And so my evident lack of deference was a disconcerting presence on that corridor. 'Yes Charles, do tell me', I insisted.

He avoided my gaze.

'You heard my words this morning', he said quietly. 'And since there is here a forum to which we both belong, I imagine you can speak your piece if you have some argument to make'.

'But, Charles, the meaning of what you had to say this morning was not clear'.

'To those with ears to hear I think it was'.

I laughed. 'You are offering generalities, Charles, which I suppose is one way of avoiding the question I asked you'.

His eyes narrowed in anger. 'I am not accustomed to being addressed in this way, Dysart'.

'Probably not, but since you have been taking steps to block my appointment and since you have not spelled out the reasons for these – at least not openly – I think I am entitled to ask what it was in my radio interview that provoked this response from you'.

'Ah, no', he said, his voice brittle. 'There you are mistaken; you have no claim to speak of entitlements. None at all! At least not here. Not among us. Because, my dear Dysart, that radio interview was the clearest evidence so far that you are not – let me repeat – not one of us!'

He slammed the door in my face, and for a moment I stood utterly astonished not only by his words, but by my last glimpse of him. For I had seen something unmistakeable in those regal eyes. It could not be missed, and it was fear.

Those words kept circling back to me over the next few days. You are not one of us. It was a kind of excommunication, for it registered something much deeper than a difference of views, and its effect on me had a power out of all proportion to the actual personal circumstances involved. I disliked Charles John O'Donnell and had done so for years, so that there was a level at which his disapproval of me was certainly a matter of indifference. But his words and the fear I had detected in his eyes could only suggest that I was not merely an irritant, that in fact I was a dangerous enemy. And that was something which greatly bothered me, especially when I recalled that John Kelly had told me how the cardinal, the other two archbishops and the Papal Nuncio had been persuaded to agree with Charles that I should not be appointed as spokesman for the hierarchy. Of course I had been chosen to be the Irish delegate on the Goldoni Commission, but I had quickly realised that this was a way of getting me to the sidelines. It was the best thing they could contrive, given that a bishop cannot usually be sacked from his diocese.

But sacked for what? For having offered in a radio interview the opinion that it was a good idea for the Vatican to have fully considered the possibility of allowing girls, like boys, to serve at the altar? But this was ridiculous. One does not gang up on a bishop for something of that nature. There had to be another reason and I dearly wished to find out what it might be, so on the last evening of the assembly I went up to the cardinal and said I wanted to talk to him in private. He agreed and we walked in silence to his room where I told him what I had heard and what I knew, and asked bluntly for an explanation of why I was deemed to have stepped out of line.

'I am very sorry about this, Conor', he said. 'But Charles insisted and the others agreed'.

'But what's it all about? I have no difficulty with the idea of not being spokesman. After all, I didn't seek the job. You're the one who approached me, having presumably thought about the matter, and now you've backed away from it, and I want to know why. What has he alleged against me? When I asked him, he just slammed the door in my face. What's going on, Jim?'

He seemed very tired and he avoided my gaze.

'It was the interview, wasn't it?' I insisted.

'Yes'.

'So what's the fuss about?'

He settled more deeply in his chair.

'Charles is fourteen years older than you are', he said gently. 'His most formative years belong to a time very different from what you've known, and this is something which you really need to understand and remember. An outlook was moulded, a career launched, friends made, and all this amid the kind of certainties that don't nowadays seem possible. I can see how it was, because I am only a few years his junior'.

He paused and for the first time since our arrival in the room he looked at me, and there was sadness in his eyes, a kind of pain which called up a kind of anxious ache around my heart.

'You know your church history better than most of us', he went on. 'There has always been the equivalent of a generation gap. Much of the time that was quite alright, because underneath it there was a continuing sense that people were on the same side, that there was a real communion in existence'.

I could feel a puzzled tension uncurling within me, because I recognised that I was hearing an example of what some of us used to describe jokingly as Jim-speak. This was a set of voiced generalities, sometimes lengthy, which criticised no one by name but which, nonetheless, amounted to a displeased cracking of a whip, a call to order. They were delivered usually with a sort of anguished kindkiness, but they arose from a tough centre, and as I looked at the cardinal, straightening slowly in his chair I knew that it was now my turn to be at fault, though I had yet to find out exactly why.

'Charles has a strong feeling for the oneness of believers. It is a core value for him, keeping in the same side as the living and the sanctified dead. That matters to him more than anything else'.

'And in some way I'm a threat to that?' The directness of my question seemed to startle him, to prevent a cloaked reply.

'Yes', the cardinal murmured, 'That's how it seems to him'.

'And what about you?'

'I didn't hear that broadcast', he answered.

'So it really is back again to that interview. For heaven's sake, what did I say that was so shocking?'

'It was not so much what you said as what lay beneath it'.

'Jim!' I began in exasperation. 'This is all vagueness and I really wish you'd get down to specifics'.

'It was the matter of altar girls'.

'So I've gathered. But do you know what I actually said about that?'

'Yes'.

'So you know I acknowledged that there had been one kind of regulation, that I observed it in my diocese and that I would observe the new one?'

'You also said it had been eminently sensible to have reviewed it'.

'Correct. And what's wrong with that?'

'A remark of that kind coming from a bishop was a great shock to Charles. As he saw it, the implication of your words was that a rule of the Church was ill conceived, even foolish. Which means, of course, that other rules could also be held to be foolish. Such as the matter of not having women priests. And it needn't stop there. Until eventually the whole fabric of authority in the church comes under question. One expects it from misguided believers. But you don't expect it from a bishop. That how Charles would see things. And so he's very upset about the interview'.

We were both silent for a moment. I could hear the tick of his bedside alarm clock.

'If you think about it', I began at last, 'this really is a quite extraordinary sequence of events. It takes a few seconds in which to give an opinion on what, after all, is not at the forefront of the world's concern. A particular implication is read into it, though in fact there are others. A head of steam is built up. An agenda is changed. There are high words at our meeting. There is a hasty backtracking about my possible appointment as spokesman, and Charles slams the door in my face when I ask him what's bothering him'.

The cardinal said nothing, and this apparent unwillingness to talk began to unsettle me, because I suddenly realised that if he were a prime minister he would be asking me to resign my seat in the Cabinet and that the word be sent forth that I was not really 'sound'. Instead, I was to be made a member of the Goldini Commission and there would be solemn talk on some well-chosen public occasion of the importance of having me there.

'Oddly, enough', I returned, 'on the evening before I drove here, the thought went through my mind that for the first time before such a meeting I had not been receiving calls from colleagues. That makes me wonder now. Is there some collective decision to put up a distance between the hierarchy and me? To suggest I am not the man you once knew? That, of course, would be a way to justify cutting me off. Is that how it is, Jim? Tell me'.

'My dear Conor', he said, 'I think you may be forgetting something. In fact, I'm sure you are. It seems to me that you should try to bear in mind that we all go through bad patches. It's inevitable. Part of the job. Especially so when you think of the responsibilities which lie on the shoulders of every member of the hierarchy. You carry them for days and months and years, and most of the time one gets by. And then a slump hits you, perhaps for no obvious reason and the old reliable perspectives don't seem to be there. So what do you do? Quit? Of course not. You remember your comrades, redouble your prayers and, eventually, you pull out of it and pick up where you left off. It happens to all of us, Conor. Believe me. I know. I understand'.

He gave me a look of warmth and compassion. It was not something he turned on for the occasion. It was genuine.

But it disturbed me. He was holding out a prospect of forgiveness, leading me towards it, helping me along so that if I co-operated I would be brought back into the fold where I belonged. In effect he was reformulating the words of Charles. But, like a good diplomat or politician, he was trying to soothe me, trying to soften the impact of

Charles' outburst. In his own fashion he was saying you are not one of us, but you were and we'll allow you to be so again. But of course that will be on our terms.

'Look, Conor, please take a few days off when you get home', the cardinal continued. 'Do it quietly, prayerfully, reflect on all this. Everyone has to take stock sometimes. You know that as well as I do'.

'Think myself away from altar girls?'

'Altar girls today, women priests tomorrow', he said.

'Ah. In other words, circle the wagons and stay where you are'.

'Conor!' he exclaimed, with evident exasperation. 'If any changes are needed, they will happen. But in their own time and in a proper manner, and certainly not by way of radio interviews. That is not how the Church moves. Never has been. If there are problems, one works at them from within an ambience of loyalty'.

The phone rang and he was grateful for the interruption.

'Jim, I'll leave you to it', I said.

'God bless you, Conor. I hope we can talk again soon'. He patted my shoulder and, at the same time, picked up the receiver.

I walked from his room and made my way out by the seminary gates into the street which was edged by shops and bars and restaurants. The evening was warm. A few hours of light still remained in the sky. The thick summer leaves stirred continuously amid the exhaust fumes from passing cars. There was the sound of a radio. There were shouts from some running, laughing youths in jeans and sweatshirts. An old man smiled at me and gave me the salute which from his boyhood days he had always reserved for the clergy. I returned the smile. Everyone else ignored me.

From the street I went into a long avenue overhung by aristocratic old trees. It was a route I had often taken in the days when I was myself a student of the seminary. In those times one was forbidden to walk alone there. We had to go in groups, and only after we had been given permission to do so. We used to walk earnestly, and our conversation was about the lectures we had attended, the oddities of some professor, or the football match at which we had cheered our classmates to victory. We passed clumps of crocuses or of daffodils in the spring, looked forward to the holidays, but spoke rarely of parents or family. After all, we had left home. Or, rather, we had moved out of home, not as our brothers or sisters had done, when, having grown up, they found their own jobs and embarked on their own lifestyles. We were different. We had found an alternative society. We had set ourselves apart, so that, as we say it, we could both leave the world and yet serve it. We had cut the usual connections, and we had found much of the courage to do so by our sense of comradeship in a shared enterprise.

Of course there were the down days. Times came when I wondered if I had made some appalling mistake. I questioned my worthiness to be a priest, felt my enthusiasm evaporate. I tried to pray, but my words and my thoughts creaked in a dried-up interior. The walk down the avenue, between this honour-guard of trees, became something mechanical like every action. I was in a mist. Mind and feelings were soaked in futility.

But the bond with the others continued to hold. I even thought I could detect a closing of ranks around me. Nothing was said. Days passed. But a moment came, then the heart lifted, when I joined their laughter, when the sense of belonging grew assured.

As I thought of this, I immediately recalled the words of the cardinal, his soothing reference to bad patches. Was I going through one of them now, as I had in my student days?

Actually, the situation was rather different. In those times my recurring fear had been that I would not be able to measure up to the demands of the special company which I had joined. Our mentors would proclaim in high seriousness that each one of us had a call from God to be out of the ordinary. The phrase often quoted was that of St Paul who had asserted the requirement to be athletes of the Lord. But given that my own background was devoid of any achievement on the playing fields whose heroics I nevertheless admired, I was troubled from time to time that in a context where performance seemed to matter most of all, I had a continuous prospect of failure. Yet my conviction that I really belonged to this company used to come back to me and I nestled into the encouragement generated by friends around me, young men like myself, with their own struggles to endure.

But now I was a bishop, selected by the institution as one of its special men and granted an authority to which many were willing to submit.

"'But you are no longer one of us!'" I quoted Charles John O'Donnell. 'So now where does that leave you, my dear Conor Mahon?'

As my voice rose towards the overhanging branches I laughed. Because once again I had detected another instance of an emerging trait, that of talking aloud to myself when I was alone. But the laugh died suddenly within me, and remembering the look of fear in Charles' face, I realised that the angry reaction to what I said in the radio interview was a cover for something else. Charles was well able to face down anyone, even a colleague, who might be an advocate of change on questions such as that of women priests in the church. His own imperious nature and his abiding connections with Vatican cardinals would provide him with all the assurance needed to deal with those he considered to be mavericks. The role of resident thunderbolt came naturally to him, but as I thought of his performance when he rampaged against me I could see now behind it another occasion and a very different theme.

I had been in the same room with him several months earlier. It was one of the regular sub-committee meetings attended by the four archbishops and by three other delegated members of the hierarchy. In the middle of routine business I began to feel exasperation taking hold of me as we droned through items which could just as easily have been settled in a round of phone calls. As I listened to the minuet of words cris-crossing the bog oak table where we had gathered, I could see a few of the reasons why we bishops had the reputation of being diffident and uninspiring men for whom a prime consideration was to protect our backs in a world where we could no longer count on deference.

'I'm sorry, Jim', I said, looking at the cardinal, 'please excuse this interruption. But it seems to me that the remaining items on our agenda can be dealt with over lunch. There's something much more drastic which we can't put on the long finger any more, and the sooner we acknowledge it the better'.

'What do you mean?' the cardinal asked softly.

'I'm referring to the all too frequent cases of sexual abuse by priests. They're a slow poison in the public domain. God only knows how many more cases we are going to have on our hands. The tabloids are circling, ready to pounce because they know well that there are lurid and terrible stories waiting to unfold, even now as we sit here. And it seems to me that so far as the public is concerned the hierarchy is perceived either to have no credible policy on the matter or else is trying to conceal as much as possible what's actually going on. In fact there are far too many people who are quite convinced that we'll go to any length to protect our own, even if that means shoving the victims into the background'.

'That's a very hard saying', the cardinal remarked.

'That's what's being said', I responded. 'Which is why I'm raising this matter now. We've not had a proper discussion of it among ourselves, and there are voices claiming that our handling of the situation has been disastrous so far'.

The cardinal surveyed the others. He began to turn the cap of his pen round and round and his head was cocked to one side as if in anticipation of a distant echo.

'We can't go on either saying nothing or else reacting after events have been forced on our attention at this meeting'.

'Well, then, what are you proposing that we do?' The cardinal sounded tense.

'I'm sure we all understand Conor's worry'. It was the voice of Jim Tallon, the bishop of Derry. He was sitting next to me and he spoke with a wheeze. 'And if I'm right in this, he's anxious that we have a worked out policy. But if we're going to do that properly we're going to need some back-up studies to help us on our way. That takes time. But it can be done, and I think we might be ready to have it on the agenda of our fall meeting. Say six or seven months down the line'.

'I agree with that', said Liam Murphy, the bishop of Killaloe.

'So do I', said the archbishop of Tuam, raising his pencil as if a vote were being taken.

'Well, then ...', The cardinal was about to sum up.

'Sorry, Jim', I broke in, 'But we've got to move faster. A decision here to establish a series of studies will be followed by a process of consultations, followed by the appointment of someone, followed by time for that someone to go to work, followed by an eventual report, followed by preliminary discussions, followed by our general meeting. It simply won't do. We can't afford to wait so long. It's too serious. We run the risk of being very badly wrong-footed any day and found to be at serious fault if we don't act now'.

'What are you suggesting?'

'That we take time out of our very busy schedules over the next two weeks and go at this issue. So that we can all have a rough and ready basis on which to act if any of us is confronted by the situation of having one of our priests shown up to be a paedophile or a rapist'.

'But this has to be properly structured'. It was Jim Tallon again. 'We can't just sit around a table and have a chat about it. We need experts, we need documentation, we have to be put in a position of being able to speak with authority if we have to'.

'And meanwhile ...?' I was getting impatient.

'I'm sorry, I don't understand the question'.

'What do we do in the meantime? Sit and wait and hope that we don't have to face up to some nasty incident. No, this won't do. It really won't'.

It was obvious that I was now a minority voice.

'Alright', I said. 'I know well that we can't arrive at some consensus overnight. But on the other hand I have something pressuring me about a situation that exists right in the moment and it involves a member of the hierarchy'. The silence around me grew poised for outrage. Nobody moved. 'I have reliable information about something that happened in diocese X. I'm naming no names in order to avoid any distraction from the essentials of what happened. A young girl, thirteen years old, was raped by her parish priest in the sacristy of his church. She's an only child, and her father, a farm labourer, is widowed. When she got home she was so distressed that her father noticed, began to question her and when she admitted to what happened her father battered her. Why? For telling lies against the priest. Can you imagine the agony of that afflicted child? But worse was to come. The father forced the girl to go with him to the parish house where he beat her in front of the priest until she apologised for what she said about him. And it might have ended there if it hadn't happened that a young man, a nineteen-year-old cousin, found out what had been done to her. He had initiative, this young man, and he phoned the residence of our colleague, demanding to see him. The secretary took the call and when he asked why the young man wished to see our colleague he said it had to do with one of the priests. The secretary obviously guessed what was in the air and said the bishop was unavailable. Over a few days the young man got the same message until he said he would go public if he wasn't received. He was immediately given an appointment for the same afternoon'.

I could recognise the crackling of the atmosphere around me.

'The young man went to our colleague, told him what had happened and demanded that the parish priest be removed at once and that something be done about him. Incidentally, I've talked to the young man and I believe every word he has said to me. His interview with our colleague was, shall we say ... not pleasant. He first tried to browbeat his visitor. When that didn't work he began to talk about the need to ensure that the priest's life wasn't spoiled forever. He tried the "I'll look into it" approach. But the young man held out and eventually laid down two demands, promising to give the whole sordid story to a Sunday tabloid if these were not met. The priest was to be removed. And our colleague was to go to the house of the father of the raped girl and tell him what really happened. Our colleague agreed to do what was asked of him. That was one month ago. The priest is still in place. As for the other demand, the play was as follows. Our colleague telephoned the father, explained that there was a scandal involving the daughter and that he would like to visit the house of the father to talk to him about it. He let this much sink in. Then he went on to point out to the father that he would be driven there by his diocesan secretary. Having said that much he went through the motions of having a considerate thought. He remarked that of course the neighbours would recognise the car, would naturally wonder what it was doing outside the father's house, and of course small towns being what they are ... You get the picture, I'm sure. The father was then asked if it was all right for the visit to go ahead and, of course, the calculation about him worked. He answered that perhaps it would be better after all for our colleague not to be seen outside the house. Our colleague then urged gentle treatment of the girl and rounded off by promising the father to take a special interest in her welfare. Naturally the father is filled with gratitude at the kindness shown to him!'

I let the facts register.

'So you can see there's more than enough reason for us to deal with this whole business immediately'.

There was no dissent. Instead, it was decided that the four archbishops would have urgent consultations among themselves and would get in touch with the rest of us within days. And of course I made no mention of the fact that the colleague to whom I was referring was Charles John O'Donnell, archbishop of Cashel.

III

'In fact, are you still one of them?' Helen McDermott asked.

'Certainly I am!' I turned to her in amazement. 'Whatever makes you think otherwise? How could I not be?'

She watched me carefully.

'You've just been telling me what the archbishop of Cashel said to you'.

'I was reporting his opinion'.

'True. But now I've asked you for your own opinion. Or perhaps that's an indiscreet question'.

I looked out over the sea. A large white bird interrupted a strong flight to plummet into the waters. It re-emerged at once and I thought I could detect the last sun-touched moment of a fish in its bill. Other birds stretched comfortable wings around the cliff top below me. There were anemones in the thin grass. Low tentacles of thorn bushes slid out from cracks among the rocks. The breeze from the Atlantic was barely a hint.

On the road behind us two cars were parked, one beside the other. She had recognised me while driving by, and she had walked down towards the cliff edge to greet me. I had been sitting on a rock. In fact I had been there for a couple of hours.

This was the only part of my diocese which opened on to the sea. It was a finger of land claimed in medieval times by a predecessor of mine whose promotion of trade and business had been a scandal to his colleagues and a boon to hungry people. The corporal works of mercy he had called it, this entrepreneurial life of his, and to all efforts to divert him to the more conventional routes of theology and public piety he had replied bluntly and unanswerably that he and his God understood one another and that so long as he remained a bishop he would continue ways of making money for his diocese. He added, with characteristic realism – or malice, depending on one's point of view – that the reason for his unpopularity with colleagues was that, whereas he had thus far earned nothing but continuing profit, they would not recognise a business opportunity even if it prostrated itself before them to kiss their feet.

It was not a subconscious effort to identify with him which had brought me here on this day of warm sunlight. I had come because it was a cherished place, a scene I invariably loved, and because my morale was low. During the week since the meeting of the hierarchy I had felt something akin to shock. I could not get rid of the image of Charles John O'Donnell, with that look of fear and anger on him. I thought too of the cardinal and of the background moves, the collective moves to render me as harmless as possible.

'No', I said eventually. 'It's not an indiscreet question. But I am not at all sure how I could even begin to think of answering it'.

I had described to her what had happened at the meeting, and I had done so because I had no defence against the way she had confronted me after she had come down from the car. She had greeted me and was remarking on the beauty of the day when she stopped, staring at me as though her attention had been drawn to an unexpected blemish.

'You look terrible!' she exclaimed. 'Has something bad happened to you? Are you sick'. She stood there, the yellow of her sweater brilliant in the light, her hair and black skirt reacting to a sudden breeze. The sea behind her was green.

I watched her. I reckoned she must be in her early forties. But I am not good at guessing age. Perhaps I have not properly developed the habit of looking closely at people. In fact, as I now think of it, such a habit was discouraged by one of our mentors in the seminary who used to warn us about the danger of coming too close to someone else. It was obviously that he was thinking about our vow of chastity, but he would cloak this by quoting a passage in Augustine where that powered saint describes his feelings of guilt at having gone into a field to read scripture and finding himself beguiled by the song of the birds and by the joy of a landscape. We were to be holy men, with thoughts fixed on God and on a realm beyond our own. To be in this world but not to be of it, such was the old maxim instilled into us, and like all maxims it had the sort of tidiness which one would not usually encounter in life.

'And you look remarkably well', I said, and was so startled and embarrassed by the unpremeditated character of the observation that I must have blushed. At any rate I hastened to find a way of answering her query about my appearance, and before I knew it I was launched on a description of the meeting of the bishops.

She sat near me on a rock and she listened, and it was when I had finished that she put the question whether I was still 'one of them'.

'This may strike you as odd', I began, struggling to deal with what she was saying, 'but what happened at the meeting, together with something you said to me when I visited you at your house after your husband's murder – these have somehow managed to come together to provoke an unsettling in me, to make something of a problem'.

A puzzled expression came over her face.

'Forgive me', I intervened hastily. 'Please bear with me. I realise I'm a bit incoherent'.

A fishing trawler had come into view, and for some moments I watched the slow rise and fall of its homeward rhythm.

'They're really not unconnected, this meeting of the hierarchy and what you remarked to me. I realise that now'. I continued to turn in the direction of the trawler, but was actually aware only of the light over the sea.

'You described my sermon as being entirely predictable, as the sort of thing any bishop could be expected to say. And my colleagues - especially Charles John O'Donnell - have put that in my radio interview I showed myself to be out of step with them. Too much like a bishop, too little like a bishop. Contrasting perceptions of me, as I'm sure you'll admit'.

I could see she was not too clear about what it was I was trying to express. But then there was a thickening fog within myself.

'On the one hand there is Conor Mahon'. I was stumbling. 'On the other hand there is his lordship, the Most Reverend Conor Mahon, Bishop of Dysart and Apostolic Administrator of Kilcolman. Outsiders do not distinguish one from the other, and furthermore, they look to him with expectation as to how he should be. But I know there is a distinction, and what you said that day and what my colleagues think of me suggest that there is very good reason to assume the existence of such a distinction'.

'Are you telling me that you are losing your faith?' I could see the expression of concern in her eyes.

'I honestly don't know what I'm telling you. No this is no mid-life crisis. I've been having one of those every six months since I was fourteen. Or maybe twelve. I don't know. I don't remember. And, yes, I do believe in God. And, yes, I am hung up on that figure who walked in Palestine two thousand years ago. And, yes, I have my bad moods, like anyone else. And, yes, I am depressed and probably hurt after that meeting of the hierarchy.

But that's not it. It isn't. Not what? Not what's causing the sense of being suddenly, somehow disconnected. Of flailing around inside myself and everything outside having stepped back from me, retreated. Even my prayers seem to be merely words circling the enclosures of my brain. I keep trying and trying and trying and keep finding myself praying in the silence to the withdrawn, and that's something that fills me with rage and frustration and I yell and shout and say can't you even once in a lifetime just give me one lousy answer, a fraction of a second's answer instead of leaving me utterly alone? And then you expect me to be a bishop! Me! A successor of the apostles, of the apostles led by Peter. By Peter! Isn't that an irony? Me. A living illustration of the Peter principle, promoted to the level of my incompetence, yet officially I am plugged into them, those apostles. What kind of folly is this? Me a bishop, creating, like those before me, the expectation that I know the wishes and the thinking of my God, that on everything to do with how everyone relates to one another I know the answers, I know the score. Each time I get up into the pulpit to preach, I am laying a claim to the implication that I actually know what I'm talking about, that I have a knowledge and expertise unavailable to my polite, uninterrupting, acquiescent audience. What have I got myself into? What am I supposed to do? In God's name, what am I to do?'

'I'm so very sorry, Conor. Conor, oh I'm so sorry, Conor'.

Her words seemed to come from a far-off place. And then I realised slowly that her hands were on my shoulders and that she was staring at me, trying to comfort me and that I was haranguing her, hurling my words over her, spilling on to her the bewilderment and the sorrow which had come to rest within my own unanchored self.

IV

A few days later I was in the meeting room next to my office at the cathedral. Most of the priests of my diocese had gathered there and by noon we had worked our way through nearly all the matters which I had wanted to discuss with them. It was a spacious room, and from my chair I could watch the faces of my colleagues in the daylight which slanted from the high windows on either side of us. I had just finished the description of a request which had come to me and which was centred on a proposal to bring into the diocese for a summer holiday, groups of Catholic and Protestant children from those parishes of Belfast which had suffered most from violence. The idea was that the children would camp together and the only problem seemed to be to find a suitable location. 'I know the perfect spot. There are fields, a river with good fishing, plenty of trees'. The eager voice was that of Tom Lydon, a curate recently ordained, indeed not a year on the job. 'It's in my parish and I'm sure we can get the owner to let us have the place. It's Mrs. McDermott, the widow of the Minister. I can go talk to her, if you like'.

'Don't bother!' said Jack McDonald, his parish priest.

'Why not, Jack? Can you think of a better place?'

'No, Tom, I can't. But she's the last one to give it to you. Or indeed do anything for you. That's one tough woman, as her poor husband found out, and she'll do nothing for you. So forget it'.

Other suggestions were considered until someone reminded us of an area at the eastern end of the diocese where picnic tables and woods and other amenities were available. But the words of Jack McDonald continued to sound within me, and at the end of the meeting I sought an opportunity to talk to him when we were both on the way to the car park.

'I was interested by your remark about Mrs. McDermott. What do you mean by "tough"?'

'Just that. I've known her for a good number of years, and I can tell you she's someone to keep away from'.

Jack McDonald was sixty-nine, thin, and bald, except for a slipped wreath of white hair. He had grey eyes and a wry smile.

'But why?' I persisted.

'At poor Tim's funeral did you notice how members of his own family, his brothers, broke free of her as soon as they decently could?'

He was right. Even when surrounded she had been plainly alone.

'Do you mean that she's difficult to get on with?' Of course I was prompting him now. But I wanted to know.

'She had hardly signed her name on the marriage register when she told him straight out that she wasn't going to have any children. What she liked and wanted was to be the wife of a politician, especially of someone successful like him, a government minister. If he had lived, he would have been leader of the party and of the government. And there would have been all those photographs of her in high places. That's what interested her. She had no use for the idea of being a wife. To be a public figure but with no work or responsibility – that was her plan. Poor Tim, I felt so sorry for him. He was a really lovely man. But at least he had his career'.

We were stopped beside my car.

'But Jack, how did you get to know all this?'

'Sure I knew Tim for years. But don't misunderstand me. He was no whiner or complainer. No, he wasn't that kind of a man. But I could tell from the things he said, from hints he dropped. I really felt sorry for him, God rest him'.

Since he did not seem to have anything more to volunteer on the subject of Helen McDermott, I did not push the matter, and I was soon on my way to lunch. But her name was uttered again later in the afternoon during a visit from a detective. He was looking for information about a family I had helped a few months earlier that had been left destitute when the father, a bank official, had absconded with a large sum of embezzled money. And now, apparently, the older of the teenage boys had stolen a car and vanished. The detective, a quiet and obviously compassionate man, was hoping to find some way of tracing him. But I was not able to give him any help, and I apologised for the fact.

'Ah, no', he said. 'No need to say that. Even negative information points us in the right direction sooner or later. Like the case of Mr. McDermott. For a while we had nothing to work with, but a few straws are beginning to come our way'.

'I'm glad to hear it', I said. 'That was a cold-hearted murder'.

'It certainly was, but we'll get them'.

'So the enquiries are going on?'

'Oh yes. Every day. Only last Thursday we ran another reconstruction of the killing and this after getting a tit-bit which was new to us'.

As we were going out he suddenly turned to me. 'How well do you know Mrs. McDermott?'

'I wouldn't say I know her particularly well', I answered, startled. 'I've met her a few times and ... Good God! You don't mean she had anything to do with this?'

'Ah no. Nothing like that! No. Not at all. But it's just ...'. He wrinkled his cheeks. 'I don't really understand her. We've interviewed her several times, and it's not as if she were unhelpful. Nothing of the sort. She's given us all the time we want. But there's something strange there.

I've had dealings with widows before. But she's different. As if somehow she couldn't give a damn that he's dead'.

He got into the car and left me on my doorstep. I slowly returned to my study where a pile of documents awaited and where I knew I must spend the next three or four hours. I have an unshakeable dislike of administrative work and I sometimes let things gather before I attend to them. In fact the truth obliges me to acknowledge that the affairs of the diocese would be in a bad way if I did not have the help of my secretary. But I worked through the papers on my desk, I stopped occasionally to think of what Jack McDonald and the detective had said about Helen McDermott. I found it difficult to imagine how I could reconcile their words with what I had encountered that day on the edge of the Atlantic where she had shown such radiant sympathy. Yet the detective had unsettled me. I trusted his professionalism and his experience and I could not convince myself that he must have been wrong to think the death of her husband had been a matter of indifference to Helen McDermott. That was an observation from which I could not escape and I had no idea how to deal with it.

However, other problems and tasks intervened and nearly a week had passed before my thoughts returned to Helen McDermott. Once again it was in a context where her name was evoked, this time during a chat with Donal Williams, the Minister for the Environment. He had come to perform the official opening of a new bridge. I had been invited to be present at the ceremony and I was beside him when he cut the tape and lifted the scissors on high. We applauded. Photographs were taken. He beamed at the television camera. His limousine, in which I rode as a guest, was driven slowly across the bridge, followed by a line of ordinary cars. There was waving. Some of the more loyal party members cheered. Of course, as we all headed towards the reception at the nearby town hall, no one had the grace to allude to the fact that the bridge had been in full use for the previous fifteen months.

Tea and sandwiches were laid out on long tables and I noticed after a while that the noise of general conversation was much more subdued than would be the case if alcohol had been served. There was less laughter, something I instinctively regretted, and the guests seemed to prefer to remain in the same groups rather than to circulate. Two girls stood near a window. They each had a pot of tea and were obviously supposed to refill cups, but they chose to come only to the minister and to me, a fact around which I could have concocted a little clerical joke about how it was that such occasions were the one time when church and state were on an equal footing. But I desisted. Anyhow, the Minister was talking to me about Tim McDermott.

'I still can't quite accept that he's gone', he said. 'He was such a presence! I loved to watch him, to see the way his antennae were always on the job, faultlessly, flawlessly. He had instinctively what I'm having to learn in small bits, slowly and by experience. It was like watching an absolutely top-notch soccer player during a very tough match in the World Cup. You're full of amazement and admiration, and you know you couldn't ever be like him'.

'You're not pausing in the hope that I murmur something about your undue modesty?' I asked, grinning.

'Ah, no'. The laugh was good humoured. 'But I miss him'.

'Of course'.

'And he was such a good colleague. I well remember a moment some years ago when I had been spending days pushing one of my bills through the house, and I was getting a lot of stick from the opposition. But I had done my homework and I figured I could handle it. But that fellow Monaghan threw a question at me from the other side. It was one, which, if I had answered it directly, would have made difficulties for the Government. I hesitated just long enough for all the opposition front benches to spot my problem and they were on to me like a bunch of hounds in at the kill. They shouted and demanded an answer. And it was Tim who came to the rescue. He picked on Joe Lawlor, who was one of those baying at me. Tim said just loudly enough for Joe to hear that he was considering the hypothesis that Joe was a constipated little hypocrite. Of course he knew his man, knew that he is very short-tempered, and sure enough Joe blew up and began to yell at Tim. Then the others beside him joined in, demanding that Tim be made withdraw his unparliamentary remarks. After this went on for a while, Tim stood up. He bowed to the chair saying that he had made no derogatory allegation about his parliamentary friend, Mr. Lawlor, that he had merely voiced the thought that he was contemplating the hypothesis that the honourable gentlemen was a constipated little hypocrite. He had made no allegations, but if the mere consideration of a hypothesis could in any way be construed as disrespect for the proud traditions of the House, then in the interest of the good name of all concerned he would gladly withdraw from the ears of everyone, including Mr. Lawlor, the thought which had crossed the private recesses of his mind. By this time I was off the hook and able to continue on my statesmanlike way when the debate on my bill was finally resumed. Ah, he sure was fun to be with'.

'But was he a good Minister?'

He looked startled.

'Don't misunderstand me', I hastened to add. 'I'm not a member of the opposition! I'm really not trying to trap you. I suppose you'd have to say it's the historian in me coming out. Because, you see, I'm fascinated by what makes and shapes and drives people. I'm always struggling to tune into what it is that people are. So that's why I'm asking you'.

But he could not answer, for we were joined by others. And we drank our tea and we chatted, and it was only later that he could return to the subject. I was in the limousine with him and the purpose was to bring me home. But before we came in sight of my house he told his driver to stop.

'I could use a quick walk', he said.

'An excellent idea'. And as we paced along together we were able to look across the countryside at the hedges and the fields and trees.

'Yes, he was a good Minister', he remarked suddenly. 'Of course he had the basics. Stamina, ability to work the long hours, the willingness to be on call seven days a week. Even bad Ministers need to have that much'.

'But why was he good?'

'Well, as you know, you can't sum these things up very easily. But let's say that he was a man of many wiles, a mixture of brilliance and low cunning, so that whether he was addressing an election rally, answering a parliamentary question, making decisions, supervising the drafting of a bill, he seemed always to hit the right way of doing it. And he did it with class and flair. He brought wonderful style into everything he did'.

'So, then, was he a contented man?'

'I must admit I really didn't think in those terms'.

We walked for a few moments. 'I'm not at all sure that he was, now that you mention it'.

'Why do you say so?'

'Not much more than a guess, I suppose. Certainly he was very successful. In fact, during his entire political career he was hardly ever out of power. He held the most important ministries. He was continuously popular. He generated a stir whenever he got up to speak ...'

'But ...?' I probed.

'Well, now that you are pushing me down that road – and I really have to admit I hadn't thought about this before – I'd have to say that there was some kind of shadow around his eyes, around what he said and did'.

'Boredom?'

'I don't think so. True, after so many years a bit of that might just begin to creep in. But no. It wasn't boredom'.

'What was it, then?'

'You're really cornering me!' he laughed. But at once his expression became sombre. 'It might have been insecurity, not that of a man wondering if he'll be re-elected next time. No, it was something else. I'm sure of that. Maybe the way to get at it, the only way, is to tell you about a tiny incident which happened about a year ago. I was at a meeting. Now don't ask me how this came up, but somebody got stuck for a quotation, and it was Tim who piped up immediately. "Always and everywhere be first". Yes, that was it. Don't ask me where he got it from, but the point is that it wasn't just any quotation. You could tell that from the way he said it, revealing himself as he so rarely did. It was something special, as if ... as if he lived by it. And was not sure he could continue to live by it'.

Not wishing to seem pedantic, I chose not to tell him that I recognised the quotation. It was a set of words which the Roman politician Cicero had taken for himself, a motto which seemed to speak of ambition, but which meant something special to him because of his own terrible personal insecurity, that special insecurity of someone who had never known what it was to feel loved. I could think of other politicians like him, politicians of our own day, especially in Britain. 'But surely', I began, 'surely Tim McDermott came from a secure family background?'

Donal Williams looked very carefully at me.

I had been thinking of parents, of brothers and sisters. It was a notion which came naturally to a celibate like me. But my companion had someone else in mind.

'There was no peace in his background'. The words came almost like a growl. 'How could there be? The fact is that at the end of every day he had to go home to her'.

'You mean, to his wife?' my incredulous tone made him stop and turn towards me.

'Yes! His wife! That was one dead marriage. Let's face it. Bishops are not famous for their willingness to admit that such things happen. I suppose that to make such an admission would be to put a bit of a strain on the position they've taken on divorce. I don't know. I'm only speculating. But in any case Tim was stuck. For life. No break. Anyhow, in our business you can't afford a scandal. So there he was. Trapped. He rarely let the truth of it slip out. But it was there. He was caught, really caught. I tell you, Helen McDermott is one tough cookie and I honestly don't like her. And I especially don't like what she did to him. The poor unlucky bastard! She was the shadow. She was the sour edge in his life'.

We had reached the gate to my house. He declined my invitation to come in, but climbed into his limousine, which had been following us, and took off for Dublin.

After I had finished my evening meal I phoned her.

'Helen?'

'Yes'.

'I hope I'm not calling at an awkward moment'.

'No. Not in the least'.

'Good. I just wanted to find out if things are alright for you. That's a rather large and empty house'.

'Thank you. How very thoughtful of you. But, yes, I'm managing'.

'Are some of the neighbours rallying around?'

She laughed. 'I wouldn't be tempted to describe it that way'.

'Surely people are coming to see you?'

'The only visitor I've had in a week was an American. And that was because he had taken a wrong turn in his car and was lost'.

'But, Helen, I don't understand this. Why?' as I asked the question I was suddenly reminded of the opinions of her which I had recently heard.

'Oh, I suppose it's because people don't quite know what to say to a widow, so they look the other way and pretend not to see you at all'.

'But that's awful!'

'Perhaps. But that's how it is'.

The finality of her tone made it impossible to dwell on the matter. So, after a few more words and a promise to keep in touch, I said good-bye.

Any thoughts I might have had about her situation were quickly side-tracked both by a phone call which I received a few minutes later and by a series of events during the remainder of the evening. The call was from the religious affairs correspondent of one of the television stations. His name was Larry Jordan and I had met him many times in the previous couple of years. He was tall, and an impression of boyishness was strangely enhanced by an undisciplined moustache.

'Hello, Larry', I said as soon as I recognised his voice. Whenever we had been alone he called me 'Bish', but in company he was careful either to omit any reference to my title or else, in rarer circumstances, he would address me as 'My Lord'.

'Hello, Bish. I have to talk to you'.

'Fine. Go ahead'.

'First of all, the interview with you is going out to-night'.

'Oh? But I had understood it would be at the end of the month. At least, that's what was said to me by your colleague, Jim Powers, when we made the recording'.

'Yes, I know. But it has been brought forward'.

'Any particular reason? Though I don't suppose it actually makes any difference when it's transmitted'.

'In fact it does, and that's why I'm phoning'.

'Tell me about it'.

'Have you received any official word about your Honorary degree?'

'Of course I have. But that was nearly six months ago'.

The letter had been a wonderful surprise. It had been sent by the Rector of one of the best Catholic universities in Germany and it had invited me to accept an Honorary Doctorate in recognition of my published work, especially on the history of the Council of Chalcedon which had appeared just before I became bishop. The degree was to be awarded at ceremonies planned for the late autumn. I was unashamedly thrilled. Historians are not famous for their kindness to one another, and now to have a group of my professional peers decide to recognise my own work was an enormous pleasure, a validation of what I had been doing for many years. My reaction was not a mark of vanity, but of great relief. It seemed after all that the research and the writing had been judged worthwhile.

'Haven't you heard anything more recently from them?'

'No, Larry. But I wouldn't have expected to until we go a bit closer to the conferring'.

There was a pause.

'You're quite sure nothing has come from them?' The insistence of his question began to disturb me.

'Believe me Larry, nothing whatever. But what's this all about?'

Again, there was a pause, and I could sense an awkwardness in him.

'Look, Bish. I'll tell you what I've got. Something in the woodwork is stirring and I have a gut feeling that it doesn't look good for you. There are vibes going – and I'm not the only one getting them – that you're in some kind of trouble in Rome. I got a hint of it when I was preparing the ground for an interview with the Papal Nuncio here. I don't like that man, Bish. I don't like him at all. Anyhow what would you expect from someone who's just a glorified spy? After I had been with him, I phoned a pal of mine in Rome, a Dominican, who works for the Congregation of the Doctrine of the Faith, and he said "yes" that he'd been hearing things along the grapevine. You know how it is, Bish. They spend so much time contributing to and analysing their own rumour mills that you'd wonder where they get the time to work, not to mention saying their prayers'.

In spite of myself, I had to laugh.

'Yes, Larry, I know what you mean. But please go on with your story'.

'Well, my source said to me that a letter had gone out from the Congregation for Catholic Education – that's Cardinal Goldoni's bunch, as you know. The letter was to the Rector of the University and it was about your degree. It was written in the usual language. All about due prudence and the need for more prayerful reflection on the matter and trusting that the Rector of this most distinguished University could be relied upon to understand the delicacy of the matter and how personally painful it was for the Cardinal and blah blah'.

He stopped, drew breath and hustled on, as if concerned about his phone bill.

'Sorry, Bish, but that's how it is. And I called the University, and it seems that no honorary degrees will be awarded this autumn. So, I guess the Rector has looked over his shoulder and has seen the hounds of heaven on his trail'.

I was astounded. 'But', I spluttered, 'why? Is there something in one of my books that caused offence? I know the Council of Chalcedon is a thorny subject, but ... but ...'

'It's got nothing to do with the Council of Chalcedon, Bish. But my hunch is that it's got a great deal to do with you'.

I looked across my desk to the windows and to the fields beyond where the daylight was showing the first signs of fading.

'Larry, would it be possible for you indicate why your sources consider me to be in trouble?'

He grunted. 'Those Curia boys might be less inclined to get their long frocks in a twist if it weren't for the fact that there was a plan to groom you as next Archbishop of Dublin. That's over now. You're going to stay where you are, so I hope you like it over there in Dysart'.

'But you still haven't told me why'.

'Because the word getting to Rome is that you're showing more and more signs of breaking ranks. Of course I've heard about the row at the Bishop's meeting. And there's that speech you gave which was reported in all the papers, the one in which you said that the Church in Ireland had far too long been a church of occupation and not a listening Church'.

'What I actually said was that to some outsiders the Church might have seemed to be one of occupation and then, later, in an entirely different context I said that a great need nowadays was for the Church to be a listening Church. I think you'll agree, Larry, that's something different from what was reported'.

'Of course I agree. But qualifying clauses don't make good news'.

'I can see that', I replied sadly. 'So what you're saying is that I'm being reported to Rome on the basis of what's in the newspapers'.

'That's it. Though I would add that so far as I can see, the reporting is being done by a few of your colleagues in Christ'.

'Ah'.

'Sorry, Bish. I don't like to be the carrier of bad tales. But that's how things are. And I'm amazed you haven't heard about the degree. Because that's going to be the main evening news tonight and that's why your interview is being brought forward. Not only that. There's going to be a live panel discussion about it afterwards. So you'd better take the phone off the hook if you don't want to be plagued by reporters like me'.

After I had talked to him, I sat for a long time and stared at my bookshelves, though I saw nothing of them except a kind of blur in which there were lines and colours. My thoughts seemed to break into fragments and around my heart I could feel the beginnings of a bruise, an ache which would have turned to bitter tears in the times of my childhood. I had a sense of being alone and empty, a thing cast from the waters. I knew I ought to be angry and resentful, but I was too shocked, too drained, and I continued to sit there like someone stricken. Names rose up in me, perhaps because I am an historian and because I am trained to remember. I thought of men like me, who had called down upon themselves the displeasure of Rome. It was no help to say to oneself that disapproval in the Vatican meant only that particular servants, ecclesiastical servants, had chosen to be hostile for reasons that would vanish eventually, like the wind. I knew that cardinals and preferred monsignors could be as cold hearted and cruel as any street corner politician. But that knowledge was no balm to the hurt of being frowned upon.

It was not the doctorate which really mattered now. Anyhow, I have three of them already. No, it was the rejection of me, the awareness that colleagues had denounced me, that far away men at Roman desks had made decisions which affected me and which, perhaps, even the Pope himself had sanctioned, that a university president had bowed to them, and that not once in all of this had any face turned to me to seek my point of view or indeed to tell me what I had done or failed to do. On the main evening news I earned the third headline, after a drop in mortgage rates and an attack on the government by a trade union leader. Against a background picture of me in full canonical regalia there was the announcement of the cancellation of the degree.

Then came Jim Powers. He shared with Larry Jordan the responsibility for covering religious and social affairs. He repeated the news about the degree and proceeded to speculate on the reasons for it. There were the usual code terms, such as 'I understand' or 'informed sources have let it be known'. There were references to what was called my radical views and then came closing remarks to the effect that the decision regarding me would suggest that no grounds would exist for the widespread expectation that after the retirement of Dr. Raftery I would succeed him as Archbishop of Dublin. And, as in the past, the reporter managed to convey the impression that the authority of his speculations about me could be guaranteed by the fact that he had just been briefed by the Pope himself, if not by the Holy Spirit.

After the news and weather forecast the recorded interview with me was shown and it was followed by a discussion. The talk seemed vaporous. Three panellists answered questions put to them by a moderator, a journalist depressingly full of himself, and conjectures garbed as certainties were piled around me until I gradually emerged not so much for what I had said about altar girls but as someone likely to harbour scandalous views on the subject of women priests. And this despite the fact that I had never spoken publicly about the topic at all. By the end of the programme the fact of the cancellation of the degree together with the punditry regarding my innermost thoughts had produced a cocktail of emphatic assertions which could do nothing but damage my status as a church leader. This could serve only to confirm the opinion of men such as Archbishop O'Donnell that I was a dangerous outsider and, hence, that the Vatican decision concerning my honorary degree was surely the right one.

And then, by a ludicrous coincidence, I reappeared later that evening on television. Because my thoughts were so emphatically elsewhere I had forgotten to switch off the set and, suddenly, there I was again, but this time in a programme of quite a different kind, one so popular that it was transmitted within an hour after the news when, seemingly, most viewers were gazing at their screens. The essence of the programme was that hidden cameras recorded the language and the expressions of people caught in seemingly ridiculous circumstances.

At once I remembered the incident. Actually, even if I had suffered a lapse of memory the programme was there to remind me as the familiar scene unfolded. I had been in Dublin for several days in early July at a time of warm sunshine and of light caressing winds. I was at a conference and during a lunch break I had brought my second pair of trousers to a shop advertising itself as Marty's Super Cleaners.

Next day at about the same time I returned to collect the trousers and when I presented my ticket I was confronted by a man with thick horn-rimmed glasses and a goatee. He looked at the ticket.

'What's this for?'

'A pair of trousers. I left them in yesterday and was told I could collect them now'.

'Ah. Right. Trousers. You're sure of that?

'Certainly!' I was a bit surprised.

'What colour were they?'

'Black'.

'Oh. Black. Of course. A good colour, black. I like it myself. My grandfather used to wear black'.

He leaned across the counter. 'Tell me something, sir. Do you have any objections to any other colour? For trousers, I mean. We wouldn't be talking about shirts now, would we?'

He gave me a light tap on the shoulder and winked. 'Is it your experience, sir, that most people seem to get stuck in a rut when it comes to colour? I often think that's a great pity. It bothers me a lot'.

He shook his head, then straightened up.

'But I have a feeling about you. And let me say at once that I trust my instincts in such things. I haven't been wrong yet. Not that I know of, anyway. But I really have the feeling that you're someone who is more broad-minded. For instance in matters of colour. What do you think yourself? If you don't mind me asking, of course'.

I was getting increasingly baffled.

'Well, I'm sure that's an interesting question', I said, 'but I really am in a bit of a hurry. So if you wouldn't mind, I'd like just to collect my trousers'.

'Ah. Your trousers. Naturally. Well, let me just ask how would you react to these?'

From under the counter he produced three pairs of trousers. One was canary yellow, one an eye-assaulting red, and one a limp mauve.

'Just your size, sir, stylish, elegant and oh-so fashionable! And ...' he hastened to add as he saw my intention to interrupt, 'and two of these are absolutely free, compliments of the company. No charge. I mean it. Yours for the taking. Now what do you think of that?'

'Very generous, I'm sure. But really I would be quite content with the trousers which I left here to be cleaned and which I would very much like to collect right now'.

A depressed expression crossed his face.

'I was afraid you might say that, sir. You see, there is a reason for our offer of two of these beautiful trousers for yours'. The emphasis he put on the word 'beautiful' created an immediate implied contrast with my own trousers. 'We feel compelled to offer these to you in compensation for a most unfortunate happening with your trousers'.

'Oh?'

'Yes, I'm afraid so. You see, those over there are your trousers'. He pointed to a corner of the area behind him. 'But unfortunately they are not in their original condition. That is, the condition they were in yesterday'.

'What has happened to them?'

'Very distressing it is. We can't understand it, but I can assure you that we launched an immediate investigation into the matter and we are still working on it'.

'I'm sorry, but I don't think I have the remotest idea what you're talking about'.

'Of course not. But leaving aside the technicalities of the process leading to this most regrettable outcome the fact is that you can't wear these trousers again'.

'Oh? Why not?'

'I shouldn't say you can't wear them. I mean it's physically possible to do so, but I doubt that you'd want to. Because, you see, while one leg is as it was yesterday, though cleaned now and beautifully pressed, the other is only three quarters of its original length. And you wouldn't want to be seen that way, now would you?

'What you seem to be saying is that the trousers are ruined'.

'I wouldn't want to go that far. Not at all. Not completely ruined. But, I grant you, they're not what they were. If you wore them you'd be going around displaying an ankle and a shin, and I wonder what you would feel about that'.

I was overcome by the image and began to guffaw.

The man with the horn-rimmed glasses stared at me, and then a grin slid across his face.

'Ah, sir. I'm glad you did that. Because, you see, you're on television. Smile! You're on the Truthful Camera'.

There was laughter all around me. I was patted on the back. My hand was shaken. I was complimented. I was told I was a good sport.

Then someone took a closer look at me, and backed away.

'My God', he said, 'aren't you Dr. Mahon, the Bishop of Dysart? Oh God! I didn't recognise you!'

'Smile!' I answered. 'You're on The Forgiving Church!'

The irony of it was too much for me now, so I reached over to switch off the television set.

A few moments before the midnight news headlines which I had hoped to hear, I was phoned by the Cardinal. He made an elaborate apology for calling, he asked me how I was, and then came to the point. He wanted to assure me that he had not been responsible in any way for the cancellation of the honorary degree.

'Thank you for telling me that'.

'Not at all, Conor. And, again, I'm sorry to have intruded at such a late hour. Good-night to you and God bless you'.

'Good-night, Jim', I answered. The click of his phone was accompanied by the thought that I had heard no hint of sympathy or regret at what had happened to me.

I sat by my window and looked out, and because I knew well that it was pointless to search for sleep in bed, I decided to go for a walk. I put on my anorak and stepped out to my driveway. There was a full moon in a clear sky and the western horizon continued to hold its midnight glow. Although the air was still, there was the unmistakeable lilt of leaves in the trees beyond my boundary wall and when I passed under them on my way to the field and to the river below me I could see my way in the silvery light and there was no one to disturb me or compel me to be sociable. I walked slowly, feeling along my shoes the texture of abundant grass. From the woods beyond the river came the long tapering cry of a curlew, a cry which could have set up echoes within myself if I had yielded to it. But I was determined, however briefly, to hold before me only the moment such as it was and not to let my thoughts go tumbling into distress. The panorama of stars in a spacious sky helped me, as did the approaching sound of water rushing between the stolid faces of rocks and pebbles. I could detect the tall grasses on the riverbank and, somewhere beyond them, the pine branches shaped moonlight.

I came to where I could see and watch the falling waters. I let the sounds enter into me, filling me, taking me over, until at last it was time to move up the river to a point where I knew there would be utter silence in the gliding stream. I looked at the streaks of moonlight on the water and because a gust of grey rising loneliness had begun to take hold of me, I bent to reach for stones and had soon a handful. I tossed one into the air and listened to its plop as it vanished in the river. I threw another one and then another and then I searched around until my hands felt a rock which I lifted over my head and hurled from me. After the first splash there was the muted sound of its grinding arrival on fellow rocks beneath the stream, and for a long moment I stared after it, trying not to acknowledge the cold sorrow growing around my heart in a spreading emptiness. I threw more stones and would have continued to do so, had I not been overtaken by a feeling of being watched. I was startled, and it was only when I gazed carefully around me that I gradually became aware of a figure standing between the opposite bank and the woods.

'Hello!' I called, feeling a little foolish.

'Hello, Conor'. It was Helen McDermott and she moved closer to the river.

'You've caught me', I said. 'I have a secret vice. I throw stones in the river at moonlight'.

'Do you?'

'Will you join me?' I asked, with a bravado evoked by embarrassment and by the ambivalent nuance in her question.

'I'll meet you at the little bridge farther up', she called.

'Right!'

We walked parallel with one another and when we reached the bridge she was slightly ahead of me and came over to my side.

'Do you often walk at night?' I asked.

'Oh yes. It's safe to do so around here. That's one of the few nice things about this area. I imagine I'll miss it when I leave'.

'You're going away permanently?'

'Yes. There's nothing to keep me here'.

I looked past her to the black handrails of the bridge on which moonlight had settled.

'Have you decided when you're going to leave?'

'I can't put a date on it, I have to sell the house and in any case there's the mess resulting from my husband's will. Or rather, lack of it'.

'That must be a surprise. I mean, the fact that he made no will'.

She laughed.

'Not really. I think I've already told you that my husband was a very tight-fisted man with money. To let a penny go, even in death, would have been a cause of anguish'.

'So you have to get lawyers working and all that sort of thing?'

'Yes'.

'What a nuisance! I am sorry'.

'Oh, it'll sort itself out in due time. I'm not too worried about it. It's the house that'll be the real headache. It's going to be very hard to sell'.

'You think so?'

'Of course. Who's going to want to buy a fortress in which there's only the most primitive heating?'

I did not know how to answer that one. We drifted along a track, obvious in the moonlight and forming an edge to the field below my house.

'I was watching the television this evening', she remarked.

'Ah'.

'What's happening to you must be very hurtful'.

I did not immediately answer.

'The only honest thing to say is yes', I eventually murmured.

'Oddly enough, I've seen this sort of business before'.

'You have?'

'Not among bishops, of course. Don't misunderstand me. No. Among politicians. The details were different, naturally, but as I watched the programme this evening, I couldn't help thinking that the essential ingredients were plainly in sight as in the Ennis affair a couple of years ago. You remember Frank Ennis, don't you?'

'He was a government backbencher, lost his seat at the general election'.

'That's the one'.

'Yes, I remember him. He was involved in some sort of political row? It happened, I think, while I was on a long visit to the US. Something to do with a heave against the party leader'.

'That's right. It was really very simple. He had an independent mind and didn't waffle. He said what he believed and when the great leader, our man of destiny, was proving particularly incompetent, Frank Ennis put down a motion of no confidence. It was not the done thing to take on the boss in that way and so there was an outcry. For a few days before the vote there was plenty of media talk about the crisis. But the party minders did a good job. The rebellion was squelched, and Frank was frozen out for disloyalty to the party. The talk was smooth, self-righteous, and he was gone'.

I stopped and looked at the river again. Helen had moved along the path before she seemed to realise that I was no longer with her. When she turned back, half of her face was in moonlight.

'So you were reminded of all that?' I said.

'Yes, Conor'.

'Am I disloyal to the party?'

'My husband would say yes. After he counted heads'.

'And you?'

'Tim and I had very little in common in recent years', she said, and, as if to emphasise her point, she linked her arm with mine and nudged me back to the path.

We walked to where the river curved into the woods.

'Will you walk up to the house so that I can make you a cup of tea or pour you a drink?'

She laughed.

'What about your housekeeper? Won't she be hanging about the keyhole of her bedroom door to find out who the strange woman is that the bishop is bringing into his house after midnight?'

It was my turn to laugh.

'Mrs O'Connell doesn't live in the house. She works for me only in the mornings, so I think I'm safe'.

'In that case, thank you for the invitation, and I accept'.

We walked up through the field to the gate which led into my garden. The air was quiet, the moonlight spread around us, the countryside silent. For the first time in many hours I felt peaceful. I took her into my study and gave her the chair at my desk. It had arms, a high back and a headrest, and had been given to me by former students to mark my appointment as bishop. It was very comfortable and I rarely offered the use of it to anyone else.

'A cup of tea? A drink? I have some wine and some whiskey. What would you like?'

'Not a drink, thanks. Would a cup of tea be a bit of a nuisance?'

'Of course not. I'll plug in the kettle and I'll join you'.

I had a feeling that if I drank whiskey, I would begin to feel sorry for myself, and that was something which I wanted to avoid.

She must have sensed this, for when I came back into the study with a tray on which I had assembled a pot of tea, two mugs, sugar and milk, she made no reference to the television programmes. Yet I could not pretend nothing had happened.

'This is something of a coincidence isn't it? I get into trouble at the conference of bishops, and you show up at the cliff-side when I'd taken refuge. Today I'm big news for being a bad boy, and here you are!'

She smiled, but made no comment.

'But let's forget about me. You said something very sad a while ago, about yourself and your husband. I'm really sorry about that. To have to go through a dead marriage and then the murder ... I can see why you'd want to get away from this place. But where will you go? To Dublin? Out of the country?'

She put her mug of tea on to a coaster.

'I don't know, Conor, I haven't really decided. But there's nothing to keep me here. In fact I'm so unpopular I'd be better off gone'.

'Unpopular? Why do you say that?' I felt slightly hypocritical as I asked the question, for of course I remembered what others had said to me.

'Oh yes, Conor', she answered quietly. 'I have the reputation of being a cross between a child-eating ogre and a fallen woman'.

'What in the world have you done to deserve that kind of name?'

She got up and slowly walked around the study, looking at my books, at the icon which was on the back of the door, on my collection of strangely shaped stones.

'My husband was a very successful politician, wasn't he?' she never seemed willing to pronounce the name Tim.

'Yes. I'd have to say that. He certainly was'.

'Well, you might say I'm living proof of how effective he was'.

'I think you'll have to explain that one to me', I remarked, as gently as I could.

Again, she smiled, and for the first time since I had met her, I noticed the sad faintly down turned edges of her mouth. I wondered why I had not noticed this before, and I decided I must have been distracted by the dominance of her eyes.

'I was the mistake in his life, and he needed all his political wiles to disguise the fact. I think it's called a damage limitation exercise. And he was good at that. Oh, yes, he was very, very good'.

The absence of bitterness in the way she spoke reduced me to a kind of crouching alertness.

'Within six months of our wedding I knew that something had gone badly wrong'. She was not quite whispering. 'I couldn't make out what I had done or what I had said to turn him away. But when we were alone I had the inescapable feeling that so far as he was concerned I was the enemy. I told him so, begged him to talk, to tell me what was wrong, but his eyes went cold and he proclaimed I was ridiculous. He spent less and less time at home. Somehow I was a threat to him, and yet I couldn't make out why, couldn't get him to open up to me. It took me years to realise that he was a horribly insecure man, that love was, if anything, the biggest problem he had to deal with, that to be loved put him at some sort of disadvantage, put him in a position he couldn't control. I don't imagine that makes very much sense to you, after all your job is to preach love'.

The sardonic shrug of the shoulders was a way of signalling that she was not trying to score off me.

'I loved him, I gave him my best and he was afraid of me. That's how it was, Conor. And because he was afraid he had to put me at a disadvantage so as to master my presence. He was a subtle man and for a long time I didn't realise what he was doing. A hint here, an implication there, a tiny well-timed sigh. That was all it took. And gradually his family began to establish distance from me. Colleagues in the government became strictly polite, said hello or good-bye to him with increasing warmth while I looked on. Even Father McDonald, our parish priest, changed. He had been friendly at the beginning. My husband often talked to him, about parish projects, about ways to help needy people. After the assassination Father McDonald came to the house. Of course, there were others there. At one moment he started moralising and talking about my husband, remarking, as he looked over at me, that my husband had been so unlucky, making it obvious he wasn't thinking of the murder. So when I challenged him, later, he rounded on me and he snapped that my husband would have been a happy man if I had been a different sort of wife, someone who made a good home where he could have what he really wanted and needed in life. Then, with great self-righteousness, he stalked out'.

Remembering how Jack McDonald had talked to me about her, remembering too what others had said, I sat silent and faintly sick.

'I wanted to have a child, and my husband refused, and one day my sister-in-law started to yell at me that she couldn't understand why I was so cruel and selfish to deny her brother what he wanted most in all the world, a son or daughter to delight him. It was useless to hit back or to defend myself. He had anticipated everything, provided for every scenario, and there was no way in which he could look bad. Which for the politician is important. I thought of leaving him, but what kept me back was a kind of obstinacy – silly, I know – a feeling that by walking out I would confirm everything he had been hinting and suggesting. I suppose it couldn't have lasted. Who knows? But some sort of pride made me think of things in that way. I wasn't going to give him or the others the satisfaction of seeing me conform to the image they had spun of me. So I stayed. How long would I have held out? Who can say?'

She gripped her mug of tea, looked into it and then pushed it aside. 'I think I'd better go home', she said.

'I'll drive you back'.

'Would you?'

'Of course. Glad to'.

'Thanks, Conor'.

We both stood up.

'And as for what's happening to you, Conor ...' She shook her head. But I knew I had an ally.

V

Over the next few days the idea of escape began to grow. I needed to get into hiding, to have a holiday, to put myself beyond knowing looks or ambiguous silence. One morning as I entered the assembly hall of the cathedral where the priests of the diocese had gathered for a meeting, there was a sudden interruption of intense conversations and, later, during discussions I noticed colleagues who avoided my gaze or developed an urgent preoccupation with the shape of their fingernails. Of course I knew what prompted this, for in the aftermath of the cancellation of the Honorary Degree there had not been the usual fadeout of public interest. Letters to the editors of various newspapers had discussed my views, real or imagined. A student society in one of the universities had announced a decision to invite some prominent speaker to confront the question of the role of bishops in the modern world. In television programmes on religious affairs there was speculation regarding who might now be the next archbishop of Dublin, given that I was apparently in disgrace with the Vatican. At a funeral mass my sermon was listened to with an attention out of all proportion to the ideas I offered, and as I looked from the pulpit at the faces in the congregation, I could feel the readiness in some of them to be shocked by anything I might say.

I suppose it was all predictable, but what I had not expected was the impact of an article published about me in an English Catholic newspaper. The headline was blunt: 'How did he get through?' Voiced by an acerbic right-wing columnist, the question clearly rose out of the notion that my appointment was the result of a serious breakdown in the system whereby bishops are chosen. I was described in terms calculated to avoid a libel action but laying unmistakeable claim to the notion that I was soft on morality and a subverter of hallowed traditions. This would have become obvious if I had been properly scrutinised. That I was unfit to be a bishop was so evident to the writer that the only real question to be faced was how I had managed to escape detection. Someone was badly at fault and the culprit was proclaimed to be the archbishop Bevilacqua who, after a decade as Papal Nuncio in Ireland as the man charged above all others to advise the Pope in such matters, ought certainly to have realised the folly of even considering me for the job. It was incomprehensible that the archbishop could have made so grievous a mistake, and what would now be a source of continuing worry was the fact that the Nuncio himself was known to be in line for promotion to a position of great prestige where as a cardinal and as a senior diplomat he would exercise abundant and decisive influence. Within two days of the publication of this article, my name was again in print, and once more in an English newspaper. The religious affairs correspondent of *The Times* had travelled to Dublin to interview the Papal Nuncio, who made quick use of the opportunity to rebut the slur on his own competence. It was a scene easy to visualise; the insistence that the distinguished correspondent of *The Times* should have lunch, the excellence of the meal, the richness of the Italian wine, the discreet elegance of the room, and the hinted sadness underlying the roundabout and diplomatic language by which Bevilacqua sought to put distance between himself and me. Names were not crudely thrown about, of course, but the message was nonetheless clear. Something had happened between the time of scrutiny and now. The scrutiny itself had been thorough. All the exhaustive procedures had been followed. Advice had been sought at every level, and the clear verdict was that I should be appointed. But who could have anticipated what followed? Who could have foreseen the changes that would occur in me? And if something had gone wrong, it was not with the system of ecclesiastical appointment but rather with me.

Here was the nub of the message, delivered in a flood tide of disclaimers and subtle nuance. For the archbishop – described as 'Informed Sources' in the printed version of the interview – went on to claim that I was not the Conor Mahon he had known. I had been pulled down by some forces, some personal woe, some crisis within the spirit, and no system, however perfect, could be expected to foresee all the havoc that might be done by human frailty. It was truly lamentable, for I had been someone of great promise. But, unfortunately, that was how things stood, and as the points were made to the man from *The Times* there was doubtless a pained expression on that face above which the hat of a Cardinal would shortly find a well-prepared home. In short, I was isolated, and when I realised the fact I was reminded suddenly of what I had been told by Helen McDermott when she described to me the way in which her husband had turned so many against her.

I decided to phone her.

'So, Conor, they're really after you, aren't they?' It was as if she had been expecting my call.

'You would understand such things', I answered.

'Yes, I suppose you're right. Have you decided what you're going to do?'

'No. All this is rather new to me'.

'And yet you're a historian!'

'Sure! But even historians think of such things as happening to someone else'.

There was a tiny pause.

'Are you busy?' she asked.

'Now?'

'Yes'.

'I haven't anything on the agenda which can't wait'.

'Well, then, come over and I'll give you a glass of wine, and you can see some of my sculptures'.

'You collect sculpture?'

'No. I make it'.

'I didn't know you were an artist'.

'Well now, in spite of having us believe the contrary, there are lots of things which bishops don't know'.

'*Touché*! Anyhow, thanks for the invitation'.

'You'll come over?'

'Gladly'.

'Good. It might take your mind away for a while from that charming species, the human race'.

And so I walked across the fields to her house. She poured me a glass of wine and led me upstairs to a studio from which there was a panorama of woods and a river. Sunlight filled the room, and I became gradually aware of figures around me, on the floor, on tables, on a stand on the windowsill. I put my glass in a safe place and began to examine them.

Most of the figures were two or three feet high, and despite their differences of theme or texture there was about them a recurring aura or note which, at first, I could not quite grasp. Heads of stone or wood, full-length portrayals of women, a bird attempting to rise sideways into something hazardous, all of them tugged unmistakably at the edges of the heart and left me silent. I looked more closely. There was a head of a young woman, her hair and features flowing with vitality, but her eyes were focused on what was forever out of reach. An old woman looking to the sky seemed appalled by the emptiness between her open arms. The face of a girl contrasted pitifully with the grained experience of the wood from which she was emerging, and as I looked at her and at the realm to which she belonged I knew then what it was that united all these pieces of work spread around that studio. It was their sadness.

Helen McDermott stood quiet and withdrawn while I gazed at the sculpture. I could feel her stillness, especially when I squatted down to inspect a piece of bog oak on which two heads had been carved, each looking in opposite directions. One face was turned to the window, smiling towards the light, rising towards celebration. The other face was a duplicate of the first, except that now it was free of the wood which had enclosed it, but the lips were tight and the corners of the mouth drawn slightly down, and the eyes, full and open, were coping with shadows.

I stood up. 'They are wonderfully crafted', I said. 'Especially this last one here'.

'But ...?' She prompted me.

I was not quite sure what to add, because I knew so little about her and I was afraid that, against any intention of mine, I might hurt her. But she was looking directly at me, challenging me to be honest. 'There's such a chill descending on their way of being'.

She smiled from within herself, and, to my relief, I could see that she had taken my words for a compliment.

'Thank you, Conor. That's a reaction which gives me a ... sense of approval deeper than you could ever imagine'.

Then, as though anxious not to dwell on this moment, she reached for my glass of wine and handed it across to me.

'Have you ever exhibited any of these?'

'Oh yes', she answered. 'For several years. In this country, in London and in Italy. But since I was a kept wife, I didn't need to make money and I always arranged to put a "sold" tag on them. I just didn't want to part with them. They're me, and unless I get tired of them, which could happen, I'll not let them be scattered until it's time to scatter my own ashes'.

As if to emphasise her relationship with her work she sat on the floor amid the stone and the wood.

When I followed her example she looked startled.

'God, Conor, I'm sorry! I'm being thoughtless. Let me get you a chair'.

'For heaven's sake, there's no need. When I cease to be comfortable I'll stand up. So once again, cheers!' I lifted my wineglass.

'I'm glad you like my work', she said.

'I certainly do. And I must admit to a touch of envy'.

'You? Why?

'To have a talent to make, and to be able to say, as you certainly can, that something you did was a success ... Well, I'm glad for you'.

She leaned forward slightly, as though to have a clearer view of me.

'They're getting to you, aren't they?'

'Yes, I suppose so'.

'A pity you haven't a thick skin'.

'Like the one politicians are supposed to have?'

She shrugged. 'Will it blow over?' she asked.

'Well I imagine people will have other things to think about, eventually'.

She considered this, her eyes narrowing for an instant. 'Conor, what have you really done? I mean, all this is so ridiculously out of proportion. You make some remark about altar girls and before there's time even to blink, you've turned into the enemy at the gates'.

I felt a sudden weariness seeping into me.

'I don't know how I can answer that in any sensible way. So I made a remark about girls on the altar. Sometimes, as of course you know, a remark is enough to reveal a whole landscape in a person. In saying what I did, maybe I showed up things in myself, things I don't even know about or realise, but which scare my colleagues'.

'Such as?'

'How can I say?'

'Yes, you can! Yes, you can! Come on, Conor, you must have some idea at least of what it is that's turning them off. Maybe you don't want to tell me, and that's fine. But you must have some notion of what's going on'.

'I think I'm beginning to feel like her', I answered, pointing to one of the sculptures. It was an old woman whose stance was that of someone who had given up.

I got off the floor and walked about the room. 'My colleague in Cashel used words, which I think I reported to you. He said "You're not one of us", and I've been turning that around in my brain until in the end all I hear are syllables jumbling together like a bell out of control. I do what he does. I run my diocese as well as I can. I pray alone and I lead my congregation in prayer. I try to help those in any sort of need. I make myself available to everyone who might want my help. I work towards making the Church a living presence in the world and not just a hangover from a dead past. For twenty-four hours a day and not from nine-to-five my life is my work and my work is my life. When I relax it's with a book, and even then I'm trying to keep my horizons open. I have to fight off the temptation to subside quietly into complacency or self-satisfaction. And then he comes along, this colleague of mine, and cuts me out. "You're not one of us". And to judge from what's being said about me in the paper and elsewhere, there are lots of others who agree with him'.

She said nothing, but watched and waited, giving me the chance to find what words I needed. 'It could be, it just could be that His Grace, the archbishop of Cashel, might be right. Certainly, the cardinal thinks the same about me, but because he's a kind man he'll make excuses. He'll say it's just a temporary little difficulty, like catching the flu, and that I'll eventually get over it, and I'll take a hold of myself and become normal again. But Charles John O'Donnell is different. He stands back and he analyses people and he doesn't allow himself to be taken over by charitable thoughts, as the cardinal does. He's cold-eyed and he's very clever and it could be that he has figured out my scene a great deal more accurately than I have myself'. I did not mention the episode involving the young girl raped by her parish priest. 'We've been through all this before, you and I. You asked me that day we met on the cliff top whether I was one of them. Your question amazed me then, as if somehow it was absurd. So I dismissed it. But now ...'

I gazed at the dark underside of some clouds over the woods.

'And now?' she asked softly.

'Now I think I'm too disheartened to have any idea what I am. Apart from being tired. That's real. And I even have some low-lying urge to run away'.

'Well, you can't vanish into the mists', she answered. 'But you might think of a holiday. Why not? An escape. A rest. A chance to quieten the bell inside your head'.

'I can't just walk out. I've a lot of commitments ...'

'Re-schedule them', she said, interrupting me. 'You have a secretary, haven't you? Of course you have. Put him on the job and go away. After all, you are the boss of your diocese, so you don't need anyone's permission. Come on, Conor. Look after yourself for a while'.

I had to laugh.

'You're very persuasive!' I said.

'Good. So now the question is where you are to go. I think you should leave the country and travel to where nobody knows you. There you can be free and can let go for a while'.

Within the next half an hour she had talked me into making use of her phone to call a friend of mine in Genoa who had a villa on the island of Elba and who had urged me for years to stay there. When he heard my voice and my request, he answered in a crescendo of delight that the villa was empty and that the key would be available to me within a day.

'What more could you ask for?' Helen was smiling.

'Thank you'.

'For what?'

'For pushing me into it'.

As I left the house she called me back. 'Conor'.

'Yes'.

'An indiscreet question'.

'Oh?'

'Have you the money to get there?'

'I'm sure I must have'.

'That's not good enough. Have you or haven't you?'

I pondered a moment.

'Yes, I have', I replied, finally.

'If you haven't, I'll give it to you. So don't do something stupid like calling off this holiday just because you don't have the cash. Remember you need that break'.

I looked at her with amazed gratitude.

'Blessings on you', I said quietly and headed home.

VI

Next morning while my head was filling up with the prospect of going to Elba I had a call from my brother Tom. He wanted to know if he could come immediately to the house, and as soon as I said that I would wait for him he promised to arrive within half an hour.

He was a senior detective at that time but he was soon to move to the more lucrative world of a major security agency. He was eight years younger than I.

'Tom! Come in. Delighted you've come'. I could see he was putting on weight. His face, too, was slightly puffy, as if he were being shadowed by bad health.

'Conor. I'm glad I was able to catch you'.

'Coming from a detective that sounds serious'.

But he did not smile, and he followed me into my study where I pointed to a chair and offered to make him a cup of tea.

'Just had coffee, thanks'.

'So how's the family? Mary was on the phone to me the other day and she sounded good. I really wish we lived closer to each other. I'd love to see you more often, after all, you're the only family I've got. Ah well. But tell me, what's up?'

'I'm on the team investigating the McDermott killing'.

'Oh, I didn't realise that. A heart-breaking business. Just atrocious. Are you making progress?'

'I think so. Of course we've a lot to do and a long way to go. But it's shaping up. At least we've been able to establish that it was not a paramilitary operation, and that's a help to us. It makes it possible for us to concentrate. It's taking the look of being a contract killing'.

'My God! Who would want that? That's awful. It's hard to get the mind around the idea of going out to buy a murder in the same way you'd buy groceries. Do you ever get used to the thought that there are merchants of death plying their trade among us?'

'In my business you have to get used to it. You might be dead if you didn't'

He looked tired, and I could well imagine that since the killing there had not been much sleep for anyone at the centre of the investigations.

'There's something I want to ask you to do for me', he said, 'Could you spare me an hour or two this morning? I wouldn't ask if it weren't very important. I know you're busy, but ...'

'Of course, Tom. What can I do for you?'

'There's a thing here I'd like you to read'. He pulled a leather-covered notebook from his pocket and reached it over to me. 'It belonged to the minister. It was on the desk in the apartment he used in Dublin. As you'll see, it's hand-written but I don't think it'll cause you any difficulty. It seems to be a set of jottings he put down whenever the mood was on him. There are no dates. But there are a couple of political references in it which make me think that a lot of the things in those pages were written in the last twelve months or maybe a bit more. I'm not sure about this, and we'll have to examine it all more carefully'.

'But what do you want me to do?'

'He seems to have been a very well-read man, this McDermott. He was very energetic and he was also an insomniac. One of his secretaries told me that there was nobody in the government who could match him when it came to detail. He had a photographic memory and every document that passed over his desk he knew backwards. You could phone him at pretty much any hour of the night and you'd get him at his desk, always reading and writing. Did you know he wrote books?'

'McDermott? No. I hadn't realised that'.

'Yes. But not under his own name. He was careful not to appear too smart in case he put people off or made them uncomfortable in his presence. Especially his constituents. He wrote under the name of Robert Leonard. Have you heard that name?'

'Robert Leonard! The historian? Of course I've heard of him. In fact I have one of his books inside'.

'Well, if there's a dust-jacket on it you won't find his picture. And I'll bet there's no information about him either'.

'I'm really amazed to hear this ...'

'So you know about Robert Leonard, then. What kind of a reputation does he have?'

'Oh I couldn't claim to know anything much about that. I can tell you however that his book about British ambassadors in Ireland got plenty of praise. And his life of de Valera is a marvellous read. That's the one I've got inside'.

'Look, Conor. I have to be at the incident-room in the village station. There's a meeting. It shouldn't last more than an hour, and I'll come back here after it to collect the notebook'.

'Fine. But you still haven't told me why you want me to read it. Is there something you want me to look out for?'

'I'd rather wait until you've read through it before I ask you anything about it'.

He was getting up from his chair as he said this and I could see he was in a hurry.

After he had driven off in his car I returned to the study and picked up the notebook. It was loose-leaf and the entries varied from a full page to a couple of sentences. On one page there was only a few words followed by a series of dots, while on another there was a long quotation squeezed into reduced handwriting. However, I soon found that every word in the entire notebook was legible. Many of the pages had comments on current political matters. They tended to focus on the personal characteristics of people McDermott had met such as the British prime minister whose policies and public behaviour he explained in part by the fact of having been an unloved child. There was a reference to a well-known gossip columnist whom he described as a salaried peeping Tom. That same columnist must have annoyed him more than once, because there was another place in the notebooks where an imagined front page of a Sunday tabloid was laid out:

> Mystery Columnist located. The creature writing under the name of John Carey has been tracked to his lair by the *Sunday Clarion*. Reports from toilet indicated where he is to be found and we reveal to the world that everything is coming out in abundance.

There were quotations from books. Sometimes they stood alone. Occasionally they were followed by comments. One, which I recognised, caught my attention.

'Words, too, changed their accustomed meanings. What used to be referred to as a thoughtless act of aggression was now described as the courage one could expect to find in a party member. To speak of the future and wait was simply another way of saying one was a coward. To talk of moderation was to try to conceal one's unmanly nature'. The quotation was followed by his own comment. 'To say "I love you" was to be accused of hypocrisy'.

At intervals throughout the pages there were remarks of this kind, as if the notes on books or current events were interludes between the real drama which he wanted to record.

'Sometimes to write things down, using whatever words that come first, might be, should be the way to stop the racing of the mind as it tries to grapple with what keeps sliding away from it into near frantic surges of questioning. The fact is I've done my best. I have tried and tried to reach out. And I refuse, refuse, refuse to allow myself to be swept away on a tide of guilt and self-recrimination. I really have been doing my best, but that despising sneer comes into her eyes ...'

'The deadly silence in the house. I listen to my shoes on the floorboards. I rattle the teacup against the saucer and it makes a bit of company'.

'Why won't she ...?'

'I really thought it would work eventually, that there might be a small measure of sharing, a bit of peace between us. Fat chance!'

'She really and truly hates me'.

'It would be the worst ingratitude not to write this down. It was good, so wonderfully good. We sat in the garden talking about the exhibition and anyone listening to us would have been sure we were kindred spirits ... So why? ... No, no, stop. It was good, that half hour on the garden bench'.

'I so wish I could understand how to reach her ...'

The notebook ended with a strange remark 'In some circumstances Achilles would slaughter even Patroclus'.

I was re-reading these words when I heard Tom arriving at the front door. I went to let him in.

'Well? Have you had a chance to read the notebook?' He subsided into the chair opposite my desk.

'Yes. And I find it disturbing'.

Tom leaned forward.

'Why, Conor? Why do you find it disturbing?'

'I'm trying to visualise the situation. He is sitting in his office, and at some moments when he is not doing his political work he pulls out his notebook and jots things down. And of course he was a very stylish writer, so a lot of his comments on the people he's met are really interesting. It'd be nice even to be free to quote some of them. But then there's something about it all which makes me wonder if this is a commonplace notebook as such things are usually understood. I'm sure you know what I mean'.

But Tom remained silent and continued to watch me.

'I can understand jotting down things you want to remember, ideas, incidents, something you've read. But those comments about "her" and reaching out and the like ... They just don't quite fit, do they? It might be a lot easier to understand them if we knew who he was talking about, wouldn't it'.

'Mind if I smoke?'

'Of course not'.

I could see the lighting of a cigarette was a deliberate act, a way of getting time to think. He fumbled in his pockets for a lighter then examined the flame, breathed in deeply, coughed and then sat back.

'We can't say beyond all possible doubt who she is', he said slowly, 'but I think we can have a pretty good notion'.

I was not going to speak her name. So he did.

'It's got to be his wife. There isn't the slightest whisper of any other woman in his life. Somebody would have heard by now if there was. A prominent politician can't keep these things completely hidden for long. No it's got to be Mrs. McDermott'.

'So?'

'So, it ties in with other things we've been hearing about her. We're turning up a lot of bits and pieces, and they are beginning to fit together. She's not a nice woman. At best that's how it's beginning to look'.

'Is it the pattern of comments in the notebooks which are pushing you towards that view?'

'The notebook and what we've been hearing are coming together. But tell me, what did you make of the remark about Achilles and Patroclus?'

'Well, I don't need to remind you who Achilles and Patroclus were. And yet the reference'. I stopped. 'My God! Are you suggesting ... Are you considering the possibility that Helen ... that Mrs. McDermott is in some way involved in the murder? That she has something to do with it? That McDermott suspected he might be the victim of it?'

'We have to consider everything, Conor', he answered gently, and I could see that he had noted my use of her first name.

'But'. I stared at him.

'Such things happen, Conor. Maybe not in this case. But I'm sure you'll see that in view of what's in the notebook we have to take aboard such a possibility'.

'You mean that since she obviously didn't pull the trigger herself she hired someone to do it?'

'You can rent a killer for as little as three hundred euro'. His voice was blunt now. But another thought came to me.

'So why have you brought this notebook to me? Because I can see now that you weren't really looking to me to help you with it'.

He sighed, and he seemed to grow visibly older in the chair. We had always had a good relationship. But we were not close, probably because I had left home for the seminary before he was a teenager. There had been years when our only contact was the occasional phone conversation or the exchange of Christmas cards. This was especially the case during my time as a student in Rome. He had come to my ordination as a priest and,

113

later he had joined me in the cathedral for my consecration as bishop of Dysart. And of course, when he got married it was I who performed the ceremony. Certainly there was ongoing affection there between us. But that was as much as circumstances permitted.

'Conor' he said, at last. 'I have a worry about you and it has to do with Mrs McDermott'.

My lack of astonishment seemed to galvanise him, because he abandoned the slouched posture in the chair, sat up straight and put his hands on the edge of my desk.

'Since the murder you've been over to her house twice and she has been here once. Now I'm absolutely sure that all this has had to do with your wish to be helpful to her. After all she has just been widowed in a bloody way and because of the kind of man you are – and in any case because you're a priest – you would naturally want to do what you can for her'.

'But ...?'

'But you need to be careful here ...'

'How do you know I've been twice to her house and she once here?'

'Because we have a twenty-four hour watch on her house. There are a few reasons for this. One is her security. Until we know why her husband was killed we have to think of the possibility that she too may be at risk. But at the same time we need to keep an eye on her in case she had a hand in it. When we can eliminate her from our inquiries we'll drop the surveillance. But we're not ready for that yet, especially because of the stories we're hearing about her. And of course there's the notebook. That bothers us a lot and I'm sure you can see why'.

'Yes, Tom. Of course I can see that. But it's a bit of a shock, this way of looking at things'.

He stood up.

'I've got to be off. I have to return the notebook to the incident room and then go to headquarters'.

'Thanks, Tom. I appreciate what you've been doing for me this morning'. We shook hands at the door.

'Mind yourself, Conor. Please mind yourself'. And he was gone.

Over the next few days the conversation with Tom began to haunt me. I thought again and again of my encounters with Helen McDermott. I revisited the details of what she had said to me. I tried to recapture the tone of her voice, the expressions on her face as she had described her relationship with her dead husband. It had all been so convincing. I had sensed pain and bewilderment and had reacted with sympathy.

Clearly she could call upon a bundle of talents, but this very fact began to dissolve into ambiguities as I thought of them. If Tom had asked me to characterise her I am sure I would have spoken of her intelligence, her irony, her creativity, her articulate ways. I would have described them as admirable virtues. But a question mark hung over them now. I began to wonder about the extent to which they had been used to impress a particular image of herself on my mind. The idea chilled me, and at the same time I felt guilty for allowing such a notion to come into me from the sidelines.

After all she had shown such kindness to me, such attentiveness when she became aware of my own difficulties with colleagues. I remembered that I had come to consider her an ally, that she had even offered to give me the money to go away on a holiday.

How could I have been so wrong about her? Actually, was I wrong? Could it be that Tom and the others were all moving to draw mistaken conclusions? But then there was the notebook with its bitter outcry against her.

I simply could not deal with it. Tiredness began to fester within me. I kept waking up in the night. In fact I was becoming obsessive over the whole matter. Or, to be more precise, the question mark over Helen McDermott seemed to draw strength from other unacknowledged issues. For if I had really been misled in my appraisal of her how much else was I wrong about? Were my colleagues on to something about me which I myself could not see? The questions proliferated madly and gave me no rest. I tried to defuse their power by facing them one by one. But there was no help there because seeping through them all was a common fog, fattening self-doubt and uncertainty. I prayed. I brooded. One night I set out for a long walk under a half-moon but as I crossed the fields beside my house I was suddenly reminded of what Tom had said about surveillance. Was I alone now? I imagined a detective watching me from behind a low bush and making a note of the fact that I was obviously not attempting to make contact with the suspect.

'Enough', I whispered 'Enough. Time to clear out'.

VII

And I did. Two days later. After a hasty conclusion of urgent business I left my secretary as a kind of rampart in front of my empty desk. I could rely on him to know what to do and what to say when the usual calls and requests came in. Only he had the phone number of the villa in Elba where I was planning to stay.

'Enjoy your rest', he said at the entrance to the departure hall at Dublin airport, and it was clear that behind his words lay the generous hope that I would find a way to face down what was happening to me.

It was a Saturday and I flew to Rome with the intention of catching a train from the city to the port opposite Elba. But I arrived to discover that there was a three day public transport strike and it would be Monday at the earliest before I got to the villa.

On my previous visits to Rome I had stayed in a convent near the Vatican. But this time I wanted to disappear into some obscure place where I could be sure of anonymity. I had my mass-kit with me, so I would have no need to present myself at some church. I found a cheap room, settled early into my bed and promptly began to dream of calls from dimly-lit phone boxes reporting my presence to someone in the Vatican bureaucracy who was in charge of the special file set aside for the recalcitrant and the unreliable.

A church bell outside my window pounded me awake at six-o-clock, but I lay under the covers for a long time. The morning light showed my room to have pink wall-paper on which there was a design so faded that I could make no sense of it. There was one framed photograph above the bed. It showed two boxers in a ring. One of them was on the ropes, his gloved fists lifted more in supplication than defence. He looked faded, his shorts a wan red, his face raised to accept a conclusive battering from his opponent.

I rolled over and tried to sleep some more, but after about half an hour I gave up and made my way to the shower. Later, having set out my kit on the beside table I said mass, tried to meditate for a while but found my thoughts wandering back over recent events and returning especially to the compassionate expression on the face of Helen McDermott when I had told her of the atmosphere which had reared up between me and my fellow bishops. The possibility that I might be completely mistaken about her seemed to acquire strength and substance, and as I tried to understand why this was so the thought flitted into my mind that perhaps at some deep level within me the question mark over her included the ideas, the attitudes and the habits, and indeed everything which shaped my own life as a bishop.

To escape from all this line of thinking I left my room and went out into the streets of the city. A late spring had just arrived. The cherry trees had blossomed. The new leaves on the trees were still fresh, unaffected yet by the complexity of life in the streets. The sky was blue and the sun was not yet too warm.

After a cup of tea in a sidewalk café I headed for the open spaces of the Villa Borghese, read some newspapers, watched the strollers, and the joggers and the cyclists. I began to relax. Later in the afternoon I drifted towards a crowd on the piazza beside the vast palace. There was a good-humoured and expectant atmosphere while control barriers were set up by uniformed soldiers. A police captain watched them as he walked past with nonchalant chic. Two high black horses came into view, their manes and tails stylishly groomed, their riders cloaked, gold-helmeted and clearly conscious of the impression they were making. Children were hoisted in to parental shoulders. A short fat woman beside me manoeuvred past a man who was blocking her view. A mobile phone rang and there was an immediate projection of a voice into imagined distance between it and the caller. A helicopter briefly hovered above the crowd but moved on quickly because, someone claimed, the wife of the president of the republic did not want her afternoon siesta to be disturbed. There was immediate disagreement with this theory. Others asserted that the lady would know there would soon be a half-hour of music from a military band. In any case this could be heard even now as it made its way up a slope before coming into view in front of the palace.

There was a stamping of feet and a shouting of orders as the soldiers were choreographed around the piazza, the broad red stripes on their uniforms flaring, their faces serious. But when one of them turned right instead of left there was sympathetic laughter in the audience. Yet officers and men could be in no doubt of the approval flowing towards them.

As the voices of soldiers and spectators mingled finally in the singing of their national anthem I gazed at the huge façade of the palace, at the rows of mostly shuttered windows, at the candle-shaped lights ready for the hours of darkness, at the balcony where a fan of flagpoles thrust into the air, at the intimation of corridors and ornate rooms behind the painted walls. And as I tried to visualise courtiers ancient or modern in a building such as this I had a sudden unaccustomed feeling, and the only way I could think of it at first was to picture myself as a dying flower stretching its neck towards the light in the last hours before falling apart. Within me grew the alarm of someone, sharply awake, from whom everything was moving away in an act of deliberate withdrawal. In an effort to deal with this I began to focus intently, almost desperately, on the countless figures who must have crossed and re-crossed the tiled or parquet floors of this palace, interacting with one another, each with a different agenda, many of them walking and talking with a demeanour customary for an elite, others hurrying to perform the tasks which would earn them something towards keeping body and family nourished and surviving. The more graspingly I tried to imagine them the more they seemed to rebuff me and to deny me any knowledge of what they truly were. And beyond those walls, stretching towards the river and the Vatican was the thrust or huddle of roofs, sheltering for better or worse the rise or slippage of other lives. So much happening, so many elusive privacies, so much in the past, and I alone, hemmed in by the few tangibles on the piazza, the passport in my pocket declaring who I was, the memory within me bulging with what I had experienced, loneliness in head and heart rending me and beating into me the ungentle awareness of how little I was and how very little I knew of the being of the world.

I felt drained and frightened on those sunnied cobbles and I realised I had to go at once in search of some distraction, of a means to break out from these enfolding sensations. And the urgency grew with the reminder of the face, and especially the eyes, of Charles John O'Donnell, hissing and spitting the words 'you are not one of us'.

I left the crowd behind me and hurried as if I had important business to transact. But as I moved I had the raw emotion of being left behind by the streets themselves as they stretched in front of me or else moved aside into networks of other byways.

'What's happening? What's happening to me?' I mouthed the questions as I tried to cope with feelings which were entirely new to me. I wondered if this was what was called a panic attack, though what such words could actually mean seemed to escape me. All I knew was that I was deeply uneasy though I could not say why.

I passed an immense sign which announced an exhibition of impressionist paintings. I could see a queue of people waiting to get in, and I decided to join them. Here at least I would be doing something familiar, and before long I was inside the building. Gazing at them, allowing myself to be taken over by them I began to feel an emerging calm, and when I noticed a very large painting by Monet I went over to stand before it and to immerse myself in it as completely as I could. There were only two or three people in the room, so that I could admire the work undistracted.

The painting was a mass of lush blues, yellows and greens giving life to a scene which included water, an embankment, trees and the opulent presence of early summer. There was an assault of massed colour until I realised I was standing too close to it all. I stepped back, and the effect was like bringing the blur of binoculars into a clearer view. I could now see the trees as they were and as the water reflected them. The embankment served to divide the canvas roughly into an upper and lower half. Buds, blades of grass, leaves and blossoms gave up their details to the scrutinising eye. The atmosphere was vibrant and tranquil, and for many minutes I was received by it and felt grateful.

At last I moved away. As I was drifting out of the room I gave a final backward glance at the painting and was startled by what confronted me. From where I was standing I could see that the view had shifted. The pond was now clearly a curving river. The bank was no longer a more or less horizontal line bisecting the view but rose from left to right like the sign of growing success on a sales chart. The clear outline of a woman emerged in the foreground. I had not seen her when I had been directly in front of this painting, but there she was now, her back turned, her gaze encompassing what her vantage point allowed her.

At other times I would not have been troubled but the effects of shifting perspectives of the same picture bothered me fiercely and they called up once again the sense of deep vulnerability which had swept over me on the piazza. And as I left the gallery and as I tried to imagine why I was a prey to these anxieties, so new to me, I travelled slowly to the realisation that mind set and life-long convictions were coming unstuck and that all this had a profound bearing on my job. After all I was someone theoretically at one with realms beyond the ordinary and I was licensed to give instruction and leadership to those entrusted to us by the church to which we belonged. My trouble now was the consuming awareness of how few knowable things had made a rendezvous with me.

VIII

The transport strike ended at two-fifteen on Monday. When I asked why that moment rather than some other I was answered by an elaborate shrug of eloquent shoulders and a hand raised to forehead level in what looked like a palsied salute.

But at least I could get out of Rome, and after a couple of train journeys north I joined the last ferry of the day to Elba. Working to push aside the memories of recent times I stood at the rail and watched the dark blue shadows on those rocky island faces which had been deserted by the setting sun.

I was one of perhaps a dozen passengers who walked ashore on the pier at Rio Marina. We were followed by a couple of cars and a min-bus. Night was rapidly coming down and I could see the lights in the high facades of apartment homes and in the restaurants along the shore. The open boats of fishermen had been drawn up on to the sand beside the point where the pier joined the town. Two young men on motor scooters were racing each other.

Strollers paused to watch the ferry. An elderly man, standing by one of the black iron bollards to which rope hawsers were attached, smoked his pipe and observed the passengers who were now beginning to leave.

From behind me came a deep gravely voice.

'Doctor Mahon?'

'Yes', I said, and I turned to look upon a plump figure in a blue suit.

'You are welcome to *isola d'Elba*. I am Alberto. I have a car and a key. I take you to your villa. It is all arranged. Come'.

He took my suitcase and led the way to a black Fiat.

In less than five minutes we had reached the villa after a climb up a steep pot-holed road overlooking the sea. Alberto said nothing during the drive and he peered out over the wheel with an expression that suggested an expectation of imminent crisis beyond the next corner. But when we reached our destination he relaxed, smiled and with a kind of old-world deference, carried my bag to the tall wrought-iron gate. From where we moved under a vine trellis towards a door, and, a moment later, with the lights on around me, I caught sight of a kitchen.

'There are two bedrooms', Alberto said. 'I think you should use the big one. The view of the sea is magnificent'. He uttered the last word with a hint of awe and, satisfied that he must have convinced me, he went towards it with my bag.

Five minutes later he was gone. Opening cupboards, doors and drawers, switching taps on and off in the sinks, pointing out coats, hats, even sunglasses in a closet, he had shown me where to find anything I could possibly need. Then shaking my hand he had bidden me goodnight, walked out the front door and, after an instant, he had reappeared.

'In the morning if you wish I come. In the night if you need anything you telephone'. And, once again, he was gone, leaving in his wake a sudden deep silence.

I had eaten nothing since the middle of the day, and I realised now that I was quite hungry. I had forgotten to ask Alberto about food, and with a sense that I might have to go to bed fasting I turned into the kitchen. Of course I knew that to fast was supposed to be good for my soul. Nevertheless, I felt a surge of relief when I discovered that supplies had been laid on for me. On the kitchen table there was fresh bread, a bottle of red wine, cheese, prosciutto, olives, tomatoes and fruit. There were written instructions about making coffee and tea, and in the refrigerator I found meat and fish. I poured a glass of wine, unscrewed the olive jar, and broke some bread, opened the window and shutters and gazed out into the night. Along the top of a dark mass of hillside rising before me there was a line of six, perhaps seven, pine trees standing alone against the sky under a brilliant moon.

I watched them for a long time, my mind circling around their untamed and unpacked shapes. There was a mysterious comfort in the assertiveness of their presence on that hilltop. Nothing was expected of them. They stood with the sky for a backdrop. They were. And that was enough. As I looked at them, at their independence, at their freedom to be nothing other than what they were under the moonlight, I could feel an ache spreading around my heart, a sense of inadequacy and rejection which I knew I must keep from getting out of hand. So I finished my meal, went to my room, unpacked as much as I needed and was soon deeply asleep in a bed which was wide enough to hold at least three very fat people.

When I began to stir again there was a grey light outside my window and a stillness broken only by the first waking birds. I listened to these, got out of bed and had a sight of the sea on which the sunlight had yet to appear. Trees and bushes sloped away below me. I could make out a zigzag path and, having pulled on some clothes, I stepped out the window, which I then pushed over to give the impression of being shut, and I made my way down. I could hear a cuckoo somewhere. There was dry grass on the path, and within five minutes I had reached a point where the land parted into fangs of rock. Tiny waves confronted my shoes.

On the headland to my right there was a house, brown and turreted, surrounded by trees. It was distant, and was the only sign of human presence. From where I stood all else was sea and shore, and I began to feel my six feet two presence as some kind of intrusion here. Although not a swimmer I took off my clothes, leaving only my underpants for decency, and I stepped into the water following descending shelves of rock until I was able at last to sit with only my head and neck rising above the Mediterranean. I remained that way until a hazy sun slid over the horizon. I looked at the almost imperceptible stir of the sea. I thought of fish and crabs and octopus. I imagined the elegant curve of a dolphin, the sunlight glimpsed on its back before it nosed into the depths. And behind me there was still the occasional voice of the cuckoo.

I sat there, head and neck above the water. 'Good morning, world!' I said loudly, but with a sense of something missing. Then more loudly I intoned, 'Charles John O'Donnell, Archbishop of Cashel, bugger off!'

Feeling content now, I climbed back up to where I had left my clothes. Slowly I made my way back up the hill, and by the time I reached the villa I was mildly out of breath. I opened all the windows, brewed coffee and, as I looked out towards the sea, I realised that a set of steps outside led up to the roof. Taking a bread roll and my mug of coffee I went to investigate and within moments I was sitting in a comfortable chair in the shadow of a tall scotch pine. Behind me and also on my right were other villas, most of them higher up on the slopes of the hill and surrounded by a profusion of flowers and greenery. All were pointed towards the wide arc of the waters on which the sunlight was spreading. As I watched I went suddenly asleep. It was almost noon before I became conscious of where I was. The sun on my face had awakened me and as I blinked in the strong light I felt my bones to be stiff and creaky. I stood up, astonished that I had slept so long, and yet I did not feel refreshed. It was as if I had managed to have only the first instalment on a long accumulated need to rest.

I was so drowsy and sluggish that after a lunch of bread, fruit and tea I stretched out on my bed and I might well have slept until the following day if the phone had not started to ring. It was Alberto. 'The shops in the town have reopened after the siesta. They remain open until eight o'clock if you need something. If you cannot get, tell me. I come. Thank you very much'. And he hung up. The only way to keep from sliding back into sleep was to go for a walk. To shock my system I took a towel soaked in cold water and held it on my neck for a minute. Then, leaving the villa, I strolled along the sloping route towards the harbour and the surrounding town. The sea was on my right, mostly greenish blue but as I came in sight of the red-bricked clock tower on the edge of the town I could glimpse a thin tell-tale line of paper and grey rubbish travelling on the water about half a mile from the shore. It was as if the resplendent colour of the late afternoon required a blemish.

Below the inner end of one of the harbour walls there was a small beach, more pebble than sand, occupied by a few women and children. They were mostly quiet, these last sun worshippers of the day. Some were lying down. Others were staring across the scene. Two children played at the edge of the water. A golden retriever barked and wagged his tail.

Reaching the start of the harbour wall I thought first of walking to the end but settled instead for a point where I could sit and see everything, the water, the light turning bronze from the western sun, the fishing boats returning to shore, the town, and the strollers. I was very tired, more weary than I had been for years, but I began suddenly to realise that in this I was not alone.

A little away from me, sitting on the wall with legs dangling over the edge, there was an old man, he was bare-headed and was wearing dark slacks and a sweat shirt. His hands were on the edge of the wall and, somehow, they looked as if they were keeping him upright, for along the curve of his back there was an unmistakeable aura of exhaustion. He was looking towards the people on the beach but I felt sure he did not see them. His entire attention appeared to be concentrated on the task of not toppling over.

I wondered if I should offer him some help or encouragement, and, as if sensing my thoughts, he turned his face slowly towards me. His eyes were very dark below a deeply lined forehead. Then, like someone who has made a resolve to pull himself together but to do so in an elaborately casual way, he straightened up, swung sideways, stood and then walked away towards the town. I watched him until he had gone from view, and my own fatigue was now in abeyance and I had a feeling, like the onset of hunger, that I had missed some kind of opportunity, though what it might be I could not have said.

During the rest of the day my mind strayed back to him and I wondered where he was and what was happening to him. In fact I saw him again on the following evening when I went for a meal in a restaurant beside the harbour. I had spent most of the day at the villa and such was the fatigue within me that I passed the hours in a state close to hibernation. I had experienced nothing like this since the aftermath of my final exams at university, and it was only when another afternoon was about to slip away that at last I bestirred myself and left my vantage point on the roof from which, half dozing, I had watched the small fishing boats immersed far out in the gentle movements of the sparkling sea.

I decided to walk into town. I would buy a paper, have coffee, return to the villa for a shower and then go out again, this time for dinner. It sounded purposeful and I thought it might shake me up. But there were no papers and I ended up in a mineralogical museum filled with specimens from around the island. They lay in their cases, inert and catalogued, and exquisitely coloured. I gazed at them in astonishment and allowed myself to be taken over by their presence and by the sheer vibrancy called out by the passage of light across them. And I was so moved by them that, as I walked back to the villa, there seemed to be a sharper, more emphatic quality of being in everything around me, in the flowers, in a pine tree overlooking azure water, in the painted housefronts, in the young woman on a flat rock looking like a goddess enclosed in unapproachable privacy. By the time I had reached the villa I felt a resurgence of life within me and when, later on, I set out for my evening meal it was with a sense of anticipation and pleasure.

When I reached the waterfront I had a choice of at least half a dozen restaurants, their white cloths on tables that reached from under awnings to the edge of the road on which the sea wall was a low margin. In each restaurant there was at least one waiter who composed himself to convey the image of someone who had been especially on the watch for me. There was a smile, a hand pointed towards a table, a few words designed to establish whether I spoke English or German. Two of the restaurants had obtrusive music and so, like some elderly grouch, I settled for a table where only voices could mainly be heard. I ordered spaghetti, seafood and white wine and I sat back to watch the passage of the evening on people and on the sea. Directly in front of me was a familiar sight, the long pole, the comfortable fold-up chair, the cast of a line, the atmosphere of unperturbed time. What was unexpected, however, was the fact that the fishing here was done by an old and regal lady.

At last and with a flourish a plate of spaghetti was brought to me, and when I reached for a spoon my red napkin was caught in a sudden eddy of wind and blown over to the next table.

'Oh, I'm sorry!' I exclaimed.

'Not at all. Don't mention it'. The words were spoken by a man whom I instantly recognised. He was the weary figure of yesterday on the harbour wall. But now he was in a grey jacket and tie instead of a sweatshirt and he was waiting quietly to be served, a glass of red wine in front of him, a bread roll broken up on a dish beside him. He had handed me the napkin.

Since the meals we had ordered were now before us, we said no more. But when the coffee arrived I felt a wish not to lose contact with him.

'Are you on holiday?' I asked.

'Yes. My first holiday since I was a boy', he answered, and because his tone did not suggest he was merely being polite I decided to extend the chat. And so I learned that he was a Czech, that he had arrived four days before me, had taken a room in a hotel and, as in my case, had spent the time either resting or strolling.

He spoke quietly, the heavy lines on his face rising and reforming as he talked. His gestures were also subdued and I noticed that the index finger on his left hand had a slight but permanent inward curve.

We both finished at the same time paid our bills and as we left the restaurant, I invited him to join me in an after-dinner walk. He seemed glad, and having gone through the town we pointed again towards the harbour and headed to the end of the pier.

'You say it's your first holiday since you were a boy?'

'Yes', he answered. 'It is a gift from my son. My wife would not travel with me, but my son insisted I had to have a change'.

The accent was heavy but the English clear.

'It has been a bad time for me, and my son who makes films is very good to me, he said I must come here'.

'Are you glad that you did?' I was thinking of my first sight of him, of the weary eyes and of the body that wished to slump.

'My son will be pleased, and that is enough'.

'But you say it's a bad time for you?'

He looked up at the sky which had grown dark.

'You are from Ireland?'

'Yes'.

'Then probably you are a Catholic'.

'I am'.

He nodded, and then sighed.

'Perhaps therefore you might understand', he said. 'I too am a Catholic. And I am a priest'.

I suppressed my astonishment. Nor did I seek to reconcile his words with what he had declared earlier regarding his wife and son. I also sensed that our conversation might end abruptly if I were to admit that I was a bishop.

'Yes, I am a priest', he repeated. 'And in the opinion of some I am a disgrace'.

'Why is that?'

We had stopped and, as though by agreement, we sat on a bench. Directly in front of us were the waters of the harbour, fringed by the boats drawn up for the night, by the restaurant and, behind these, by the apartment buildings from whose lighted windows came the muted sounds of talk and television sets.

'I am seventy-five years old', he said. 'When I was a young man I wanted only one thing, to be a priest. At that time my country had been taken over by the communists and we were a satellite of Moscow. We were all poor, and there was a rule of terror. People spoke only to those they trusted, and often it was to discover that a supposed friend or even a younger brother might betray you to the police. All they had to say was that you were an enemy of the people. They came for you in the night, and you would only be seen years later. Or not at all. Oh, it was so terrible that there are no words for it'.

He paused, and as I looked at him I could have sworn that he was ageing visibly.

'I know that countless people who have gone through such times prefer never to speak of them', I began. 'Perhaps you'.

'No. I tell you. I come from a very religious

background, and so it was not strange that I should want to be a priest. Especially when the Church was being so terribly persecuted. Not that I wanted to be a martyr. No! I have always been too cowardly for that. I don't remember a time in those days when I was not afraid. I hated myself for it but I couldn't help stop it. But I told my bishop what I wanted, and for two years, on and off, he trained me. He trained others. But the others and myself never met. In case one of us was arrested and tortured into betraying comrades. Only the bishop knew how many of us there were. Six months after he ordained me he was found in a canal, his hands tied behind his back with wire, his body battered. A few weeks earlier he told me to keep the flame alive, no matter what happened. Ah, he was good and brave, a true saint'.

My companion's eyes filled with tears.

'He said to me, my bishop, that no matter what weakness I fell into, there is a God to forgive me and a God to beg me not to forget him or the people who need him'.

My companion paused only long enough to gaze at the shimmer of light on the waters of the harbour.

'So I tried to be faithful to those people', he said. 'I got a job in a factory. I had to work because I had to eat. Anyway if I didn't work I would have been arrested for being a parasite on the economy. That was the way they talked. A parasite. But, of course, through my work I made contacts. I got to know people who needed a priest, who wanted him to pray with them, to help them, to be there to give a blessing when someone was dying, to the baptise their new-born. I offered Mass in the strangest places, in a coal-store, inside a goods wagon on a railway siding, in a garden shed. Sometimes for communion I had to use old stale crusts of bread. And so often there was the smell of fear, and the smell of those who were taking great risks to come and be with me. And it went on for weeks and months and years, and usually at nights. Often after my work in the factory I would slip away to meet some of my parishioners. Winter was always safer because the nights were long and cold and the rain made it easier to get around. I was like a mouse in the undergrowth, darting in terror from place to place'.

He shook his head. 'Only for Lisa I would have died of fright. We lived together, she and I and we had children, and she gave me the strength to continue the work of the Church. My parishioners knew about us. But they understood. Oh, how well, they understood! They did not point the finger at me. No. They came looking for my blessing and my prayers. They sent for me when they needed confession. They put their arms around me to thank me when I buried the ones they loved'.

'Then why did you say a moment ago that you were in disgrace?' I asked.

'I'm not in disgrace with them', he answered quickly. 'No. Not with them. Never with them'. He went silent. At first I assumed he was deep in thought. But I understood suddenly what was happening. He was trying to control his grief. 'I'm not an important man', he murmured. 'I am too weak to be anybody special. But at least in the bad days I never refused the people who needed me. I risked my life to bring the consolation of God to them. I never gave up on them. Never! But now I'm an embarrassment to the Church'.

'An embarrassment! But this is ridiculous!' I exclaimed.

'The new bishop has called me in to tell me I can't be a priest anymore. I can't say mass. I can't hear confessions. As a grudging favour I can do the work of a deacon. But no more. Because I won't give up my Lisa. I am giving scandal. That's what he says. Oh, I don't blame him. He is only doing what Rome tells him. He's a good ecclesiastical bureaucrat and he obeys his masters. And Rome says that people like me are a scandal. They want me out of sight, so they can talk comfortably about the rules. Always the rules'.

He became silent again, and I began to wonder if perhaps he might have finished what he wanted to say. But he stirred suddenly. 'One of the hopes I had during the bad days was that a time would come when the Church could be open and free again. I imagined meeting my fellow priests instead of having no colleagues to talk to. I imagined the sort of things I could learn from them. I thought that because of my own experiences I might even be useful to them. What a dream that was! Not to be alone any more. But it was not to be. Because I am a scandal. I still want to do God's work. But I won't throw away the woman I love'.

He sighed. 'But shall I tell you what is the worst part? It is the way they are putting a distance between themselves and me. A television reporter had a programme about people like me who had struggled along in the evil days. And he told about Rome's orders. People started to ask questions, so the bishop spoke out and also some of the younger priests. And do you know what they said? I tell you. They spoke about what a betrayal it was for a priest to break his vow of celibacy. They asked for prayers. They said that what had happened to people like me would make them all reflect on their own weakness and on their own need to be humble. They said that people of my kind showed the human face of the Church. So they are moving on inside the system and leaving me behind. Of course they kept saying they love me. But from a distance'.

He stood up. 'Good-night. Thank you for listening to me. If you are a Catholic, try not to be scandalised by me. I have never wished harm to anyone. But Rome says I'm a disgrace. Of course, maybe God doesn't agree with them'.

And he walked away.

IX

I packed up and returned to Ireland and to my house. I had decided to cut short my visit to Elba, and had done so mostly out of shame because when I thought of the conversation beside the harbour it seemed that any grievance of mine was trivial by comparison to what had been done to that Czech priest. What I did not realise until later was that something more than shame was at work, that the conversation was not settling into me as just another memory but was reaching into some depths within myself where insights are won and plans made.

At first I seemed to have come back to accustomed routines. My diary was full. I had many visitors. I took advice on ways to improve the finances of the diocese. I attended funerals. Colleagues phoned to discuss various problems. I gave an interview to an American journalist. I answered queries from Rome and I tried to withdraw regularly into moments of prayer. But it was all like the hush which precedes a change of weather.

Three weeks after my return from Elba I got into my car early one morning and drove off to attend a meeting of the bishops. There was a clear sky, and the trees had about them an opulent look. Traffic was light and I was able to enjoy the scenery.

But after about an hour my rear left wheel went flat and when I got out to change it, I discovered I had forgotten to pump the spare. So I began to walk towards a village which was a couple of miles ahead of me. I would have enjoyed the walk if I had not been bothered by the sense of eventually arriving late at my meeting. Still, it did not take me long to get help, but when at last I reached my destination the bishops were well launched on their agenda.

I listened carefully, made notes and said nothing. The topics for discussion were mostly prosaic and some of the talk did not rise much above a murmur. But then came a change of tone. 'Item eight', the cardinal announced. 'I think I should explain the background to this one. The issue of women priests is something that is being brought constantly to public notice. I think myself it's being whipped up by the media who never miss a chance to make things difficult for us. I believe the faithful would have hardly any interest at all in the matter if it weren't for all those journalists. But, then, they are one of the crosses we have to carry'.

He paused and joined his hands together.

'Now after those opinions polls of the last year which suggest that over sixty per cent of Catholics in this country favour the idea of women priests, I decided to ask Father Michael Moloney to devise and administer a survey which would establish for us the extent to which the newspapers polls are accurate. He has done so, and his findings are included in the documentation which you have received for this meeting. Without going into the fine print, the result is bluntly simple. It is indeed the case that more than six out of every ten Catholics think we should have women priests. So the question before us is what, if anything, we feel we should do in defence of the well established tradition of the Church'.

He sat back and looked along the room. He had on him the expression described in one newspaper as that of pained charity, and it was one which crossed his features whenever a subject under discussion was personally disagreeable.

'I can well understand your feelings, Jim', Tom Reilly said, looking towards the cardinal. He was the Bishop of Achonry and was the tallest member of the hierarchy. 'Those media people bring out the very worst in me, blathering on about subjects in which they have no competence. The fact is that if Christ had wanted women priests he'd have chosen some. He didn't. So that's that. End of story. And no journalist is going to change that. And when they go around troubling the faithful about matters of this kind, then I have to confess that only the fear of God keeps me from reaching for my hurley stick to belt a few of them around the back of the head'.

There was a sympathetic chuckle around the table, not least because of the fact that Tom Reilly had instinctively thought not of a crosier but of a hurley stick with which to wreak mayhem. For he was a devoted follower of the sport, and before entering the seminary he had earned two All-Ireland hurling medals and had been a major contributor to the three-year success of the Galway team in the national championships.

'But what in fact are we to do?' Joe Higgins asked. Nearly sixty-five and blind in one eye, he had been bishop of Killala for almost a decade. 'It's getting worse every week. Contraception, abortion, women priests, disrespect for the Pope – it's crowding in on us from every side. We've given a clear lead. Our teaching has been expressed over and over again. There can be no ambiguity about our position. And still, as you say, Jim, the media are blowing all these things up as if the Church had never spoken'.

His anguish was evident. It was the distress of a man trained to be a monarch or a martyr, but not to be ignored.

Others spoke, but the topic seemed not to be moving in any particular direction until Charles John O'Donnell let it be known that he had something to say.

'Your Eminence', he began, nodding to the cardinal with the formality which he practised for as long as I had known him. 'I have to declare my view that this discussion seems to have taken on a character which is clearly unfortunate. I can understand why Father Moloney was asked to conduct this survey which we have before us. He is, after all, an academic and a sociologist, and he should certainly be given something useful to do. But I am troubled by the fact that you chose to introduce this matter of women priests by way of reference to the state of public opinion, whether or not this is accurately set out by the media'.

The Cardinal joined the tips of his fingers in a way suggesting that he was either about to pray or else tap into the sources of patience.

'Let us remind ourselves', the Archbishop resumed, 'that while public opinion may be of some slight curiosity for those interested in the vagaries of humanity, such opinion is completely irrelevant in the present matter'.

He looked around him imperiously.

'The issue of women priests is for the Church to decide. Indeed the decision has already been made, as we all know. And the approval or otherwise of the general public is of not the slightest concern. His holiness Pope Paul the Sixth was once obliged to remind us that the Church is not a democracy. Of course he was doing no more than his duty when he recalled us to a tradition stretching back to the earliest days of Christianity. The great Saint Cyprian once pointed out that he who is not in union with the Bishop is not in union with the Church. So let the politicians worry, if they must, about feeling the public pulse. All that is of no concern to us. Our God-given business is to make known the mind of the Church, and on the question of women priests, the Church has taken its stand, and there the matter rests. I therefore suggest that we pass to the next item on our agenda'.

I could sense in the room a disinclination to resist him. But something within me moved to protest.

'I wonder if things can be that simple', I said, and at once I could see faces turn towards me, though not that of the Archbishop.

'The fact is', I said 'that we have no choice but to keep the issue of women priests on our agenda, however uncomfortable that may make the inhabitants of a seminary or indeed of the Vatican bureaucracy. We can't banish the issue. An increasingly sophisticated world is pushing it at us. And if we can't even talk about it among ourselves, what sort of credibility are we likely to have when we engage in our pastoral activities outside? What are we to say to the increasing number of women who are asking blunt and direct questions of us, as they have a right to? Are we just going to declare, sorry but St. Cyprian says you have to agree with us?'

The silence in the room became deep, and within myself there was a strange mixture of surprise and relief. I could not have foreseen earlier that such bluntness would spill out of me. But some urgent need was bubbling up and I was speaking as much to myself now as to the others.

'There are important life-giving truths which are in danger of vanishing from the earth', I said. 'Each one of us here is what he is because of a belief that there is a God, and that this God was manifested in a loving figure who walked and talked among fellow human beings and who offered us a prospect of something more than brutal extinction in some minuscule corner of these spinning galaxies. That's what it's about. That's the news we're supposed to bring to an increasingly unlistening mankind. And if we get side-tracked into lesser things, how can we expect to win an audience for what really matters? Even our own followers are beginning to get impatient with us. Many of them are openly questioning and the talk among them is of elderly celibates out of touch with life and, especially, so unable to deal with the realities of sex and of women that anything we say on such matters should be listened to tolerantly but without any need for attention'.

I looked around me and noted the numbers of those who were studying the polish on the table.

'The issue of women priests is important in itself', I added. 'And it is important because of all the other questions it brings into focus. If we're to be effective pastors, then, like it or not, we have to talk about it. And I propose that we do so'.

It was a challenge, of course, and everyone understood it to be such.

'I am sure we ought all to be edified by the concern expressed by our colleague Dysart'. The Archbishop of Cashel had still not deigned to glance in my direction, and his theatrical hesitation before uttering the word 'colleague' conveyed its own message. 'Nevertheless I have proposed that we move to the next item on our agenda. Since Rome has clearly indicated the continuing status of the question of women priests, I think our duty is to abide loyally by what has been decided. I repeat, loyally. Anyhow, a discussion here and now is pointless and might even convey the wrong impression. So I move we pass on'.

'Maybe there's another way'. Liam Hurley, the Bishop of Ferns, was sitting across from me, and I could tell that he was upset by what was happening. 'Dr. O'Donnell has quite rightly pointed to the fact that there is growing public discussion and pressure on the subject, especially now that some of our separated brethren are ordaining their own women priests. And since we're going to be asked about it increasingly, then it might be useful to have prepared an up-to-date pastoral position, while continuing, naturally, to abide by what Rome has decreed. Perhaps what we need is a small committee to look into the matter and to report back to us'.

This was a peace-making effort, and it was resorting to the classic device of postponing disagreement by having a committee which need be in no hurry to complete its work.

'We have more than enough to do without having to be involved in the creation of yet another committee', Archbishop O'Donnell growled. 'And, besides, I rather think that Rome would be displeased to learn that we had done so in regard to a matter which in fact is closed. So I now suggest, Your Eminence', turning to the cardinal, that you invite a 'yes' or 'no' from each of us regarding my proposal that we proceed to the next item on the agenda'.

It was a power play, disdaining to conceal itself, and the outcome was predictable, one 'no' and a multitude saying 'yes'. In different circumstances seven or eight of my fellow bishops would have accepted the need to face up to the problems posed by the issue of women priests. But not now. Not in this room. Not when the cardinal and the three archbishops were so clearly taking my words as a defiance of the system which they determined to uphold. And there was, of course, the matter of Rome, the knowledge that an account of our proceedings would be forwarded as usual to the Vatican and that a tip-off from Charles John O'Donnell and, probably from the Cardinal, would evoke moves to counteract any signs of unreliability in the bishops of Ireland.

So we moved to the next item, and the talk continued until late afternoon when at last we had completed our business and it was time to go home. On the drive back to my diocese I felt bruised. But also peaceful.

X

This, however, changed during the following day. When I collected my morning paper I saw the usual photographs of a few soutaned bishops engaged in an after-lunch stroll. I was not among them, but my name appeared in the report underneath. Listing the main items on our agenda, the writer went on to say that he understood from reliable sources that there had been disagreement at the meeting and that in a vote I was the one to dissent from my colleagues on an important matter of discipline. No reference was to be made to the topic of women priests. To have mentioned the theme would doubtless have earned me some measure of sympathetic interest among readers of the newspaper. Instead, I was presented as out of step with all my colleagues, the guardians of morality, and the use of the term discipline was enough to hint at a softness in me, all the more troubling for its being unspecified, in issues that truly matter.

I looked at the other main newspapers and they too carried reports which pointed to me as someone out of step and under the shadow of disapproval. By the time I reached my office in the cathedral the first phone calls from other sections of the media were beginning to come in, and I could see on the face of my secretary an expression of concern.

'I've made you unavailable for the moment until I had a chance to find out what you meant to do', he said. 'Of course they're not really interested in getting the full truth of things. Just scandal mongering to sell more copies'.

'I've been a bad boy', I answered. 'I made an inopportune suggestion'.

'Good for you!' He smiled encouragingly. 'So I'll keep you unavailable for comment, will I? After all, if you talk to any of them they'll just select what they want to hear'.

'Right and ...'. He stopped, glanced out the window and grunted. 'Bastard!'

'My dear Father!' I exclaimed with mock severity. 'Such language in these holy surroundings!'

He did not answer, but pointed to the car park. There was a van there from the local television station.

'I see what you mean', I said. 'Do your best'.

And with his help I managed to get through the day without having to face the questions of a reporter. But I was wary, and when the phone rang at home late in the evening I was tempted not to answer it. However, since it might have been a call from someone in need, I picked up the receiver.

'Conor?' It was Helen McDermott. I had not contacted her since my return from Italy, and the sound of her voice made me uncomfortable now. On the couple of occasions when I thought of her I had instinctively resolved to postpone any impulse to get in touch with her.

'Yes, Helen?'

'I hope that Elba was kind to you'.

'Oh I managed to get some rest. I actually needed it. The weather was good and the villa where I stayed was quiet'.

'Are you alright?'

'Thank you, yes'. There was a slight pause.

'You sound cautious'.

'Cautious?'

'About talking to me'.

'What makes you say that?'

'When I was at school the older nuns used to tell us that as good Catholics we had a special obligation to behave. This was at the time of our lives when our hormones were beginning to act up. And one very old nun put it to us that if we were anything less than pure the bishop would know about it. The implication was, of course, that bishops know everything. Could it be true Conor? Do they? Do you?'

'You're losing me Helen'.

'Ah, yes. Maybe. But it's that note of caution in your tone of voice'.

'I'm still unclear as to what you're referring to'.

'I'm assuming that you feel you have to be careful since the detectives investigating my husband's murder have put me on their list of suspects. They haven't arrested me for questioning. But it is pretty obvious that they're constructing a theory about me'.

'Oh Lord, this is awful'. I could say nothing which might indicate that I knew she was quite right to think I felt the need to be careful about being in contact with her.

'So you do know something about it. The nun was right. Bishops knew everything. Even those who have been on holiday in Italy'.

'Helen ...'.

'No, Conor. It's ok. Anyhow that's not the reason for the phone call. No. I decided to get in touch because I've been listening to the radio and reading the paper. They're really after you, aren't they?' Her perceptiveness and her concern embarrassed me. 'I don't like it, Conor. It has a too familiar ring about it. Brings me back to the days of my husband and his political goings-on'.

'In what way?'

'A trap is being baited for you'.

'Oh, come now, Helen! Isn't that a bit dramatic?'

'No, it's not. And, what's more, I suspect you know it, since it's so obvious. The word is out and spreading, that you're not in step. No issue is mentioned, for this might distract attention from the main objective'.

This thought had already occurred to me. But I was startled to hear it plainly put.

'And what do you see to be the objective?' I asked.

'To put you in a position of having either to declare yourself to be the most loyal of the loyal sons of the Church or, alternatively, by your silence or by anything you might say, confirming the truth that you're really no longer one of them. It's a classic ploy for gaining control of someone or turning him loose into the wilderness. I've seen it done by my husband and his cronies, and I can think of no reason on earth why the bishops wouldn't do exactly the same if their power or position comes under threat. Incidentally, if I may ask, what's the bone of contention?'

'Women priests'.

She laughed.

'I should have guessed! Well, that settles it. You're going to have to toe the line very publicly. Or else ...'

And she hung up, leaving me upset and with the guilty feeling that I had somehow not measured up to the generous instincts of a supporter.

XI

I had a visitor during the same week. It was Archbishop Bevilacqua, the papal nuncio, and he phoned to say that since he had planned to pass through my part of the country he would like to drop in for a chat. I invited him to have lunch with me in my house and he proclaimed himself delighted to accept.

I asked my part-time housekeeper to prepare the meal, and when the black Mercedes came into my driveway she let out an exclamation.

'But he has a chauffeur! You didn't tell me about him'.

'No', I admitted. 'To be honest, Agnes, I forgot that the nuncio would be in the diplomatic car'.

'And what's the chauffeur supposed to do? Sit there in his grand Mercedes while you two eat?'

'Well ...' I began.

'No! He'll just have to come in, and I'll give him something in the kitchen'.

And so it happened, although I had an impression that the nuncio was slightly annoyed at the fact he had not been consulted about the takeover of his chauffeur.

'Ah, my dear bishop', he said, settling into my armchair. 'It is good to be here. Your house is in a quite charming location. That field, those woods!' He pointed elegantly towards the window. 'Glad you like it, nuncio'. I answered, beating back that sense of the ridiculous, which grows in me whenever I get trapped in the archaic rituals of empty decorum. But from previous experience I knew that the niceties bulked large in the mind of the nuncio, especially when from his viewpoint a reminder of his status appeared to be needed.

'May I offer you a drink before lunch? I asked.

He shook his head. 'No, thank you. But please don't let me stop you from having one'.

He settled further into the armchair, as though getting ready to become a permanent fixture. He was sixty years old, with a round face, black hair and the inoffensiveness of expression which, I suppose, is the outcome of long practise in diplomacy. He was also a big man, tall and bulky. But this was not to his disadvantage. He knew well how to create an impressive image on major public occasions when his gleaming cummerbund, the swish of his cloak and his purple skull-cup under the light of a chandelier turned him into a figure of theatre.

'I have not been in this area since the day of Mr. McDermott's funeral. A terrible affair that! Such a wicked murder. And, unless I've missed something, no one has been charged with the crime'.

'You're quite right. One of the detectives on the case told me recently that they have made very little progress'.

'Terrible!'

At this moment the housekeeper opened the door and summoned us to lunch. She was a good cook, but I had heard somewhere that the nuncio was not much interested in food and that the products of takeaway or haute cuisine were equally a matter of indifference to him. Certainly at lunch in my dining room he ate mechanically, took no more than a sip of wine and seemed really to want only a cup of coffee. On this occasion, of course, his mind was perhaps on what he would have considered to be something of greater importance, and his small talk was kept to a strict minimum.

'You must miss the opportunity to do research for your books', he began, as he finished his soup.

'I haven't much time for that nowadays', I answered. 'It's not really possible any more. Or at least not until I retire. If I live that long!'

'I read your history of the Council of Chalcedon. I enjoyed it. A very fine work'.

'Thank you'.

'Clearly you are an accomplished scholar. I admire that'.

The housekeeper brought in the main course, baked cod and vegetables, and as the nuncio and I sat back in our chairs to make way for her I wondered increasingly about the reasons which had brought my guest to my table.

'Have you ever worked in the Vatican library?' he asked.

'Not extensively. I visited it on many occasions. But that's all'.

'A truly magnificent library!' he exclaimed, opening wide his arms, as though to welcome the entire world. 'Such resources! Those manuscripts! Hundreds and hundreds of them waiting to be catalogued and studied by the best scholars. Such peace there! It seemed to be a perfect refuge'.

Knowing as I did the old prayer which speaks of the refuge of sinners I was tempted to imagine that the nuncio might be thinking of me. But he changed direction and began a process of trying to make me feel that he was taking me into his confidence. It was a bit obvious. But, then, he was not a particularly bright man. If he were, he would hardly have been posted to what some nuncios considered to be a backwater.

'For someone like you, my dear bishop, a historian who knows the past, it must be extraordinary to compare how things were for the Church in earlier days and how they stand now. Such similarities! It's almost like being back again in the times of the Roman Empire when we were just a minority trying to survive as we spread the word of God'.

He paused, as though expecting a comment, but since I was certain he had some ulterior motive in speaking this way and since I could not tell what this might be, I decided to be non-committal. So I smiled benignly and waited for him to continue.

'Yes!' he declared, stoking up his theme. 'I feel increasingly that in today's Church we have more than usual to learn from our brethren of the early days. Think of the hostility they faced on all sides, the competition from ideas and practises completely at variance with their own. I sometimes try to imagine what it must have been like when you were surrounded by incomprehension, by the readiness of your neighbours to rise up against you, by the cold hostility with which you had to make some sort of accommodation. No! Not accommodation! After all, people in our position had a duty to go out and spread the word of God, no matter how uncomfortable it must have been'.

He took a mouthful of cod and paused. I waited. Politely, of course. 'But I'm at a disadvantage', he returned. 'I mean, I know something about those times. But I have nothing like the feel for the situation which you would have, you with so much historical research done and so much left to do'.

That last phrase intrigued me. Was there a hidden dimension here? Or was I getting slightly paranoid?'

'Tell me, my dear bishop', the nuncio went on, pushing away his unfinished plate, 'if you had to isolate the single most important source of the courage and the endurance of our predecessors in the early Church, what do you think it might be?'

I considered the question.

'I think you're asking me to make a large generalisation', I said eventually. 'I rather imagine you would have to specify cases and situations before I could feel free even to guess'.

He was obviously disappointed with this answer. He rested his left hand lightly on the table. The fingers were pudgy.

'But isn't there some constant, something that reappears regardless of particular circumstances?' he insisted.

'If there were, what would you expect it to be?' I was determined to flush out the real reason for this conversation.

'Well, my dear bishop, even though I am certainly not an expert in the history of those times as you are, I'd say it was the recognition among our predecessors that they must stick together, present a united front, subordinate personal agendas to the common good of the Church. Surely you would agree?'

He looked intently across the table. His large brown eyes filled with the unmistakeable objective of bringing me into acquiescence.

'Of course I understand the point you're expressing', I answered. 'But if you'll pardon my saying so, you appear to be formulating a principle in a vacuum. To talk of the good of the Church is like proposing the excellence of apple pie and motherhood. Who on earth is likely to raise objections? Nor can I imagine a bishop, past or present, who would openly denounce the notion of subordinating personal agendas to the good of the Church. The difficulty, however is that at any given time what's good for the Church is not always self-evident. And I have an uncomfortable feeling that there have been occasions when the insistence of bishops on affirming what's good for the Church has meant not much more in reality than stating what's comfortable for them. I would even suggest that in some quite specific cases the good of the Church, as proclaimed, has actually only amounted to a roundabout way of forwarding one's own consecrated whims'.

I spoke rather more strongly than I had intended or, indeed expected. But it was in response to an instinct within me that my visitor was about to sketch an expansive image of camaraderie where bishops, conscious of marching together in the face of a hostile or indifferent world, dampened down any of the exigencies of personal opinion or of private unease. I was anticipating reference to team spirit and to a common glorious enterprise. And I thought that a forceful pre-emptive strike might head him off. But, as I have already mentioned, some blessed ingredients had been withheld from the make-up of the man, and so he went on anyway, though perhaps not quite in accordance with his original scheme, and, to his credit, he did not waffle but came rapidly to the point.

'My dear bishop', he murmured, 'I have to say to you that I am troubled by the account I have received of the recent meeting of the hierarchy. Of course, as is my duty, I have forwarded it to Rome'. He glanced at me, paused, and seemed to invite a reaction. However, I merely resorted to the old trick of remaining non-committal by repeating the last sentence.

'You forwarded it to Rome', I said neutrally.

'Yes. And, as I say, I am troubled'.

I asked no question, and waited.

'You will not misunderstand me or take offence if I confess to you, my dear bishop, that I have an impression, a distinct impression, that you are out of harmony with your colleagues'.

'You have that impression as a result of reading the report of our meeting?'

'Yes'. He showed no signs of mentioning that some of my colleagues had, doubtless, also talked of me.

'Of course, I've not seen that report', I said. 'Obviously, then, I'm not in a position to comment on it'.

'Nevertheless, I have the impression which I have just mentioned', he came back, looking closely at me.

'The Dean in a university where I once taught used to say to me that he never knew what happened at a staff meeting until he came to write the minutes. It was an interesting observation, which I've never forgotten'. I smiled at him.

'What are you implying?' the nuncio asked.

'No more and no less than that reports of meetings tend to select those things the composer wishes to emphasise. And since you have, as you say, formed the impression that I am out of harmony with my colleagues, I can only conclude that the report did not go out of its way to dispel the possibility that you might indeed acquire such an impression'.

'Are you suggesting that the report is inaccurate?'

'How can I suggest anything when I haven't even seen it? But I notice that you did not ask me a question. You didn't say "are you in disharmony with your colleagues?" You made a statement which you softened slightly by referring to an impression. It was as if the basis of whatever discussion we might have now is in fact an established accusation, with me in the situation of a defendant. Forgive me for speaking bluntly, nuncio. But we might as well understand each other'.

A glow of anger came into his eyes. My directness was unwelcome, and in particular, my unwillingness to be deferential had clearly annoyed him. For he was a man conscious of rank. Unlike me he was an archbishop and even the colour of his socks proclaimed the fact. He was also the representative of the Pope and that, in his view, gave him a status which invited, even from a bishop, the bow of acknowledgement and the suspension of assertiveness.

'At the recent meeting of the hierarchy you were in a minority of one', he said.

'More coffee?' I asked, conscious of my duty as host. He shook his head.

'There were eighteen items on our agenda', I continued. 'Most were dealt with on the nod. Dissent was voiced with regard to few of them. On one of these I was in a complete minority, as you rightly point out. However, I think we should keep matters in perspective. Don't you?'

'The item in question was hardly a matter of routine business, was it?'

'If by the item in question you mean the suggestion on my part that we talk among ourselves about the matter of women priests – a topic which won't disappear – then the situation is that my colleague of Cashel was opposed to the idea that we would even speak of it in the privacy of our meeting room. I thought otherwise. And presumably the report of the meeting mentions that'.

'And why did you want to disagree with your colleague of Cashel?'

'Am I not permitted to disagree with him?'

The nuncio made an impatient gesture. 'Actually you stood against all your colleagues!' he snapped.

'So?' I was beginning to get annoyed. Something in my chemistry reacts strongly to bullying.

'My dear bishop, you know as well as I do what the position of the Church is on the question of women priests, and what troubles me is that, as I said earlier, you appear to be out of step with your colleagues on this subject'.

'Well, now, aren't you being a little presumptuous? You describe me as standing against my colleagues. That's a rather emotive way of twisting the matter. It also suggests that you have put me on trial for something and have found me guilty without bothering to hear my side of the story or even telling me what I'm supposed to be guilty of'.

He pushed back from the table and took no trouble to disguise his rage.

'No!' I persisted. 'Let us be quite clear. You have come here with an agenda of your own, and that, of course, is your affair. But when you start speaking as if something discreditable about me has been established as fact, then, to put it gently, I am rather unimpressed. And I look forward with mild interest to your next homily on the subject of elementary justice. Ah, no, if you have come to browbeat me, then I suggest you forget it. And let me say for the record that in my opinion the question of women priests will not evaporate and that it seems to me now, as it did at the meeting of the hierarchy, that if we bishops are to maintain a credible position then, given the times that are with us, we should at least talk about it among ourselves and in all seriousness. The only proposal I made at that meeting was that we should talk, and I offered no opinions of any kind on the question itself of women priests. I therefore suggest that you stop jumping to conclusions'.

'Then let me ask you a simple and direct question', he said. 'What in fact is your attitude to the matter of women priests?'

I looked at him sitting like some predator ready to pounce. All the diplomatic polish had been set aside. 'As you have said yourself, nuncio, the Church has taken a position on the question, and if I am publicly asked about it, I will refer all questions to the Vatican and will act accordingly'.

'That is not what I asked you'.

'I know'.

'Am I then to take it that you are evading an answer?'

'Evasion is a loaded word'.

'What other description am I to use when you fail to respond to my question?'

I smiled at him.

'Did it ever occur to you in the midst of your self-righteousness that I might choose not to answer a question simply because of the tone and demeanour of the questioner?'

He started, as if I had hit him across the face.

At that moment the housekeeper, who had obviously been listening to us outside the door came in, her face inscrutable. 'Can I get you something else? Fruit maybe. Or some kind of sweetener?' I managed not to laugh.

'No, thank you', I answered. 'You've looked after us very well'.

She nodded and went out again.

'I have to tell you seriously that you ought not to underestimate the extent to which you are causing unease'. The nuncio was speaking quietly now. 'Anxious questions are being asked here and also in Rome. Yes, certainly in Rome. There is some disaffection at work in you, my dear bishop. We have all noticed it. And after a certain point there are ... there are steps which have to be taken, however reluctantly'.

I studied his face.

'When you talked about the Vatican library a while ago, were you offering me a job? Trying to get me out of the country?'

He shrugged.

'Well, then, let's put it another way', I said. 'You speak of questions being asked about me. Earlier this year my honorary degree was withdrawn following some behind-the-scenes activity in Rome. Shortly before that the cardinal switched me from being appointed spokesman for the hierarchy, and he nominated me instead to be a member of the Goldoni commission. The effect of that would be to require me to spend a good deal of time in Rome. One would need to be a bit dense not to conclude from all of this that I am, as they say, under something of a cloud. What interests me is that no one has had the moral courage to tell me why'.

He lifted his napkin from his lap, folded it carefully and placed it beside his coffee cup. 'I have a feeling', he said, 'that this conversation is not leading to productive results'.

'I take it you mean it's not going the way you wanted'.

He looked at me, his face expressionless now. 'My dear bishop, let us not play games. There is an attitude growing up within you which, someday, your conscience is going to acknowledge. I pray that acknowledgement will come soon, before any scandal is caused. You may wish to talk to me about it on some other occasion and in a rather different atmosphere'.

'For my part, I will readily talk to you when and if I am given something specific to talk about. So far I have only heard hints of rumours as well as vaporous generalities couched in distantly threatening form'.

He stood up.

'Thank you for your hospitality', he said, and left.

XII

Over the next week or so I did my usual work as if nothing had happened. I attended the opening of a parish community centre, visited patients in a hospital, dealt with routine diocesan matters. There were calls to me for help and advice. I had a meeting at the cathedral with the priests of the area and learned with satisfaction that plans we had laid to improve the effectiveness of local charities were taking on the appearance of success.

But the background was different. Like the inescapable piped music of public places, there were the words spoken at my lunch with the nuncio. And there was all that had happened in the previous days.

There was also the silence of my colleagues. None of them phoned me, or sought to get in touch with me. It was, perhaps, the merest whiff of persecution mania which made me conscious of this now, because in other times I had noticed that there was very little informality within our group. We had our regular meetings and were pleasant to one another. But I had always the feeling that the expected answer to the question 'How are you?' was 'Oh, fine thanks, and you?' It was as if we had some unspoken collective fear of getting to know each other.

So, early in the morning I went for my usual long walks and tried to sink into the immediacy of things, the white peeling bark of the birch tree at the corner of my garden, the uninhibited run of water in the river, the gradations of light on the woods before sunrise. But my thoughts were fringed by anticipation. I was waiting. Yet I could not say for what.

Then came the letter from the cardinal. It was hand-written and seemed to have an unusual spattering of exclamation marks. He spoke of wonderful news. The Vatican had agreed to his request to make me a member of the Goldoni Commission. It was a signal honour for Ireland and there was more, much more. I had also been chosen to be secretary. This was certainly an unexpected bonus, and I was to be most warmly congratulated for having been elected to so influential a position.

I folded the letter, and as I stuck it back into its envelope I could not help smiling. I should have been annoyed by the fact that the cardinal imagined I could not see what he was trying to do. It was a classic move. Bishops cannot suddenly be made redundant and the only way to deal with somebody deemed to be troublesome is either to install an assistant to whom all the powers over a diocese are transferred or else to have him moved. The first possibility is inclined to be messy, and as there is always the risk of turning a disgraced bishop into a media martyr. The second is much smoother because one can dress it up as a promotion and as a call to higher things. Since the secretary of the Goldoni Commission was likely to be needed in Rome for several years my tenure of the position would obviously keep me away from my diocese, and clearly this was the bonus to which the cardinal referred. I would be removed from a scene where, it was feared, I might cause embarrassment.

It was all very obvious, but no fast talking within myself could smother the hurt of it. The cardinal and others, including the nuncio, wanted me out. Not because I was a heretic or because I had been photographed cavorting with topless women on the beaches of St. Tropez. They wished to be rid of me because they had come to distrust me. In earlier days they would have known which were the pressures that would have reduced someone in their ranks to silence. But I was in demand. Journalists wished to talk to me. Television presenters sought my opinions. Lay people could no longer be intimidated into keeping clear of me by a well-organised bush telegraph. I could not be isolated.

'But what have you actually done?' The question returned to my memory and I thought of the day when it was put to me by Helen McDermott on the cliff top above the Atlantic.

'I haven't done anything!' I murmured to the empty room. 'Or rather, I seem to have said a few unwelcome things. As a result I'm perceived to be unsound. They can't trust me not to speak in a way which will put them in an awkward position. They're afraid of me'.

I stopped, picked up the phone and had dialled the first couple of digits of Helen McDermott's number when I paused, laid down the receiver and sat on my desktop. Why was I calling her at this moment? Was it because her name had come with the memory of that day on the cliff top? The obvious answer was that I needed to hear a sympathetic voice. When I had arrived in my diocese I had left my own friends behind me. They were in other parts of the country or on the continent and what I had around me in Dysart were, at best, some pleasant acquaintances. I needed to talk. Or at least to put some distance between me and what was happening. And I had an instinct that Helen would understand my predicament.

So why not call her? Because I had turned cautious regarding her and another indication of her formidable intelligence was that she had instantly spotted that fact. For of course she was right. I had felt the need to be careful. Suppose what was said after my session with Tom and suspected of her proved to be true? An ugly picture of her was certainly taking shape and the parting words of Tom urging me to mind myself rang clear in my mind. But what if they had all got it wrong, the husband, his family, the neighbours, the detectives? What if a reading of her to which all assented was, nevertheless mistaken? My own reaction to her had been one of respect and admiration. Had I completely misunderstood the signals, like the Italian soldier on the Piazza who had turned in the direction opposite to that of his comrades?

Once again I was confronting the matter of my own judgement. The doubts and the hesitation continued to seep through me. But the thought also came that if by some chance I was right in my view of her, then my caution was no different from cowardice. If Helen McDermott was not the nasty woman portrayed by gossip and by that notebook, if she had nothing whatever to do with the murder of her husband then to draw back from her now would be to abjectly and unfairly run for cover.

So I dialled her number and she answered immediately.

'I've started talking to myself', I said. 'And that's a bad sign'.

'Not necessarily. The talk might be interesting'.

'How are you?'

'Are they after you?'

'As a matter of fact, yes'.

'Ah. Come over and see the piece of sculpture I'm working on. I'll get some wine out of the kitchen'.

'Thank you', I answered, but she had already hung up.

I sat in my armchair for quite a while. Occasionally I looked out the window to watch the afternoon glow on the field beyond me. I could feel the ebb of morale, and recognising it to be such, I knew that I would not be able to think myself out of it. So I took the phone off the hook, then replaced it because there was no sense in doing otherwise, shuffled some documents on my desk, and left.

When I reached her house the door was open. I steeped into the hall, and speculated on the possibility that some detective was watching me.

'I'm here in the studio!' The voice was ahead and above me. Upstairs I saw her sitting on a bar stool in front of a table on which there was a rough grey block of stone.

'I was beginning to think you had changed your mind', she said. 'I was just about to put the wine back in the fridge'.

'Sorry. After I phoned you I just sat there and didn't notice the time going by'.

She had been in profile, but she turned to gaze at me.

'You're not very thick-skinned, are you, Conor?'

The question surprised me.

'I don't really know. At least, not immediately. I'd have to consider it. Anyhow, why do you say that?'

But she seemed not to have heard me.

'You may not realise it', she said, 'But you and I have a lot more in common that you might think'. I assumed she was going to talk about the suspicion surrounding her.

She got off the bar stool and sat on the floor. 'When my husband and I were married, the priest made the usual after dinner speech at the wedding reception. There were the bits about the sanctity of love and the blessing of the Church. And he ended up by saying in a slightly plumy voice that two young people had found each other and were all set for a God-given relationship in the coming days. It was very sonorous and the words came comfortably. Of course he meant them, and he had probably said the same things at dozens of other weddings. Sometimes I think of those words, and of the complacency out of which they grew. Ah well! How could he know that my husband would soon come to look on me as the enemy and that he would spread that same impression to others around him so that people would start to be very wary of me'.

She looked up, and I wondered what I would say if she remarked that I too was tempted to be wary of her.

'I can imagine the time you were made bishop. The sense of occasion. The solemnity of it. An archbishop, maybe a cardinal, maybe even the Pope standing above you and talking about how God had called you and how together with your fellow bishops you would blah blah blah etcetera etcetera. And just as my husband turned against me they've turned on you, Conor. Of course, in my case it took me years to begin to imagine why. I suppose my husband got it from his mother. Anyhow he expected me not to be any kind of a threat to him, and without my ever meaning to or wishing to I became just that in his eyes. And you know what, Conor? I could be talking about you'.

She rolled over on to her knees and reached for the wine bottle. There was a glass beside her and, having filled it, she handed it to me.

'I don't know what to do'. I said. 'Of course, I could just live with it and carry on. They're stuck with me until I resign or retire to die. And yet ...'

'And yet you'd like their approval?' The question was put with such gentleness and courtesy that I felt a surge of gratitude.

'Yes', I admitted. 'Yes, I would'.

She nodded.

I walked around the studio and when I stopped, I found myself in front of a stone figure, eight or nine inches tall, clearly a woman, and with the stance of someone utterly disconnected from any haven.

'Coincidence', I said.

'Sorry?'

'A coincidence', I repeated, pointing to the figure. 'She says it all. I'm unanchored'.

There was silence.

'So, are you going to work at winning back their approval?'

Her words jolted me.

'Do you mean, am I going to look for chances to say things they want to hear? Jolly them until I'm made feel that I'm back in the club? So the cardinal can say, "actually Mahon is sound, he was just going through a bad patch?" Is that what you mean?'

'Maybe I shouldn't have asked that question. Sorry, I didn't mean to upset you'.

When she said this I recognised at once the vehemence of my reaction to her.

'Oh, Helen, please don't apologise. I need someone to shake me up, because, to tell the truth, I'm floundering'.

She smiled and then seemed to withdraw into herself. I sat down on the floor, sipped my wine, and gazed around. The air was warm, but I could feel desolation in my bones.

'I don't know if you remember it', she began suddenly, 'but years ago some man, whose name I've forgotten and who made a fortune conning people, went off to his Swiss home and wrote a book. It was the title which interested me at the time. He called it 'Do you sincerely want to be rich?' – that was clever. Most people, I imagine, would say yes if you asked them whether they wanted to be rich. But sincerely? That was the smart bit, the dividing line between sheep and goats. Because only those few willing to give up everything for riches would be likely to think in terms of sincerely'.

I waited, and a moment later she was on her knees again, this time in front of me and looking at me so that I could not avoid her eyes even if I wanted to.

'Do you sincerely wish to get back into their good books? Do you sincerely want to give up everything that you are so as to win their favour? Do you? Do you really?'

I could not avoid the intensity of her look. And yet I felt no inclination to think of her as something of a threat, a presence to be warded off.

'You must bear with me, Helen, I am not one of those who can walk down a road of logic to a conclusion which must then take over one's life. I'm no good at that sort of thing. Actually, I'm a very disorganised person, and it gets worse as I get older. Wishes, hopes, plans, convictions – call them what you like, they all cohabit and take up squatter's rights in what is really a jerry-built, ramshackle tenement of a mind. In the days when I was professor I used to think regularly that the hour would surely come when I'd be found out. And it's even more so since I became bishop'.

I could see her attentiveness.

'The fact is, Helen, I'm the wrong man for this job'.

'Why? Because you don't live inside a crust of certainties? Is that it?

I did not know how to answer her, but words she had used earlier came back to me.

'That priest you were talking about, the one who performed your wedding ceremony'.

'Yes? What about him?'

'You were remarking on how comfortable he seemed to be in what he said'.

She looked at me.

'It reminded me of something', I went on. 'Of my first time here in this house'.

'Oh?'

'Yes. You've probably forgotten. Not the occasion, perhaps, but what you said'.

She raised both eyebrows.

'You were referring to my words at the funeral mass for my husband. You more or less accused me ... well, accused is probably too strong a word, you described what I had said as being so predictable. That was your comment. And it really registered with me. I thought about it for days afterwards'.

'I'm sorry, Conor. I didn't mean ...'

'No! You were right! You were quite right. You mustn't apologise for saying what was quite true. My words were indeed predictable, and for a long time I kept asking myself why this could be so. It was important for me to understand this'.

The phone rang and, startled, I looked at it and then at her.

'Let it ring', she said. 'They can try again'.

'Are you sure?'

'Of course. Carry on with what you were saying'.

'Well ...' The phone went silent. 'Well, you see, if I was so predictable, then that could only mean that I was operating from force of habit'.

'And that bothers you?'

'Very much'.

She smiled.

'Even though part of your job is to give stern warning against bad habits. Which of course implies that good habits are to be recommended. So what's your problem? What's wrong with your kind of habit?'

'I don't think you were saying that I was boring. Or was I?'

'No, you weren't boring'.

'That's a pity'.

'A pity! Why, Conor, what are you on about?'

'Well', I began, sadly, 'if I knew it was just a case of putting my congregation to sleep, I'd know what to work on so as to improve my sermons. But you reacted to something else, to something that was missing from what I said, to some lack, so that those I wanted most to help, the mourners, I mean, you, the family – you were left on your own. By me. By my failure to say what would reach you. I find that very upsetting'.

She looked carefully at me, and slowly shook her head. 'I don't know about you, Conor. You're the first bishop I ever met who didn't walk tall in his purple. Why, I bet you even squirm inside yourself when people speak of you as "His Lordship". You don't need to answer! I can see from the expression on your face that it's true'.

'Maybe it's my age', I said. 'Maybe because I'm sixty, but something has happened. I think maybe it's a case of not wanting any more to be some kind of tribal chief. When a procession moves solemnly up the aisle of the cathedral and I'm at the end of the line with my robes and my mitre – some child called it a funny hat – I have to work hard not to think of the sort of figure I cut. I have to push aside the old story about the bishop in front of a firing squad who remained standing after they shot him through the head and then through the heart until at last someone had the bright idea of shooting him through the mitre. And then he fell down'.

I began to walk around the room again. 'Of course if I showed up in a tracksuit, did cartwheels up the aisle and vaulted over the altar rails, there would be no end of people scandalised and upset'. I rested my hand on the solid head of one of her sculptures.

'So, as your husband once said, I have to put on a good show. Only ...'

'Only what, Conor?'

'Oh, I suppose it's a case of something being broken inside. And I'm not sure what it is. Or maybe I know and am afraid to face it'.

She said nothing, remained motionless on the floor, a presence around which my thoughts gathered.

'The fact is, Helen, that I have a hunch I'm at a point when I no longer want to tell people what to do. I have enough making sense of my own scene without setting myself up as someone on the inside track, someone who has real knowledge and who must be followed. It's too much, Helen. Too much for me. Too much to impose on others. In the days when I was a professor I gave lectures and wrote books about various aspects of Christianity. I told people what it was about and I did it to the best of my ability. But this ... This business of pounding the rim of the pulpit – though that's a bit old-fashioned now, one is supposed to employ the latest PR techniques – and all this so as to tell people how they must live ... No I don't think I'm really able for it any more'.

I looked at her in astonishment because my words had come so simply. It was as if they had been biding their time, waiting for their proper moment. They were out now and the simplicity of this truth overwhelmed me.

'Yes, that's how it is', I said. 'I'm a transmitter of other people's words, and because that makes me sound like an expert and because the institution has given me a high profile, I have about me an aura of authority which I don't feel I really possess. So in a way I'm a fake. I'm a professional holy man, and yet I know what I really am. Lord, do I know!'

I sipped my wine.

'I'm going to write to the cardinal', I added. 'For a start I'm going to tell him that I won't be taking on the job of secretary to the Goldoni's Commission. I'm not going to be put out of the country. No. I'm not'.

XIII

My phone rang and I heard the familiar voice of John Collins, a former student of mine and current minister for the Arts.

'I'll be in your area within the next half hour or so. I'm on my way to a couple of appointments, but I'd very much like to see you. Just a social call. It's a while since we met. Is there any chance at all that you might be free?'

'Well, in fact, I can see you. I'll be at home for the rest of the morning and I'd be delighted to have you drop by'.

'That's great'. And when he repeated that it was just a social call I had the immediate feeling this was something he wanted to stitch into any future record.

Half an hour later I heard his car in the driveway and I went out to meet him. He was dapper, thin, tall and well groomed.

'I'm surprised that as minister for the Arts you are not wearing long hair and Levis', I said, shaking his hand. I was glad to see him.

'Ah well, the respectables have a lot more votes than any artist so I have to look like them'.

'Come into the kitchen while I brew us a cup of tea'.

'That would be wonderful'. And as if to undermine my welcoming comment he took his jacket off, laid it over the back of a char and sprawled nearby. Then he looked carefully at me.

'So, Prof, how are you?'

'In excellent health, thanks be to God', I answered.

'I read in the papers that you're making waves'.

'Now, John, you shouldn't take in everything you read in the papers. After all I never believe three quarters of what they write about you'.

'Good thing too. Anyway unless you're a complete mouse as a bishop somebody somewhere is going to disapprove of you. Sure didn't you say so yourself years ago in class?'

'I did?'

'I was listening. For once!'

'What did I say that was so memorable to someone who was usually a presence absent?'

'Oh, so you noticed, did you? Well, you told us how the Roman aristocracy were shocked by the fact that when Pompey got an itch in his head he scratched it with one finger instead of five'.

'I must remember that for the future. Sugar and milk?'

'Both please, Prof'.

There was a brief pause. We were comfortable with each other.

'I have to confess to a sin of omission'.

'Of? What's that, Prof'. I was oddly pleased at hearing my old title, or, more precisely, I was happy to see that he thought well of the days when I was the teacher and he the student.

'When you were appointed to your post I was going to write you a letter of congratulations, but I'm afraid it went out of my head. But I was really pleased for you'.

'Thanks, Prof. I value knowing that'.

'So, you're on your way to various engagements'. It was more comment than question. What I was really waiting for was the reason for this unexpected but very welcome call.

'Goes with the job. It must be the same for you'. He selected a biscuit, and then looked at me. 'I don't know if you can be of help to me. In fact it's just a long shot that you might'.

'What are you referring to?'

'You have a neighbour and she's on my agenda'.

'I suppose you mean the wife of Tim McDermott'.

'Exactly'.

'So?'

'She's an artist. And a very good one. Or so I'm told by people in the know. Some months back an application from her ended up on my desk. Now I should explain that it's usually the Arts Council that dispense patronage. Which is very useful for a minister like me because it means they can be blamed if some artist puts on a show that has people like you thundering from the pulpit'.

'Plain speech was always one of your virtues. When it suited you'.

'Oh I'm telling you Hamlet or some Shakespeare character got it right when he said you must assume a virtue if you haven't got it'.

'Minister, you're blathering'.

'Of course I am. Can I have another cup of tea?' He threw a couple of sugar lumps into his cup, and his expression became serious again. 'She wrote to me because she knew that there are some funds available which only I can dispense. The Arts Council is not involved. So there I am with this application for help in setting up an exhibition first in Dublin and then in Edinburgh, where there will be an Irish contribution to the festival'.

'But you have a serious problem about it?'

'Exactly. There's no question about her deserving the help. She's a first rate artist, and in normal circumstances I wouldn't hesitate to give approval. But, unfortunately, the circumstances are not normal'.

'Because of the murder? Why would that be a difficulty for you? If she has made the application and deserves the help what is the obstacle in your way?'

He sighed and for a moment looked out the window.

'This is where I'm hoping you can help me. I'm just clutching at gossamer and wishing for some way to get around this'.

'You mean, to refuse her?'

'Look, the business of cancelling the honorary degree which you were supposed to get must give you a special feel for the unfairness of things. And I don't want to be unfair to her. But ...'

'Yes?'

'There's a cloud of suspicion settling around her. Maybe you heard about the piece in the English Sunday tabloid when Tim's brother belched into a reporter's ear that the detectives should not be wasting time chasing after subversives but ought to look a lot closer to home'.

'My God! But that's terrible!'

'It's not something isolated. There are others saying the same thing'.

'So you feel the need to be cautious?' I had hardly uttered the words when the irony of it swept over me. I could imagine a sardonic gleam breaking into the expressive gaze of Helen McDermott.

'I don't want to jump too quickly to conclusions on this. And I've said, I want to be fair. After all think of the stories that spread about Jim O'Leary when he was minister for Justice. It never got into the papers. But everybody knew, quote unquote, that he was in a relationship with a blonde twenty years his junior. They were always sneaking off together. And she went to England. And everybody knew it was to have his baby. There wasn't a pub in the centre of Dublin that didn't know it all. The gory details were there for the asking. And even if you didn't ask you got them anyway. Only it wasn't true. There was no blonde, and anyone with a half ounce of wit would have known that a minister for Justice is on the job seven days a week and regularly into the small hours. If it ever happened that he had a couple of free hours he'd be much more likely trying to get some sleep instead of getting it up'.

John Collins gave a disgusted snort and emptied his cup.

'No, Prof. When the chips are down for her that's the time to be very careful, to be fair. If everyone else is out to crucify her for having her husband killed I don't want to join the posse until I'm a bit more sure of the facts. Which is I'm here'.

'Oh? Perhaps you'd explain that'.

'Look. I know you've been neighbours since you arrived here. She and her husband have a house right nearby. I'm hoping, just hoping that there's a chance, an off-chance maybe, that you know something, anything about her which would help me to be a bit more informed when I come to decide on the application. Of course I can refuse her, which might be horribly unfair. I can waffle and delay a decision, which might also be unfair. I could say yes and then on the day after the opening of the exhibition she gets arrested for murdering her husband and the opposition can have a field day laying it on thickly about my incompetence and about the proven fact that I am not to be trusted with decisions involving public funds'.

I could easily understand his situation. But it was no consolation because he had now created a problem for me. I had privileged information, since I knew about the notebook, the surveillance on her house and about at least one theory doing the rounds among the detectives and I had also seen the attitude of the McDermott family towards her on the day of the funeral. I had listened to the various harsh descriptions of her by people who would claim to be in the know regarding her. I even had her own testimony of what her parish priest had said to her. All this added up to a formidably nasty picture.

And yet from my own limited experience of her company I had an admiring impression of her. I remembered the haggard dignity of her words and demeanour when she spoke of the isolation created around her by her husband. The hurt of it was genuine. I was sure of that as I could be of anything. I could not believe that it was simply a performance for my benefit.

But was this belief of mine the product of hope rather than of reality? If, as she had said, her husband had distanced himself from her was this anything other than a bid for some kind of self protection on his part? The private thoughts set down in that notebook clearly implied that this was the case. I could not get away from those pages, from their bewildered bitterness and, especially from the remark that Achilles would be willing to kill even Patroclus. That in the madness of the world lover could slaughter lover. So what could I say to John Collins? There was a bond between us and I had an obligation to honour it.

'John', I began finally. 'I'm not sure I can be of much help to you. Like you I know something of the stories swirling around her. But I'm grateful to you for reminding me of the situation of minister O'Leary when he held the justice portfolio. I remember thinking at the time that it must have been a monstrous experience to be helplessly enmeshed in an endless stream of falsehood and casual slander. I don't know how one would cope with that'.

'And Helen McDermott?'

'I've met her a few times. My reaction to her has been – and continues to be – one of admiration and support. In spite of all that's going on, or is said to be going on, I'll hold to that until I'm proved wrong'.

I could see relief in his eyes.

'Thanks, Prof. That's encouraging. You see, I've met her a few times. Always with Tim. And I too was impressed with her. And yet there was something about them I couldn't quite describe exactly but which still managed to bother me. There was some ongoing tension in the air around them and ...' He wrinkled his nose and grimaced. 'Well, it was as if it were always her fault. I know that's not very intelligent as a comment. But yes, as if it – whatever it could be – as if she was to blame'.

I listened intently, wishing not to interrupt or distract him.

'And, you know, a funny thing. I feel a kind of ... solidarity with her. Yes, that's it. I'm on her side. Ah, this is getting too obscure. But I can't express it any better'.

'Solidarity? That's a strong word, John. That's very striking. Why would that be the word that comes to your mind?'

'We were good colleagues'.

'I'm not the media'. I said, laughing. 'You can safely be more precise'.

He smiled an acknowledgement.

'OK, Prof. Yes, we were good colleagues. But we weren't pals, either. I didn't have warm feelings towards him. In fact if you were exercising your priestly duties and were hearing my confession I would have to admit that I harboured bad thoughts about him and that I'd find it hard to go down the love-your-enemies road where he's concerned. Even in death'.

'What had he done to you?'

'Not so much what, but how'.

'You've lost me now, John'.

'It's straightforward, actually. As you know the boss is on his lap of honour. He'll retire about a year before the next election so as to give his successor the time to marshal the party before going to the polls. There's nothing secret about it and the manoeuvres to succeed him have been going on busily. With Tim and myself long regarded as the front-runners. We both knew this and did things accordingly. We both knew well of the cabinet reshuffle last year that it mattered a lot which ministry either of us got'.

'Why so?'

'Because some ministries are backwaters with little opportunity to catch the public eye, and good publicity, as you well know, is the lifeblood of political careers. Who's going to notice the minister for the army, for God's sake?'

'Sorry. Silly question on my part'.

'So the cabinet reshuffle was hugely important to each of us, because it could be the stepping stone to the top job for one of us. I wanted either Finance or Health. Tim had his sights on Finance. On the day of the announcement the boss didn't call me in for the usual little chat. Instead, he had one of his minders take a couple of political correspondents aside to whisper confidentially that I was to be minister for the Arts. The word went all around before I heard a thing. And of course I was left with no choice but to accept what I had been given. And Tim got Finance, and he's been handing out goodies ever since. Until he got killed, that is'.

He paused, got up and walked around the kitchen as if to inspect what was in it.

'He shafted me, Prof. It was weeks before I was able to see how he had done it, and I have to say, even if I was the victim, that it was masterly. We each had a solid body of supporters. That is, from the point of view of numbers. But then there were the opinion makers who in my case ranged from the definitely hostile to the undecided. And that's where Tim went to work. He left no fingerprints. He hinted an argument to one, knowing it would reach the ears of someone else he didn't want to approach directly. He never specifically asked for a vote against me but with a well positioned word here and roundabout hints there he got the bush telegraph to start forming a picture of me which bothered certain potential supporters of mine. Question marks began to appear over my views on the North and on the social welfare situation. Even the fact that I'm living with a partner was pressed into service. But always discreetly, always with the effective pause in mid-sentence or the roundabout waffle. He passed his insomniac nights spinning a web which encircled me without my noticing it. And of course the boss began to hear things and started to wonder if it would be prudent to appoint me to either Health or Finance. And, ironically, when Tim saw how the boss was leaning he suggested that the Ministry for the Arts was shaping up to be so very important that only a senior minister could be counted on to handle it. That settled it so far as the boss was concerned. And the description of me as a senior colleague gave the final push to send me where I am now'.

He was silent for a while.

'So the rumour mill really works', I said. 'First, the Minister for Justice in the government and now you'.

'Yes, except that in my case it was directed and co-ordinated by Tim who left nothing to chance, oversaw all the details, and ensured that his objectives were attained without anyone knowing that he was the choreographer of the entire dance. So you can see why I have no kindly feeling for him and why it is that on the rebound I'm open to the idea of helping his wife. Because I think she got his number and didn't like what she saw. Which of course is far from saying that she had him bumped off'.

He held out his hand.

'Good to see you, Prof. It's been a help'.

I waved to him as he was driven away.

XIV

During the days which followed the visit of John Collins I had little time to think of Helen McDermott. There were too many chores on hand, but above all I was preoccupied with my own situation. Although I am usually a good sleeper I found myself constantly awake. Sometimes I got up in the night, walked for a few miles along the fields and roads of the neighbourhood, fell back into bed and, even then, turned and twisted until morning. Tiredness built up and my thoughts grew obsessive. Prayerful quiet went out of reach. I had no idea what to do.

One day I was glancing through the correspondence page of a newspaper when my attention was drawn to a familiar name. It was that of a young priest who clearly liked to go public as a defender of the Church. He was unusually articulate and had a talent for memorable condemnation. In fact, denunciation seemed to come as naturally to him as breath, and his targets ranged from priests who disagreed with him to the lay people who exercised their freedom of conscience. I occasionally speculated on how he would preach a sermon on love of neighbour, and I could even imagine the sort of words which would pounce on the shortcomings of the Pope.

He was in righteous spate yet again like some febrile agent of the inquisition with his slingshot of words. My revulsion grew with every honed phrase, and I thought of the studied clarity which would be expected of me if I were ever to be asked in public to comment on some utterance of his. I would have to act like a bishop in case a gentle soul might be upset or even scandalised, and my honest opinion would have to be wrapped in camouflage or else in fulsome orotundities.

'Too much. Too much. I must talk to someone', I said loudly.

And within days I had gone south to a monastery where I had a long conversation with a monk. 'It's a bit like losing weight', I said at one point. 'You give some things up and one morning when you stand on the scales you find that you have shed some pounds. You didn't feel their departure. But they're no longer there'.

I was sitting in a room which had a view over parkland, at the edge of which were masses of great trees, all in their summer fullness. Sunshine on the morning haze gave a slight shimmering tone to the woods, and the slow wings of a passing heron hinted a peace entirely beyond my own grasp.

'And you don't wish to put the lost weight back on', the monk suggested.

'No', I answered.

We were sitting opposite each other on straight-backed chairs in a spacious room. There was a polished wooden floor, a table, a fireplace, a high decorated ceiling and, on one wall, a bare crucifix.

We had been talking for over an hour and I had told him all that had happened to me in the previous weeks and months. He listened with the anxiety of someone afraid to miss any word, and I felt a quiet ease in his presence. It was what I had expected, for I had known him a long time and it had been my custom to come at least once a year to the monastery in search of a few days of quiet prayer and meditation.

'But it can't be the fate of that priest you met in the Elba which has brought you to this point. Such things are not new. You are a historian and you know about the follies which can be done in the name of God'.

'Of course I know'.

'The reality seems to be that you no longer want to be a bishop'.

'That's how I feel'.

The brown eyes of the monk were unwavering now.

'Was the word "feel" a slip of the tongue?'

'I don't follow you'.

'I would have thought that one should more properly be talking of God-given duty and obligations, and that feeling have not much place here'.

'You are saying, are you, that I have been called by God to be a bishop and that, therefore, my own sentiments are irrelevant? Is that it?'

'Isn't that the case?'

I went silent. He waited.

'That's too simple', I said at last. 'Of course I know about duty. But I haven't the duty to be an ineffectual bishop'.

'No. But is it for you to decide whether or not you're effective?'

'Meaning that I'm an instrument of God and must let him decide how to use me?'

'Yes'.

'I've thought of that. But it still doesn't take away my main problem'.

'Which is ...?'

'Which is that since I no longer believe in part of what I'm supposed to preach, I'm left with the situation of not being able to be a leader for the people of my diocese. How can I exhort them to be good Catholics and to live as the Church wishes when I myself have lost the conviction of the Church's rightness on certain matters? And when you lose convictions on some things, then others take on a question mark'.

His hands, protruding from his habit, rested lightly on the outline of his knees.

'Can you be precise?' he asked. 'Can you specify what you have lost in the matter of conviction?'

It was there now, clear, unmistakable.

'Something has gone badly wrong in the way we treat people', I said. 'You mentioned that priest I met in Elba. He's a sign of something amiss. Why should an ordinary good man in his later years be made feel somehow dirtied because he does not fit in with a policy devised by ecclesiastical bureaucrats in the Vatican? They were glad enough to have him in the years when they needed him. And why should people who find themselves to be homosexual have to carry a burden devised by us because they do not fit into schemes we have forged to make moral situations tractable? We are cruel there, and no amount of dressing up in the finery of principles can alter that fact. And look at how we treat women. Until lately we banned altar girls and the notion of women priests sends us into spasms. We use the weakest and hoariest of arguments, the argument from silence, to keep women out. We say if Christ had wanted women priests, he'd have ordained them. But we don't ban marriage on the ground that he didn't marry. So while we keep women out, we grow starry-eyed in our public declarations about them. The fact is that when elderly celibates begin to coo in well-rounded generalities about the dignity and glory of women, I have the distinct feeling that throughout the world there are people reaching for their guns or else dissolving in torrents of laughter. And I can scarcely blame any one of them'.

The monk seemed to be considering this.

'So you want the Church to make the kind of changes with which you will be able to live comfortably?' The faint hesitation over the last word was unmistakeable.

'You are challenging me now', I said. 'I accept that. I didn't come here just to get a pat on the head'.

His face remained expressionless.

'I am in a rather special situation', I went on. I'm not an outsider wondering whether I'll join the club'.

'Exactly you're Conor Mahon, Lord Bishop of Dysart and a direct successor of the very apostles! You are one of a small select band, chosen by God himself, and now you say you don't want the job. What demon is laying hold of you?'

'Not the demon of boredom! Not depression or egotism! None of these things. If you really wish to talk of demons, let us simply mention honesty. Let us talk of concern for the people of my diocese who have a bishop who honours their individuality, their insights, their truth and who out of deep respect for them does not want to pretend to hold ideas out of which he has grown'.

'How is it that you had none of these sentiments before? I mean in regard to the Church?'

'I don't know. Laziness perhaps. Dullness. Too sheltered a life. How should I know? All that's clear to me is that I don't think I can climb into the pulpit and pretend that I haven't grave doubt about some matters which are at the centre of the Church today. I can't for instance speak about homosexuals having a disorder of nature. Even if it were true, it would be a cold-hearted and pitiless thing to say in public. And, in any case, I don't believe it to be true, even though I don't understand it. Any more than I understand what it is to be a woman'.

He said nothing, as if to allow me the time to smooth my vehemence. He had been forty years a monk and he had learned the art of tranquillity. Through discipline, studied routine and constant meditation he had acquired a way of slipping into the peaceful centre of his self. I could imagine the hours when he sat without a stir, his eyes lightly closed, his face unclouded, his lips ready to welcome the presence of his God, and I almost envied him for it.

His next words came, therefore, as no surprise. 'But one must take the long view', he murmured. I did not move.

'The Church has accumulated a vast experience', he went on, 'and neither the good days nor the black days can lay a shadow over what it knows. The Church uses human words, which sometimes fail, but it knows the truth of things. Oh, it knows. And if you tamper with what it knows, then you put obstacles in the way of God'.

He stared at me.

'My Lord! Who are you, who I am to rise up against what the Church knows? We have the words of our founders to direct us and whatever our private wishes, we must submit. The Church is not a debating society. It is the home of truth and, since you chose to speak of such matters, that truth includes women and homosexuals, and it is not for you nor for me to tamper with that truth'.

He had not raised his voice. He had no need to do so because years earlier he had found his home in a serenity which had distanced itself from the particular, from the ache of loneliness, from fright, from hazard, from perplexity. He had moved beyond all individual moments to bask in the continuing light of consecrated words from a secure past. If ever he spoke to others of the crucifixion of Christ, it was, I felt sure, to drain that event of blood, of battered bones and of anguish so as to open up instead vast panoramas of precisely articulated significance and translucent meaning. He had found a route out of the here and now, out of hurt, perversity and bewilderment, and was living his days in expansive calm.

'But I have a problem which does not confront you', I exclaimed. 'I have to spend every day in the world. People look to me. Some depend on me. Others feel they have to touch base with a living example of integrity.

They'll forgive me and make allowances for me if I'm backward, dim-witted and unimaginative. But only on condition of my being honest. I can't preach selectively. I can't skip over parts of what the Church says and pretend by my omission that I have no deep-seated doubts. That would be to cheat them. As it is I have enough trouble with the idea of my telling anyone how to live. But to pretend that I'm at one with the Pope and with those of my fellow-bishops who hold forth so easily on the subject of women and indeed on all sexual matters – ah no, I don't think I can do that. Not now. Not when I can no longer slide away from having to confront the matter. I know now that I have been turning away from it. At least until the issue was picked up by my colleagues. Especially by the Archbishop of Cashel'.

He sighed. 'Am I to take it from the way you circle round the theme that you are or have been having a sexual relationship with someone?'

I was tempted to tell of a Presbyterian friend of mine whose pastor had thundered that clearly he had been wallowing in lifelong sin. My lonely sad friend had replied gently that he wished to God it were really true.

'I'm interested to hear you put that question', I declared. 'The old saying: look for the woman. Though nowadays, I suppose, one would need to amend it to read, look for the partner. That was the first rule in any counter move after a cleric had strayed from or had actually left the Church. Such a cleric had to be put in the wrong. The well-being of the Church required it as a minimum. The vocabulary was "lust", the "flesh's weakness", "the appetites". The voice dropped at the mention of appetites. There was the half-sympathetic nod which kept open for the cleric the road back. It was understood though rarely stated that, given the nature of women since the time of Eve, a woman was surely the villain behind any clerical lapse. That doesn't work quite so well nowadays, though of course it's still tried'.

He was staring at me.

'You sound very cynical, my lord. Nevertheless you have not answered my question'.

'Ah. My apologies. The direct answer to your direct question is no'.

'Then things really are worse for you than I had realised', he murmured.

'Were you half hoping', I asked, 'that what I've been saying to you was being played out against the background of a sexual relationship of my own?'

'My Lord! What you've been saying to me this morning has been said in one form or another since the days of the Apostles. But in the end there is a simple choice. You have to throw in your lot with the abiding truth handed down by the Church or else you go down the road of turning your own experience and your own way of thinking into the measure of things. But since you are a bishop of the Church, the second choice is closed to you. You are excluded from it. To go that way would be to fly in the face of God himself!'

His words were passing over me rather than into me, and I knew why. They came out of a venerable pattern of discourse which had been created over many centuries. One leapt on to it as to a passing train. One made one's way aboard, found a comfortable seat and then settled down to watch and to measure the passing landscape from a point of view made possible by the type of windows installed into one's own compartment.

I had been doing the same for many years. It was what Helen McDermott had referred to when she described my sermon at the funeral of her husband as something predictable. She had voiced a truth deeper perhaps than she knew. I say 'perhaps' only because, unlike a full-time cleric such as myself, she had other preoccupations in life. But she had called up in me the awareness that, ultimately, I was a spokesman, the purveyor of words around which I had made myself a life, but words, nonetheless, which were not my own. I had settled into them, I had sometimes articulated them in unpopular fashion and, over the years, I had rationalised my way past the occasional roadblocks among them.

But now I was in trouble which I had managed to ignore. The sanctioned view of a central aspect of human relationships was something which my job required me to proclaim and yet it was one which the mind and heart in me combined to see as badly flawed. I might be wrong, of course. But my opinion was an honest one.

'My Lord, if our way of speaking about sexual matters seems to you to be in need of improvement, could you not make it your mission in what remains of your life to show the manner if such improvement?'

Of course, it was a logical move for him to make, since I had shown the reason for my unhappiness. He was looking for a means to rein me into my job.

I shook my head.

'No. Sorry. I wish that were possible. But it isn't'.

'Why not?'

'Because I would disturb and confuse people if I were to stand before them and say, "I am very uncomfortable with what the Church says on this and this and this. And I can't deal with it by the way of double-talk. You do what the Church tells you and in the meantime I'll see if I can find a way to get the Church to change". That would be the wrong thing to do. Just as it would be wrong for me to go through a public pretence that I am on the same wavelength as my colleague of Cashel. No, I'm caught and I was too stupid to realise it. In fact it's only now, this morning, here, that I can finally see with full force the implications of what I've been thinking and saying in recent months. That's pretty slow-witted, isn't it?'

A knot of sadness pushed up within me and I felt a desolation of such power that I had to grip the sides of my chair.

'Just think of it!' I said, almost whispering. 'If I had remained in academic life, a priest engrossed in the history of early Christianity, none of this might have happened. I would have been among my own kind, with a sense of belonging to them'.

'And you can't remain that way?'

'How can I? After all, I am a bishop. At the time of my appointment the talk was of the honour done to me. The public speculation was that I was being groomed to be the next Archbishop of Dublin. I was thrust into the front line! That's why my colleagues are shrinking away from me. A bishop who has a sexual problem or a drink problem – that's something they can cope with. But a celibate bishop who has been hinting up to now and who must for the future admit openly that he's convinced there's something badly wrong in the Church's understanding of sexuality – no, Abbot, this can't go on. I'm stuck. I'm alone'.

He allowed my words to fade away in the austere room. Then he spoke.

'The obvious advice would be for you to talk to someone, to anyone who could help you look back to where you would see the point of view of the Church. But of course you will have thought of that'. He was saying good-bye. This word 'back' showed his thoughts about me. For him I had left, and unlike the case of the prodigal son, there would be no happy ending.

He stood up. So did I. He bowed deeply.

'I wish you well, my Lord'.

On my way home from the monastery I turned the car towards the sea, and when I came to that part of my diocese which opens on to the Atlantic I stopped and began to walk. I followed a sloping path and was soon pointed towards a cove hidden from view. The water below me was clear and azure. Under its surface I could see fingers of rock pushing out from the base of the cliffs. Some rose to be garlanded by white foam and spray, and in one cluster I saw rusty sheets of metal, all that remained of a freighter which the sea had casually flicked against the reefs.

The angle of the path became steeper, hugging the cliff where bunches of anemones grew pink, white and purple in a background of wild spinach and new ferns. The path itself was stony and I stopped a while to watch a solitary gannet wheeling above the sea. The white body and the black wing tips glided on the wind and then suddenly dived, hitting the water with a splash and thrusting under until it snatched its prey.

I continued until I arrived at a narrow strip of sand, dark and clinging to my shoes. There was a swish of breakers and at the shoreline there was a churning of undertow.

I stood and looked out. I watched the eddies of wind and water, the changing patterns of colour, the blue straight horizon. There were no boats in sight. The sky was clear. From somewhere beside me came the boom of water on its ancient business of extending the hollow of the cliffs. There was an echoing cry of a gull. Another wave fell apart. I felt very alone and small.

Beside my right shoe and pushing out of the sand was a stone. I picked it up. It was a fossil. I knew a little about such things and recognised that a living creature, enclosed within its shell, had once thrust out a thin tube by which it anchored itself to the floor of the sea. It had swayed in harmony with the waters around it and when its time had come to die the grip on sand and rock had dwindled and then let go and over millions of years the shell had turned to stone, to be gathered now by a man spoken of commonly as 'His Lordship'.

I began to laugh. Here I was, a tiny figure in a tiny corner of a spinning globe at the edge of uncounted clusters of stars, and I was a lord. When I appeared in public dressed in my episcopal regalia, there were people still who wished to kiss the ring on my finger. I had a title which implied that I was the purveyor of knowledge deeper than anything available to the common run of mortals and I was trained to demand acceptance of what I supposedly knew. People were expected to live by what I said, and predecessors of mine, certain of their mastery, had promised hell for the recalcitrant.

I looked out at the sea with its hidden depths and I remembered that I was supposed to interpret the mind of God. Not for myself, but for others, and I was bothered by those others. I had lived my life so far praying to an unspeaking God, and on that shoreline of a huge sea I was ready still to do so. But to proclaim the nature of God was to impose what, after all, might only be an idol, fashioned of course from our holy books but constructed, nevertheless, by me and by human beings like me.

I thought of the old Jewish story of how Moses begged a reluctant God to let him return to earth for a week to spend time in the classroom of a brilliant rabbi whose students had come together from all the known world. Eventually and with a great sigh God agreed, though on condition that during the lectures Moses would be invisible. Moses accepted the condition gladly but he listened with growing discouragement for he could understand nothing of what was being discussed. He was not able even to recognise the subject of all the talk until a moment came at the end of the week when the Rabbi announced that he had nothing more to say for the present concerning Moses.

It was a story which had made me uneasy from the moment I had first encountered it. But now within sound of the sea it had the force of demoralising mockery. It would not have registered so much with me if I were merely a kind of spiritual plumber, establishing the right connections as I administered confirmation or laid my ordaining hands on someone wishing to become a priest. But I was something more. I was a 'lord'. I was set up to be a leader and this implied a competence and a knowledge which to my eyes looked increasingly threadbare in the immensity of this world where I stood. Perhaps others in my position, feeling the same, had managed to cope by busying themselves with details, immersing their minds in minutiae, like framers of insurance policies. One could get passionate over particulars. For instance, one could say that the texts and the practices on which we based our way of life would never allow paragraph five sub-section three of our documents to make room for women priests.

I felt a need to sit down. The nearby rocks looked uncomfortable but I saw a patch of dry sand and I settled on to it, drawing my knees up until they were almost under my chin. I stayed there for a long time, gazing out to sea, sensing the nonchalant power of those stirring waters.

Of course I would have to quit. Honesty required that much of me. The well-being of the people of my diocese could not be subjected to the evasions, the compromises, the concealed opinions which would be my portion if I remained as their bishop. So I really had no choice.

But as I thought of resignation I remembered the day when I became a priest. I called up the image of my father, standing beside me. He had the smile of a man trying to come to terms not only with the fact he had to let go of me, as all parents must, but also with my new status. I was no longer ordinary. I was somehow above that now. I was irrecoverably apart, and in conversation with others on that day he began to refer to me as Father Conor. And to block off the sad shadow which had passed over his loving eyes he fussed about my mother's misplaced handbag and he explained the workings of the camera to my well-informed sister. The three of them had seemed uncomfortable, and out of place, and were gone, dead within a couple of years of each other. I could not help wondering how they would react if they were still here and able to see the cul-de-sac in which I found myself now, and, sadly, I acknowledged to myself that they would probably not understand. They would be loving and very puzzled.

And ahead of me now was that distance of those reacting to my decision to resign. A bishop is not supposed to quit, and when he does it is usually in circumstances attracting the gossipmonger and the prurient. And even here some measure of sympathy reaches out to him because the usual reason for going is a background of sexual involvement so that only the most self-righteous and the most pharisaic will ultimately refuse to murmur 'there but the grace of God ...'.

But mine would be something different, an open declaration that I had doubts about the very system which had created me. A bishop is not allowed to be uncertain. Not in public at least. He can be dim-witted, impervious, stubborn but he may never openly confess to being anything other than very sure of the ground on which he has taken his episcopal stand.

I looked at the sea and watched the patterns of its stirring expanse, and around my heart an ache began to unfold, threatening me with my own useless tears.

So I stood up and began to walk back along the cliff path to where I had left my car. As I came around a corner I felt the wind coming in gently over the rocks and over the wild flowers, and I listened attentively to the far-off barking of a dog. Its owner was just above me, standing on an outcrop of shale and grass. I had not noticed him previously and I wondered how long he had been there. Clearly, he was a local farmer, a man in his sixties, wearing an old brown anorak, and with navy trousers tucked into Wellingtons. He nodded to me.

'Good day, your Lordship! You've picked a grand spot for a quiet walk'.

I smiled up at him.

'Yes, it's a lovely place'.

'I've seen you come here before', he said, and he sounded pleased about it. 'I suppose you like to get away sometimes from the responsibilities of your job. A man needs a break now and then'.

'You're right'. Looking at him I could imagine now, as he lifted his pint of Guinness in the local bar, he would say that he had met me just before the announcement of my resignation. I wondered about the extent to which he would embroider the story. Would he conjure up lines of worry on my face or hint at the possibility of my having sought his advice?

'Are things going well for you?' I asked.

'Not bad now, mind you'.

'I'm glad to hear it'.

'It's eleven weeks and two days since I had the hip operation and its grand to be able to get around again. The walk was bad to me, and I was nearly crippled'. Then he added, pointing to the sheep-dog which had joined him. 'But I'm nearly as good as himself now!'

We talked of the weather and of current affairs, and then, having gone back to the car, I completed my journey home. A gleaming sunset was filling both the hall and my study when I opened the front door, and for a moment I stood, blinking and slightly disoriented.

The housekeeper had left my mail on the hall table and when I glanced through the envelopes I immediately recognised the handwriting on one of them. It was from the cardinal and when I opened it I drew out two pages appealing for a reconsideration of my decision not to accept membership of the Goldoni Commission. There was nothing new in his words but the emphasis was upon his own disappointment. Polite regret shaded into something personal and he pressed me to phone him as soon as possible.

But I had no wish to talk to him. At least not now. Besides, I was hungry, and, having boiled a kettle and made some toast I sat in the kitchen and listened to the silence.

I remained in the kitchen for what must have been an hour, and a growing awareness of shock went through me, like mist seeping into a forest. It was one thing to know I was going to resign but to realise it was something else, and as I continued to sit there a sense filtered into me of some other man, another bishop, my successor, moving around this furniture. I was now almost an intruder here and, half apologetically, I began to wipe toast crumbs from what was no longer my table.

The phone rang, and when I picked up the receiver I heard the voice of Helen McDermott.

'Conor?'

'Yes, Helen'.

'Is this a bad time to call?'

'Of course not'.

'How's your social calendar? Full, I suppose'.

'That depends. Anyhow it's adjustable'.

'Great! The Arts Minister is sponsoring an exhibition of my work'.

'He is!' I felt a surge of pleasure at the thought that John Collins had decided to support her.

'The official opening is in Dublin in two weeks and I was wondering if you'd like to be invited'.

'Not to the official opening!' I answered with unintended haste. 'But I'll certainly go. In fact I would like that very much. I must say I really admired what I saw in your studio. Particularly that small piece, the woman with her arms open to emptiness. I think that is quite marvellous. Yes, it should be seen. And I'd be interested to watch how your work is exhibited in a gallery. Thanks, Helen. I'll go to that exhibition'.

'I'm glad to hear it'. She seemed to hesitate and then hung up.

I put my dishes in the sink, washed and dried them, and wondered all the while what I would do when I resigned. Because of course I had not really looked beyond that event. And the problem looming in me was whether it would be enough to quit as a bishop. Would matters end when I left the diocese? Where would I go? Would another bishop allow me into his area of jurisdiction to do what a priest does, say Mass, pray with the congregation, hear confession? In fact, once I ceased to be a bishop, was I not stepping out of the system entirely? Would I not be an ordinary layman in need of a job?

The questions began to spread like some mad growth and I felt less and less able to deal with them. I had no example to guide me. Bishops who resigned suddenly for reasons other than health or age were usually hidden away in a very private and expensive clinics or else in remote mission fields of South America or Africa. A resignation was an embarrassment to be managed as well as possible by an institution which could in any case rely on the willing co-operation of the man who was stepping aside. But something unformulated as yet within me hinted that matters would not be so simple as far as I was concerned, that I would not join in the manufacture of my own disappearance. Certainly I was going to resign but, equally so, I had the compelling instinct that regardless of what happened I would not run away.

But what if I didn't and what was I heading into? Was I to go on the dole until I found a job? I could well imagine the scene at some office where the unemployed stand in a queue waiting to sign themselves into the welfare system. I could picture what would happen when it was my turn at the grille when a new kind of confessor awaited me. So you want to sign on? Yes. Why? Because I've no work. What happened? I had to quit, honesty demanded I resign. You mean you left your job? Yes. Were you sacked? No. Just walked out? It wasn't as simple as that. Is it ever? So what kind of employment did you have? I was a bishop. My voice is lowered. There is a long pause. Others behind me in the line seem to be eavesdropping. Ah yes, well I'm President of the United States, so what was your job? I really mean it, I was a bishop.

My reverie was interrupted by the sound of a doorbell. I went out, and found myself looking at Helen McDermott.

'Have you visitors?' she asked.

'No'.

'Good. Can I come in?'

'Of course'. I stood aside and she entered the hall.

'Let's go down to my den', I suggested. 'How about a drink for you?'

'Alright. If you'll join me'.

So I poured us each a whiskey while she sat into the chair at my desk. I settled on a small sofa which I normally used as a resting place for the less urgent among my papers and books.

'I wanted to see you, Conor. As soon as I put down the phone a while ago, I realised that something's wrong. Can I help?'

I set my whiskey glass on a dictionary beside me.

'You must be very perceptive', I murmured. 'I didn't realise things were showing. Yes, I am in trouble. I've decided to resign'.

'That figures'.

Startled, I looked up at her.

'Why do you say that?'

She gazed at the whiskey in her glass and frowned as though she had discovered that it was not as mature as claimed by the label on the bottle.

'A politician's wife learns a lot in her time', she said. 'You get used to looking at people not as big or small or fat or thin but as voters at election time. It does something to your perspectives. Believe me'.

She sat back and smiled.

'Conor, did you notice that when my husband was alive, he never tried to socialise with you? Here we were for several years living next door and yet you were never invited to our house. Did you ever notice that?'

'To be honest, I'd have to say not really. It didn't occur to me to think about it. But he did come to see me here'.

'Of course. But that was when you first arrived. It was to size you up. He wasn't being neighbourly, if that's what you imagined'.

'Oh?'

'Certainly not! You might have noticed he didn't bring me on that visit'.

'Yes. That's true'.

'It was a reconnaissance trip, purely'.

'And as a result he kept away from me. Is that what you're saying?'

'He came home after the visit and remarked, "He's supposed to be the next Archbishop of Dublin. Well, he won't be". And that was all he said. So he lost interest in you. Not because he didn't like you but because he decided you wouldn't be part of a power structure, and in that case he was too busy to think about you any more'.

'Did you? Think about me, that is'.

'I didn't meet you before he was murdered, did I? But when you came to visit me after his death, I could see what he meant. And of course all that business about the withdrawal of your honorary degree only confirmed things to me'.

'You're going to have to explain that one to me, Helen, because right now you have me thoroughly puzzled'.

She laughed.

'I don't mean to add to your problems, Conor! But the truth is that an organisation like the Church can't afford to have people like you in situations of authority'.

'Why ever not? And what are you on about with your "people like you"?'

'Conor', she said patiently, 'in the old days the Church burned people. Why?'

'Mostly because the victims were said to be heretics'.

'And what's a heretic?'

'Someone who publicly goes his or her own way on what the Church affirms to be the truth of things'.

'Exactly. And if the word heretic is now out of fashion and if the Church doesn't burn people anymore, the reason is it's bad PR and not that the Church has changed its attitude regarding its own authority to lay down how things should be'.

'That's a bit cynical isn't it? Not to mention being a great over simplification'.

She grinned.

'Thank you, Conor. You're making my point for me!'

'What point, for heaven's sake?'

'In the last thirty seconds you've twice shown your hand. You instinctively described heretics as victims, and out of your sense of the complexity of things, you've accused me of over-simplification'.

I finished my whiskey, shook my head and stared at her. But she broke in before I could say anything. 'And remember what you told me about the effect of what you casually said about altar girls during that radio interview. The Archbishop of Cashel went gunning for you because of it and he ended up telling you to your face that you weren't one of them. Do I need to remind you of that?'

'No. I suppose not'.

'And why aren't you one of them? I'll tell you. Because while the Archbishop of Cashel owes his first allegiance to an established overview of things into which particulars have to be fitted and squeezed whether they like it or not, you speak publicly from within the same overview but your primary respect is for the reality, often messy, of ordinary everyday things. You don't allow yourself to drain life of its presence in order to secure some long-standing system of explanation or doctrine or theology or whatever you want to call it. It's against your nature to do that. And that's why, to your fellow bishops, you're shown up to be a subversive'.

I was shocked.

'A subversive? Me?'

'Yes, you, Conor. Exactly, so. You have it in you to stand over a sanctioned view. But only up to a point. For many years you've been sheltered from having to reach that point. Probably because you were a scholar before they made you a bishop. But now it seems you can't dodge it. And because you're too honest to hide that fact from yourself, you have to go. You're not going to be bailed out. Certainly not by your colleagues'.

Her words were not to be evaded and what most upset me about them was the recognition that speaking as she did she had barred me from an escape route. Uppermost in my conscious thoughts had been the notion that I could no longer continue with my job of telling people what to do, for my sense of knowing less and less about more and more had caught up with me. So I kept repeating to myself that I must resign for the sake of the people entrusted to me. But what Helen was forcing me to acknowledge now was that there were deeper reasons for being as I was, that more was at work in me than concern for my congregations. A central cause of my reluctance to continue my career as a preacher was that I no longer believed that the humanly created and humanly refined doctrines of the Church represented the full and authoritative account of how things are and how things must be.

Suddenly I remembered an encounter with a young woman who had accosted me one Sunday morning at the cathedral. She was tall and fair-haired, and I recognised her from a photograph in the local newspaper. She was a lawyer, recently qualified and she had joined a prominent business establishment near the cathedral. But what I particularly recalled now was the rage in her eyes. 'Can't you stop him? Can't you shut him up? Do we have to have him inflicted on us Sunday after Sunday? It's too much!'

'Please! Who are you talking about?'

'I'm talking about Father Woods'.

'In what connection?'

'Obviously you've never been a captive listener to his sermons!'

I knew that to comment would be like trying to stop a tide. So she went on.

'He was on yet again like an old stuck record on the subject of contraception. He's from the Dark Ages! It's clear he thinks women are a lower form of life and it sticks out that he's abysmally ignorant about human love. But then he's like most of you lot, yammering on about sexuality and dedicated to knowing nothing about it. You bleach out the reality of love-making of people and you natter on in stupid generalities which are driving more and more of us to stay home'.

And with that she rushed off.

Of course I was aware of the fact that she was one of a vast throng of Catholics whose lives were neither evil nor wicked and she had nevertheless, concluded that the position of the Church on contraception was flawed. Like every bishop, I was well versed in the party line on the matter and, on occasion, I had enunciated it publicly. But I never been faced by anyone in anguish over it. And as I thought about this and as I watched that lawyer striding across towards the cathedral parking lot, I began to wonder if my life had been so protected for so long that crucial segments of human reality had been withheld from me. Could it be that I was precisely the kind of person envisaged in the proposal of a maverick archbishop that when the most solemn moment came in the consecration of a bishop, there should ring out the words 'Remember, My Lord, after this day you may never hear the truth again?'

'You need another drink', Helen suggested.

'I think you're probably right'.

She came out from behind the desk, took my glass, poured me a whiskey and handed it to me.

'So, Conor, you really are going to resign?'

'Yes. It's all been moving in that direction. I have to go. I see that too clearly'.

'And what will happen?'

'Well, I must call the Cardinal and the Nuncio to let them know'.

She was still standing beside the desk.

'That's not quite what I meant. I was thinking of you. What's ahead for you?

'To be honest, Helen, I just can't say. Obviously I'm going to need a job. But I've no idea what that might be. I haven't thought that far. But something will turn up. At the moment that's the least of my worries, though of course I'll be singing a different tune when the time comes to put bread on the table. I've a few hundred euro in a savings account. I imagine that will keep me going for a while. I don't know'.

I was awash with exhaustion.

'Can I make a suggestion?' Her voice was gentle and it amazed me.

'Please do'.

'Take the phone off the hook and let's go down the field so you can listen to the river for ten minutes. Then you should go to bed and have a very long sleep'.

I thought about this for a moment.

'It's not that I'm unsociable', I said finally, 'but I think I'll skip the river and fall into bed'.

'Then I'll be off. But I'll call to you to-morrow, if that's alright'.

'Of course it's alright!'

I could see her compassion and I could only give humbled thanks for it. She was too intelligent not to know the suspicions which had descended on her. Yet instead of fretting she was ready to make room for concern about me and about what she could sense happening within me.

'Is it allowed to give you a hug?'

I gazed at her. 'Yes, indeed. It must be thirty years since anyone gave me a hug'.

XV

There were no hugs on the afternoon a few days later when I closed the front door of my house for the last time, got into my car and drove away. My bags were in the boot. Whatever I had not been able to push into a suitcase lay now on the back seat.

My books were in crates at the cathedral. The priest in charge there had agreed to take care of them until I could arrange to collect them. He had been as helpful as his feelings permitted. He had avoided looking at me and his discomfort rose off him in a barely concealed current.

'Yes, I'll see to it that your books are minded', he said, waiting for me to leave. He had turned formal and I could see the thumb of his right hand circling repeatedly over the side of his index finger.

I wondered if the Cardinal had talked to him. They had been fellow seminarians and had kept in touch.

I myself contacted the Cardinal a few days earlier.

'Jim! Sorry I haven't been in touch with you before now, but there's something I've been turning over in my mind'.

'Ah, yes, Conor. The Goldoni Commission'.

'No. Not that. Jim, I've decided to resign as bishop of Dysart'.

There was a fraction of a pause.

'This is rather sudden, isn't it?' His voice had gone into neutral.

'For you possibly. It's not something I'm doing lightly'.

'Of course not. But why? Is there ...? He stopped, and at once I could see what he was thinking.

'No, Jim, I haven't had a sexual relationship with a woman, with a man or with a boy. I haven't a drink problem. It's nothing like that'.

'Then?'

'There are other reasons besides these for going. In essence, I want to go out, and with as little upset to everyone as possible. I don't think I have any choice but to go. I realise I have my own journey to make now. Away from the Church. It's a complicated story, but if I'm to preserve some sense of integrity, I have no choice but to leave'.

There was silence. It was obvious he was thinking quickly.

'And you can't be persuaded to change your mind?'

'No'.

'And how are you going to explain this to the Holy Father when you send your resignation to Rome? He will have to be given some explanation, of course. And then he may not permit you to leave. Have you thought of that?'

'Jim, I'd better make one thing clear. I don't plan to spend six months, a year, five years in correspondence with Rome about the matter. I am not looking for permission to resign. I'm not going to wait for some bureaucratic paper shuffling in the Vatican to be gone through. I'm going to tell the Nuncio and the Pope, just as I'm telling you now, that I'm leaving. And that will be the end of it'.

'But you can't do things that way!' The anger came bursting through, and he tried to restrain himself. 'Now wait. Wait. This is all wrong. There are procedures to be followed. Above all, the Holy Father has to be given the opportunity to consider whatever it is you say and then to make his decision in his own good time. Leaving aside for the moment the question of your own thoughts on this situation, the Holy Father must be given the freedom to arrive at whatever resolution of the matter he thinks best. Any other way of acting is unthinkable. It's unheard of! You must surely see that, Conor'.

'What I see, Jim, is that I'm going to be fended off or kept hanging around or put into some kind of administrative limbo or stuck into a sin bin'.

'So you're going to deny the Holy Father the right to consider what you have to say? You're just going to walk out, without even a by-your-leave?'

The outrage refused to be held down within him.

'Jim, I don't think you understand'.

'No, Conor, I don't understand! I don't understand wilfulness of this kind, not to mention the discourtesy of it and the refusal even to contemplate the scandal of it'.

'Ah yes, the scandal', I said, with a bitterness which surprised me. 'Appearances. Is that it? Save the appearances at all costs. And in the meantime ask no questions about what's happening to me'.

'But of course what's happening to you matters! That goes without saying'.

'Yes, I notice it hasn't been said'.

'Oh, Conor, don't misunderstand me. But the fact is you simply can't pick up your bag and walk out. I wish you'd see that'.

I could feel myself getting tense and angry, so I knew the moment had come to end this phone call.

'Now, Jim, I've made up my mind about what I'm going to do. And this is why I am talking to you now. I'm resigning. That's final. And I'm leaving as soon as I can organise things. Before I go I shall announce my decision. I'll issue a statement'.

'A statement? What kind of statement?' His alarm was palpable.

'That's something I haven't quite fully decided on'.

And with that the conversation ended. I sat back in my chair, looked at the phone, and began to go over what I had just said. Of course I would have to make a statement. Yet why the 'of course'? Because it was the usual procedure. Because it was expected. Because one could not slip quietly away. But why not? Why did one have to make a pronouncement? The questions bubbled one after the other and suddenly I remembered the change of tone in the cardinal after I mentioned a statement, his evident alertness in regard to what I might proclaim. He could already visualise the enquiries from reporters, from the nuncio, perhaps even from the Pope himself. He too would have to consider and measure the terms of his response, and since he had not the instincts of a politician, even though his job often required in his eyes that he behave like one, he would fret and become uneasy. Which was why in public he was often very dull.

So there would be two statements, mine and his. Positions would be staked out and, as a result, other heads would nod in the certainty of knowing how things were with us.

The tyranny of it all struck deeply into me. Unthinkingly I had imagined myself to be the custodian of the facts of my own life, but of course I was not, since others would decide for themselves what these facts were, regardless of whether they corresponded to the way I saw myself. A statement would therefore be a conscious effort on my part to secure a particular image of me and to defeat what others might assert. It would be an attempt to influence or even to control how people thought of Conor Mahon, and yet this very urge to devise a public utterance could itself be understood by others and indeed by myself as ultimately a pathetic token of a need to be approved, of a vulnerability which sought to be assuaged or shielded.

'That settles it! There won't be a statement!' I muttered. I would resign, and the Catholic Press Office in Dublin could say what it wished about me.

And so I wrote three letters, to the cardinal, to the nuncio, to the Pope. The words were few. I declared that I was resigning at once as bishop of Dysart. I offered no explanation. I voiced no sentiments. Indeed the only concession I made to the system, for the last time, was to sign myself Conor, with a cross in front of my name. Then I went to bed and slept late.

In the morning I stopped into the post office and sent the three letters by registered mail. The finality of what I had done reached into me as I watched the envelopes drop into a special bag. I felt a pang not so much of sorrow as of dullness. I was conscious only of a grey here and now, of jobs to be done as quickly as possible so that I could go away.

And then, at last, I was on the road, my destination Galway, a vague project in my mind to stay a few days in a bed and breakfast establishment while I made plans for the next stage in what was now, suddenly, a very uncertain future.

But I was not afraid. Something would arrive, and my life would continue to run.

Strong light under a grey cloud was spread over Galway when I arrived. I made my way through heavy traffic and pointed towards the cathedral, not from force of habit but because I felt I had a good chance of parking my car nearby. But the area was thronged when I got there and it was only after I had driven around a few times that I found a place at last. I was grateful.

'Ah, father, I wouldn't leave them there if I were you'. The voice belonged to a low-sized man in his fifties with ginger hair and the splotched face of someone long acquainted with abundant alcohol. He was pointing to the jumble of clothes and bags in the back seat.

'This town is full of gougers. No respect for anybody or anything. And certainly your being a priest won't protect you at all. They'd steal the altar wine from you in a second if they thought you weren't looking. So I'd mind them clothes. I really would, father'.

'Thanks for the warning', I said, although I was not at all sure what to do about it.

'You're from out of town', the man said. I could see he had no immediate thought of leaving.

'And you?' I asked, thinking that if I started to put questions to him he might move off. But I quickly saw my mistake. He took my words as an invitation to autobiography, looking directly at me, and put on the expression of an earnest mentor.

'Ah no, I'm from Tuam. I'm sure you know the Nally's of Tuam. They run the hardware shop near the post office. They're cousins of mine. I went to school with Joe Nally. We were at the Christian Brothers. Great place. The discipline was strict, very strict. I'm telling you. No nonsense allowed. That's something the youth of today are missing. Don't you agree? If they had discipline, would I have to warn you about leaving them things in the car? No! That's as sure as you're there. Don't you agree with me? Man, isn't that the case, father?'

To have to agree with him might have evoked more confidences. But on the other hand a debate could have gone on without any prospect of a conclusion, and so I smiled, mumbled unintelligibly, looked at my watch, smiled again and began to slide away.

'You forgot to lock up, father', he said.

'Ah, yes, thank you. Silly of me!' I was slightly embarrassed, but I grasped the opportunity to go to the other side of my car, wave my keys and bid him good-bye.

I went across the parking lot and turned onto the bridge. The river was in full flow, its waters dark green and striped occasionally with foam. I stopped to look around me but when I was ready to continue my walk, I felt a strong tug at my sleeve. As I turned I was nearly pinned to the parapet of the bridge by a man who had stumbled against me and who was trying with great effort to straighten up. He was very drunk and his watery eyes sought to focus on me.

'Hello, father', he said, staggered, and would have toppled backward into traffic if I had not grabbed him.

'Will you pray for me, father?' he mumbled. 'And for me mother. She's just died. God rest her. And I have to bury her. Oh, it's terrible. And I haven't the money. Isn't that a bitch? Oh excuse the language, father. Can you give us a bit of help, and I'll pray for you in the chapel. I really will. God bless you, father. You're a grand man, and you'll give me a small bit of help, won't you? You will so! Of course you will. A small bit of help'.

Knowing well that in all likelihood there was a mother somewhere in Galway who would indignantly reject the notion that she had died, I nevertheless gave him a few coins. I propped him against the bridge and then hurried off.

But he and the ginger-haired man had done me a good turn. For they had helped to remind me that black clothes and a priestly collar draw certain types of people in the way an open jam jar in summer attracts the buzz of wasps. So by then I had crossed the bridge, and I knew that my immediate task in Galway must be to find a shop where I could buy ordinary clothes. This would be the first step on the road to my new life.

I was soon gazing at a window display. The pink faces on the models were designed to suggest young and trendy men. They wore bright blazers, shirts open at the neck to reveal richly coloured silk scarves, slacks with sharp creases and shoes gleaming below elegant socks. There were no price tags and when I went inside to inquire about these, I was shaken by what I was told. I retreated, and decided to look for a side street catering to more moderate ambitions.

I eventually found a small shop whose owner seemed depressed and where the stocks were lined up against a single wall. There were slacks, suits, jackets and overcoats, and the colours among them seemed to reflect the oscillating moods of the proprietor on a journey from grey with interludes of rusty brown or bright tan. The prices were low.

'Can I help you, father?' The voice suggested no great hope of making a sale.

'I'm looking for a pair of trousers and a jacket'.

'I've no clerical clothes, father'.

'That quite alright. It's not clerical clothes I need'.

'Is it for yourself, father?'

'Yes'.

'What size?'

'I don't know'.

He nodded slightly, as though acknowledging once again the daily manifestation of stupidity. He sighed and pulled out a measuring tape from which the first two and a half inches were clearly missing. However, it seemed enough to hold it in his hand.

'A thirty-six, I'd say', he remarked before I was able to find what I wanted. Then I selected a jacket, a green tie and a few shirts.

I noticed a corner rack on which there were second hand clothes.

'I'd like to sell my black suit', I said. 'Would you take it?'

'What's wrong with it?'

'Wrong? Nothing'.

'Then why would you want to sell it?'

'Because I have no further use for it'.

He pondered this. 'It's a good suit', he murmured, stepping closer.

'I know it is. So what would you give me?'

'Nice cloth. Well cut'.

'Yes. I agree with you. So, how much?'

He shook his head.

'How would I ever sell it again? That's the problem, father'.

'Perhaps some priest would buy it'.

'A priest? Buy a second-hand suit? I don't know any priest like that around here. They're all red rotten with money, and only the best will do them'.

'Never mind. Forget I mentioned it'. I could see his tone had shut off any likelihood that one could defend the clergy from the charge of being fat plutocrats. 'It doesn't really matter. Let me pay for these'.

He made up my bill, handed it to me and then looked at the door as if he expected me to run for it.

'If you'd like to leave the suit here', he said. 'I'd put it up for sale and if someone took it I'd give you the share of the money that was coming to you'.

'No, thanks', I answered. 'But if I may use your changing room, I'll get out of the suit and put these others on'.

He shrugged and seemed to lose interest in me, and when I left him a few minutes later he was bending over the racing page of his newspaper, a pencil in hand, a frown on his forehead. I was now wearing grey slacks and a jacket, and under my arm, wadded into a ball, was my black suit which I threw into the boot of the car as soon as I had returned to the parking lot.

I sat behind the wheel, looked around me and felt a sudden pounding onset of desolation and loneliness. I had half expected some kind of reaction within me to the decisions I had taken in recent days, but nothing had got me ready for what I felt now. My earlier feeling that all would be well, that ahead of me was the excitement of a glowing liberation drained out of me in a shocking rush, and if someone had chosen then to speak of growing old in minutes I would have understood fully. Whatever resources I had within me seemed gone and I was left with a dry sense of being irremediably on my own, with nothing to sustain me, nothing to look forward to. I was a bubble on an endless storm-shadowed sea. I felt bereft.

'Come on, Mahon, you're too old to cry. Move! Get out of here. Let's go. Let's start the car'.

The words gurgled out of some kind of breathlessness within me, and so I pulled away into the traffic. I had no specific destination in mind. I just needed to be on the move. I followed the car in front of me and when we came to a halt at traffic lights a glimmer of purpose began to appear in my mind and I decided I must look for somewhere to live during the coming few days.

I drove around the city with no clear sense of where I might stop to look for accommodation. It was not until a bus carrying elderly tourists came to a halt that I realised I was on a street in which all the homes, though obviously new, carried signs advertising bed and breakfast. They had about them the aura of daunting mortgages, and their red brick, white windowsills and television dishes seemed to promise anonymity. I parked outside one of them and rang the bell.

A heavy-set man with thick black hair and horn-rimmed glasses appeared at the door which led from a sun porch into the house. There were potted plants on all sides of him so that he looked a bit like a garden gnome which had been afflicted by giantism. He examined me carefully, and then slowly opened the door.

'Yes?' The voice was gruff.

'I was wondering if you had any vacant rooms?'

'For how long?'

'I'm not sure yet. But to-night at least'.

He seemed to ponder over this.

'No', he said finally.

'You have no free rooms?'

'I have. But I don't want any reporters hanging around here'.

'I'm not a reporter', I said.

'I know you're not. In fact I know who you are. On the run, I see. Well, not here. I'm not having the gutter press hanging around and taking pictures of my house. I don't need your sort. In fact I don't mind telling you I think we've had more than enough scandal in the Church. Let you be off now'.

He shut the door but remained behind the glass, looking at me.

I was so amazed that I made no move. Then I rang the bell. The man did not stir, but continued to frown. So I rang again. This seemed to disconcert him. He opened the door halfway.

'What are you talking about?' I exclaimed.

My question surprised him, and for an instant he was speechless. Abruptly he turned aside to a wicker chair on which there was a newspaper, a British tabloid, and when he held it up I could see that in place of a nude woman it carried a picture of me. It was a colour photograph, and above my skull-cap was the headline: Bishop Mahon Mystery.

'I've read all about you', the man said.

'Can I buy this from you?' I asked, fetching some coins out of my pocket.

'You're going to pretend you don't know, are you?' The self-righteous sneer was like something on a billboard. 'You're going to tell me that you're not trying to run away from the condemnation of the bishops and the Pope, are you?'

'I really would like to buy that paper', I replied, as evenly as I could.

'Well, I'm not going to give my paper to someone who's brought shame on the Church'.

'Fine. I won't trouble you any more'. I began to turn away. 'And in the future whenever I have any reason to think of someone who is a shining example to us all of Christian compassion and love, I shall think of you'.

As I walked away I felt sorry and guilty about that last remark. I ought not to have hit out. But he had slammed his door and there was nothing to be done now about it. I looked up at the sign outside his gate and had a laugh, for I half-expected it would say 'Virgin Mary - Bed & Breakfast'. Instead, the chosen name was 'St. Jude', the patron saint of hopeless cases.

And if I were to pray to this saint it would be to tell him what presumably he knew already, that my hope of living unnoticed was a naïve one. For the country was too small, the love of a good story too pervasive, and, in any case, at least one newspaper was on my trail. I could expect to be recognised again and again.

So I went to look for a small hotel and on the way I stopped to buy the newspaper which carried my photograph. No one paid any attention to me. Perhaps my change of clothes had helped for the moment. And when I found myself at a desk, filling the name Mr. Conor Mahon on the register, the girl who gave me my room-key was preoccupied by other concerns and barely glanced in my direction.

I climbed a narrow thinly carpeted stairway to the third floor and was shortly at rest amid drab furniture, brown curtains, a window overlooking rooftops, a phone book, and a discarded issue of Playboy. Since I had left most of my possessions in the car at the back of the hotel and had brought only a medium-sized suitcase, which I laid on the end of my bed, I was quickly able to relax.

I examined the wall-paper, the cracked ceiling, the pink globe on the overhead light. The mirror above the dressing table had replaced a larger predecessor, of which the marks were still visible. A plastic ashtray wore an advertisement for beer. On one side of the window there was a nail, and from it a spider was lowering itself, swinging on the thread. I could imagine someone before me watching it from the bed in dullness or despair.

I took up the newspaper and recognised the photograph. It had been taken two years earlier on a July day of teeming rain when I had consecrated and declared open a new church, designed and built by a socially prominent Dublin architect. He was a man regularly quoted on the subject of art. One could see him at well-publicised exhibitions, a gin and tonic in his hand, a knowing smile on his lips, and he had been commissioned by my predecessor to build a church in a valley overlooked by low rocky hills. When the job had ended the duty to conduct the appropriate ceremony came my way. I found myself surrounded by umbrellas, and because of the rain and because the architect had failed to be aware of the presence of natural spring wells, the new church stood like an exotic boat in a lake twelve to fifteen inches deep. The photograph of me had been taken while robed, mitred and croziered I waded to the front door in Wellingtons loaned by a nearby farmer. What remained of that day was the tetchy grimace under my increasingly damp mitre, and the text below it, untroubled by consideration of accuracy, offered some reasons for suggesting that I might not be a loyal, meek and mild servant of the church.

> The sudden resignation of Bishop Conor Mahon from the diocese of Dysart has surprised many, though not all of his colleagues.
>
> No statement has yet been issued by the Catholic Press Office. But it is known that the resignation has come at the end of a series of events in which the controversial Bishop was at loggerheads with the other members of the hierarchy.

Although he has made no public comment so far, Cardinal Flynn, the Archbishop of Armagh, is known to be particularly angry with Bishop Mahon. Relations between them have been strained for some time.

Demands by the Pope that Dr. Mahon should tone down his public utterances on the subject of women priests have been ignored by the Bishop.

Attempts to contact Dr. Mahon have so far failed. He is thought to be in hiding.

XVI

Next morning I woke up early, sat on the edge of my bed for a long time and decided finally that I must look for a job. I felt sure I would need many weeks, months perhaps, to settle on what I ought eventually to do with my life. I realised that inside myself a reaction would grow to what I had just done. I could not simply opt out of my past and I knew that I must be ready for bouts of uncertainty and regret. I would have to work my way through it all before I could be ready to decide on a future for myself. But in the meantime I would need money, and although I had a few hundred euros in a savings account, I did not want to turn to this unless I was without choice. So after breakfast I went in search of a local newspaper and turned to the section dealing with jobs. I read the columns slowly, and what became clear to me at once was the scantiness of my qualifications. The situations on offer were mostly for mechanics, assistant butchers, electricians and security men. A city bar was looking for what was, unmistakably a bouncer. A night-club offered auditions for entertainers. A hospital sought an experienced gardener.

By the time I had finished my study of the paper I could feel a slight edge of anxiety floating on to me. For only two positions seemed to be available for someone like me. Both were as part-time assistants in take-away food stores but when I phoned the numbers supplied in the paper I was told the jobs were gone already.

I remembered that the biggest store in my cathedral town used to have a notice board inside the door, and I wondered if the same might be true of Galway. I got into my car, drove to a shopping centre and began to look around. There were newsagents, a video library, shoe shops, a hairdresser, a boutique, a couple of hardware stores. But in a large super-market I found what I needed, a wall-panel on which filing cards had been posted, some hand-written, but most of them printed. I looked at each of them. Babysitters were much in demand. There were advertisements for language, yoga and cookery classes. Several associations of residents provided details and dates of future dinners and dances. A jam-making session was announced for the last Saturday of the month. A pink card gave the phone number for pregnancy tests. But no jobs featured.

Discouraged, I turned around to leave and noticed two men outside the door.

'Imagine, just walking out of this place!' one was saying to his companion. 'I mean good jobs are scarce and he walks out'.

'When was that?'

'This morning. An hour ago'.

'Well, that was plain stupid. And what's he going to do now?'

I did not wait for the answer but went towards a middle-aged woman who was the supervisor at the check out counters.

'Where's the manager's office?' I asked.

'Over there'.

I walked to the end of the meat section and turned to a set of doors, one of which had a brass plate bearing the word 'Manager'. I knocked and went in.

Behind a desk gazing at a computer was a grizzly-haired man. He was working a toothpick and seemed disgruntled.

'Yes?'

'I understand a job became vacant this morning'.

He swivelled to face me directly.

'News travels fast'.

'I'd like to ask what the job is. I'm looking for work'.

'Can you drive?'

'Yes'.

'Show me your licence'.

I handed over the document and realised suddenly that the photograph showed me with a clerical collar.

'Ever drive a van?'

'Yes'.

'If I take you it'll be Tuesday to Saturday'.

'That'll be fine'.

He stood up.

'Alright. Follow me'.

We went to the emergency exit behind his office, out into the parking lot and over to a blood-red Volkswagen van. The manager unlocked the door beside the steering wheel, pointed me towards it and then got in the other side. As I made myself comfortable he mentioned the wages in a voice that seemed a challenge.

'That would be more take-home pay than I've ever had'.

'Start her up!'

And for the next twenty minutes or so I drove around the parking lot stopping sometimes, reversing, squeezing between cars, jamming on the brakes at a grunt of a command. Finally he waved me back to where we had begun.

'I'll send Joe Quinn, our despatcher, to go around the city once with you. Then you keep the van for the afternoon. Find every road and alley. Get to recognise them. Be back here by five. You can start to-morrow. But see to it you get to know this whole town. I don't want groceries delivered to the wrong places'.

'Thanks', I said, and as he began to get out of the van I added, 'there's something about myself I'd better tell you ...'

'I know who you are, and I don't care if you're the Ayatollah of Abu Dhabi. Just deliver my groceries where they're supposed to go'.

'Again, thanks. But there might be press-men'.

'So what? Can't you put up with having your picture taken?'

'Of course I can'.

'Well, then ... And if you're worrying about pictures in the paper of you and the van, forget it. I can save a few pounds on advertising'.

He walked off, changed his mind and came back.

'By the way, you'd better watch Joe Quinn. Don't get me wrong. He's a good man. But he's a joker. He sends out our three delivery vans each day. But he'll try to point you to Mrs. Edel Martin. She sends for stuff every morning. But if she sees you she'll want you to carry the groceries into the kitchen for her'.

'And am I not supposed to do that?'

'Customer-pleasing is our business, and she'll even ask you to put things in the cupboard. And while you're doing it she'll take all her clothes off. Which might or might not please you. But with them press men around ... Know what I mean?'

'Oh, Lord, yes'.

'Good'.

With that warning in my mind I waited for Joe Quinn. He arrived after about five minutes, sat beside me, and for the next hour or more we drove around the main areas of Galway where customers of the supermarket were likely to be found. He made little conversation and seemed content to give his attention to names and landmarks. I could not tell from his manner if he had received from his manager a firm warning to behave. Nor could I decide if he knew who I was. But I was wary and perhaps he sensed it, so that when we returned to the parking lot, he merely said that he would expect me to hand over the keys of the van by five o'clock.

And when I began my rounds next day as deliveryman, Joe Quinn caused me no trouble and the routine proved to be straightforward. I carried boxes of groceries to doors, rang bells, greeted customers and went on my way. I got a word of thanks here, a remark there about the weather. At one house a pale and anxious woman begged my help to push a stalled car. A baby threw a plastic horse at me. Indeed during the first two days the only drama in my new life came when a man in his thirties crossed a road, rushed towards me and yelled. 'What do you think you're looking at?'

'Sorry?'

'What are you looking at, you old prostitute you?'

And he strode off.

At no time was there any suggestion that I bring groceries to Mrs. Edel Martin. Perhaps she had caught cold as a result of disrobing once too often, or could it be that Joe Quinn kept her in reserve for his favourite deliveryman. I continued to deal with housewives, most of whom were pleasant and none of whom appeared either to recognise me or, if they did, to think it odd that their supplies were handed over to them by a former bishop. By the end of the week I was beginning to think of my first packet of wages and when on Saturday morning I was told by Joe Quinn to leave a hamper in the house of a parish priest in the suburbs near the sea I thought nothing of it. But when the door was opened in response to my knock, I immediately recognised the man whose expression, at the sight of me, was already slipping into outrage.

Father Desmond Meehan was now in his late sixties, white-haired, blue-eyed and with a face deeply scarred by morose lines. He had once been short-listed for appointment as bishop but had been passed over, and the experience had evidently soured him. But he maintained a recurring prominence as a writer of bluntly conservative articles in religious magazines and journals. A sign of his outlook was the frequency with which he quoted a passage in St. Irenaeus which claims that despite the extensive choice of foliage in the Garden of Eden the fig leaf had been chosen by Adam and Eve because it was sufficiently scratchy to be a disincentive to the deployment of their sexual organs.

'Come in! Come in!' he said, and as I entered the hall he tried to take the hamper from me. But I held on until I could lay it on a chair.

'There now', I proclaimed and started to turn back to the door.

'No, please. Wait, wait!'

I looked at him.

'Couldn't we sit down for a moment and talk? I'll make you a cup of tea'.

'That's kind of you, but, you see, I have deliveries to complete. I just don't have the time now'.

'My Lord, this is terrible!'

'What is?'

'You'.

'What about me?'

'You're ... a delivery man!'

'What's wrong with that? It's a job. It pays me a wage'.

'No, no! That's not the point'.

'Then what is?'

'Can't you see? Can't you see the scandal of it all? What are people going to think? How are we to continue with our work, to have influence, to set an example, if you ... if you ...'

'If I what?'

'If you're doing this?'

'You mean working in a supermarket?'

'Yes!'

'Ah. You'd prefer if I were a bank manager or a prominent businessman. Well, I'm an ex-cleric and I have no qualifications and no experience of the kind that would make me employable at the present time. I consider myself very lucky to have been taken on by a supermarket. And I'm inclined to suspect that the main reason I got this job was because the manager practices what you preach and is offering a helping hand to someone in need'.

He shook his head.

'My lord ...'

'Yes?'

'My lord, would you not take account of people's feelings?'

'Regarding what?'

'This, my lord! This! You're a bishop ...'

'An ex-bishop'.

'No! Active or not you're a bishop and nothing will change that. And the sight of you driving around every day for a supermarket ... Why, you must see what I mean! You must!'

'Are appearances important to you, Father Meehan?' I was staring at him and I remembered at once the expression like his own which I had seen once before. The touch of fear and the controlled rage were exactly the same as in the face of Archbishop O'Donnell on that evening when he had hissed that I was not one of 'them'.

'Why are you so angry?' I went on. 'We have never met, you or I. Of course I've heard of you and obviously you recognise me. But what is it about me that makes you barely able to control yourself? Men have driven vans before and I'm sure that's not something that bothered you. But as soon as you see me you become barely coherent. Is there some deep moral principle which says that ex-bishops can't be employed by supermarkets?'

'You are giving scandal, my lord'.

'To whom, apart from you?'

'You are letting the side down!'

'Ah! Now that's honest'.

The hall door was suddenly pushed open and a priest, a parish curate, came in and stopped as soon as he saw us.

'Oh, I'm sorry. I didn't know I was interrupting'. Then, realising who I was, he continued, 'why hello! You're welcome. Is that your van outside?'

'It is'.

'So you're come to live in Galway?'

'Yes, I have'.

'And you're even managed to land a job! Good for you. That's really great. Anyhow, I wish you lots of luck, and if I can be of any help, make sure you let me know. But sorry for butting in. I'll wait in the kitchen'.

I moved to the door.

'Good-bye, Father Meehan'.

'My lord!'

'Yes?'

'Don't do it'.

'I have to. I need the job. Can't you understand that?'

'Well, then, get a job somewhere else. But not here. Not where everyone can see you'.

'Out of sight, out of mind. Is that it?'

The anger seeped away from him and he grew visibly older.

'You can sneer about appearances mattering', he said. 'That's fine for you. But don't forget that for some, when appearances go there's not much left'.

The grief in his bones showed through and I sensed at once what he was really saying to me. He would have to retire soon and he had chosen his way of life in the days when to be a priest was not only to have a feeling of purpose and of well-articulated objectives but also to have these validated and bolstered by public esteem and status. But that was all crumbling, especially so for a man who knew only how to look backward to a receding world. To find on his own doorstep now a bishop who delivered groceries was something for which he had never been prepared.

'Father Meehan', I said, 'I'm really sorry to be a cause of hurt to you. But I can't help it. I am what I am, and at the moment I need this job. Please try to understand that'.

But as I drove away from his house I felt something close to guilt. Father Meehan was not a man to call out warm feelings in me. He was a type I had met too often, righteously moored in his little domain, easily arrogant, something of a bully. But a world changing too quickly had made him vulnerable and he possessed few of the resources needed by those who are stranded. He could remember the days when he was deferred to, when he was saluted on the street, when his assertions, wise or ignorant, had about them the resonance of a confident oracle. Not now, however. Not any more, and the sight of me must have cut far into his bewildered spirit. I felt sorry and sad, and as I drove back to the supermarket at the end of my rounds I wondered over and over if after all there might be some nugget of wisdom in the idea, natural to Father Meehan, that someone like me should vanish into a very dark corner of a far off place.

But I stayed in Galway and the weeks slipped behind me. I delivered the groceries. I worked overtime when I was asked. Nobody bothered me. The manager of the supermarket appeared to be satisfied with my performance, and as I crossed and re-crossed every part of the city and suburbs I began to think that if I were ever to lose this job I could turn to being a taxi driver. I was acquiring qualifications, visible expertise, and when I remembered my time as a bishop, especially the recent couple of years, I felt something quite new, a confidence born of the awareness that now at least in one level I could, on demand, not only find my way but be seen to be able to do so. My competence could be trusted, and this was a comforting thought.

One result of my daily travels around Galway was that I came to know where every kind of accommodation was to be found. I could quote prices. I knew which places were in or out of current favour or which were especially noisy on Friday or Saturday nights. I learned about landlords, good and bad, about the alleged difference between a flat and an apartment. If someone had remarked to me that rents seemed unusually high in one side-street where the houses were jerry-built and of poor quality, I would have been able to provide a reason, the immediate proximity of what was held to be the most desirable address in the city. When an elderly timid lady mentioned to me that she was looking for a retreat in a safe district, I pointed her towards a road inhabited by three detectives and a fearsome dog. At the door of a prostitute I was told the going rate for rooms in the houses nearby, and as she took her box of groceries she remarked with a very wide grin that it was getting harder and more troublesome each day to make ends meet. And around the corner another woman, recently widowed insisted on showing me a converted garage where she had two spare rooms into which she was trying to entice a suitably respectable lodger.

This knowledge acquired as I traversed Galway in the van made it possible for me at last to settle on a flat for myself. It was about five miles from the middle of the city and was well furnished. My bedroom looked out to the hills of Clare and towards a line of bushes and of eastward-leaning trees below which, and out of immediate sight, was a corner of the bay. In the morning I could see gulls rising in the sky, and I followed the march of clouds as, sometimes bunched and black, sometimes rushing, they come off the Atlantic. There were sloping fields, grazing cattle and boundaries of willow and of rough stone. But when I left the bedroom and emerged on the other side of the house I was confronted by hundreds of rooftops lying between me and the city.

The landlord was a gruff man in his mid-sixties. He had a bad limp, a florid complexion and horn-rimmed glasses. He had no inclination to chat and in all my dealings with him he managed to practice an economy of speech requiring the concentrated attention of anyone disposed to listen. He addressed me as Mr. Mahon when I handed him the rent. Otherwise he restricted himself to a nod if we happened to meet. Nothing about him suggested he knew of my past or, if he did, that he was in any way interested in it. He seemed preoccupied and dour, and when I delivered groceries to a neighbour one day I was told that his wife and daughter had walked out on him. In the evenings after work I returned to the flat and had my main meal. I cooked on a new electric stove with its panel of knobs and lights which reminded me a little bit of the dashboard of a sophisticated car. For several weeks I ate badly. Sometimes the food was as dry and tasteless as I imagined straw to be. Once when I picked up a macaroni and cheese concoction from the freezer and put it in the oven I ended up with a dish that was lukewarm on the fringes and ice cold in the middle. I mastered the techniques of grilling mainly by watching the change of colour on meat or fish. I fried as little as possible, not because of worries regarding cholesterol but because I had no patience with the subsequent need to wash the wall over the stove. But I was not discouraged and I made up my mind that expertise in cooking was something I could eventually acquire.

I also recognised that a day would come when I might wish to expand my life beyond the boundaries of cooking, doing my job and minding my flat. Of course I had my books which I had retrieved from the reluctant guardianship of the priest in charge of my former cathedral. They were mostly in boxes in my bedroom, and in the evenings I enjoyed the experience of reading without pressure, of being able to linger over what interested me with no accompanying thought of sermons to be prepared or speeches composed.

But I also knew that this was not enough. There was a life to be made. Though I was long accustomed to being alone, it was not in my nature ever to think of turning into some kind of recluse. I had a sense of gratitude for being alive and I tried to give an appropriate outlet to this in the years when I was a student, a priest, a bishop. But I was a van driver now, and for eight hours a day. At the moment I was enjoying it, but something would have to be added sooner or later.

Of course I realised that considerations of this kind were a reflection of the sort of career I had followed up to now. I had been obliged then to think of such things, and had a professional interest in getting others to do the same. I was accustomed to focusing upon a grand scheme within which every sinner had a place and purpose. But since I was no longer a bishop, my mind was a bit like a disconnected flywheel going round and round out of a past momentum. I could not imagine any of my work mates sinking into worries about the extent to which their lives fitted into some cosmic arrangement. Certainly the boss did not appear to be the sort of person who because of a decision to go out for a drink would spend time in philosophic speculations on the question of how man best fulfils his potential as a social being. Yet here I was one evening walking to the pub, my head full of earnest thoughts about ways of life and modes of existence. And all arising from a notion that it might be pleasant to have a leisurely pint of Guinness.

I had to cross a main road before I reached the extensive parking lot which channelled the thirsty, the lonely and the bored into Nicky Langan's Bar. I had been there a few times with my van and my groceries, and I had met the owner, who was once a champion footballer. He had wiry black hair, a fluid complexion and an unending sniff as though some internal plumbing had suffered permanent damage during his sporting days. He was friendly, and the bar, clean and bright, was popular.

Although there was a crowd I had no trouble finding a seat and table for myself. My Guinness was delivered to me and, as I looked around, I thought I recognised some of the faces. But I was beginning to settle in my chair when I acquired company, a low-sized man whose blue eyes showed him to be overflowing with alcohol. My morale began to falter and I wondered if, despite the absence of black clothes and a collar, I still had about me the unmistakeable look of a cleric. 'Thought you'd like this one', he remarked bronchially. 'Yes, it's real good. Real good. You know what I mean?' His cigarette was lying on the ashtray, its smoke reaching over to me, but he lighted another one. 'I heard from me mate. About the priest and the donkey. You haven't heard it before, have you? He did not wait for an answer, and he started a guffaw which was interrupted only by a long hawking cough. But at least he chose not to spit on the floor.

'Yes. The priest and the donkey. You'd think a priest wouldn't come within an ass's roar of such things, would you? An ass's roar!' His eyes filled with tears and I was glad to be out of range of the poke in the ribs which he would certainly have given me as he contemplated his witty, punning self.

'An ass's roar! You get me, like? Well. You see, Father Murphy went to his bishop asking permission to enter his donkey in a race and because the bishop thought it was for charity – do you know what I mean? – he said yes. So next day the sports page had the headline, "bishop gives the go-ahead to Father Murphy's ass". My entertainer began to shake. 'And, when the bishop read this he was very angry and he sent for Father Murphy and Father Murphy said he was going ahead with his promise to run the donkey in a race next week and the bishop said no. And do you know what the headline said next day? It said, "Bishop scratches Father Murphy's ass!" Get it?' he spluttered and gasped until I thought he was going to fall on the floor.

From the way he eventually rallied I could tell that he had many more jokes of this kind for me, and I began to wonder if my Guinness was worth the ordeal. I had almost resigned myself to an ignominious retreat when a voice behind me muttered, 'Ah, no', and Joe Quinn, the despatcher at the supermarket, came around to where my companion was sitting, took hold of his arm, lifted him on to his feet, smiled pleasantly and said. 'Jimmy! The very man I wanted to talk to! Listen. Come with me. No it's got to be now. It's important'.

I watched the two of them as they snaked towards the exit, and nearly ten minutes passed before my rescuer came back.

'Sorry about that', he said disgustedly. 'He's a right half-wit when he gets a few pints into him. He doesn't mean any harm, but after one drink he turns into a big child with the stupidest stories'.

'I must admit I'm grateful to you. I thought I was stuck with him'.

'Sure, I could see that', he hesitated. 'A few of us are finishing a jar over in the corner behind you. If you like to join us, you'd be very welcome'.

'Of course I'd like that', I answered. I got up, took my glass and followed him. Three men were at a table beside the cigarette machine, and after Joe had introduced me to them a slightly awkward silence ensued. I realised at once that all of them knew me to be something more than a recently recruited van driver. But there was an unspoken determination to make ease for me, and a conversation came gradually into being. If they asked questions, it was only about my present situation, and I marvelled at their tact.

Later, when it was time to leave, Joe turned to me.

'We usually have a drink here on Thursday evenings around this time. So if you're ever free why don't you come along?'

The kindness elated me, and on the walk to my flat I kept thinking about those four men, all in their fifties, all married, all settled. Aware that I had been a well-known bishop they had clearly sensed that I must be going through a strange time as I groped my way into a new life, and what I felt most about them now was the lack of reproach in them. I was not yet well enough acquainted with them to decide if they were the sort of pious Catholics in whose world bishops never resigned. But as we drank our Guinness I had encountered only tolerance. Thinking of this I could imagine the reaction of Archbishop O'Donnell if he met me now, with the smell of beer on my breath, me that lapsed man who had once been addressed with the deference granted to age-old titles.

I restrained my urge to laugh and was still smiling within myself when I got back to my room. The house was silent, the air warm. I undid my shoe-laces and sat into my chair, which was the one piece of furniture from my former life. It seemed always to make me comfortable, holding me as no other chair had ever done, and I half sighed as though anticipating a quiet nap after a good day. But some opposing current was at work and the well-being I had felt on the walk from the bar seemed all at once to be pulled upwards through me into the ceiling and the roof and the overhead sky. And I was left with a desolation like that of an awakening tree ripped suddenly bare in springtime. I could not understand what was happening and I was slow to realise that I was caught up in a whirl of bleak loneliness.

At that moment the delivery of groceries moved on to some lower plane in my mind. The knowledge opened to me of Galway, of varied people, of arenas in which I could be competent seemed all to step back from me and to leave me barren. I was dry and achingly on my own. The days had passed, the hours had glided away as I drove around the city. And I remembered how it had been with me, how for others I had sketched possible worlds of sanctified deeds and holy action. I had been enthusiastic. There had been times when I could see the stirrings of openness to what I was saying. But now it was as if something had been broken within me, or else had faded. Perhaps it was a simple case of departing energy and that it had left me now with a sense not of wide horizons but merely of being in the day, drifting with the passing minutes, neither despairing nor apathetic, just there, living out of a suitcase of accumulated memories, capable of being taken over by emotion, articulate when I had to be.

Since childhood I had been accustomed to pray and I was still doing so. But always with the consciousness of the unreplying, addressed voice. I needed more than this now. I longed for ballast of some kind, a responsive centre, a welcoming home. Yet there was only my head and the thoughts within it and the things outside which, sometimes, could absorb me for the longest moments. But it was not enough, though what I could do about it remained out of sight beyond some horizon which, once, I used to point out to others.

The irony of it all overtook me. Sitting in my chair in the fading light I was still, technically, a bishop, inoperative of course but a bishop nonetheless. And 'His Lordship' - as some textbook of Canon Law would be obliged to describe me – was alone and, from the point of view of larger schemes of things, he was unmistakeably rudderless.

I phoned Helen on Friday evening. I was not sure why I did so and had no plan beyond hearing her voice.

'I'm glad you called', she had said, and the conversation evolved somehow to the stage where she promised to come to Galway the following week, on my free Monday.

I met her at the cathedral parking lot. I had borrowed a helmet for her and she sat behind me on the new scooter for which I had already made three weekly payments. I had sold my car and had put the money aside for emergencies. Now as we pointed out of the city, with the wind in our ears, I heard her laugh. I could guess what was in her mind.

'So what, if people see us?' I shouted.

'Couldn't agree more', came the answer.

'Are you warm enough?'

'Yes'.

We gradually left the city behind us and were soon passing by stone walls and scattered bungalows until we came to a neck of land which thrust itself into the sea. Wan fields held down some of the massed rock and a returning tide moved into a channel where seals swam and birds dived.

The sun was shining and the breeze off the Atlantic blew gently on Helen and me as we came to a halt behind a grey hump-backed bridge.

'I brought a few sandwiches', I said. 'I thought you might be hungry'.

'Thank you. That was a nice idea'.

We walked in silence for a while. She linked arms with me.

'And how are you, Conor? I'm glad you called me, because I really wanted to know if things were well with you. But I didn't want to intrude'.

'I've got work, that job I told you about. I was lucky. And it keeps me busy and pays my way'.

She said nothing.

'That's not a brush-off to your question', I added. 'But the job gives me a context. So you're asking how I am'.

I looked at the changing colour patterns on the sea.

'Oddly enough, I'm not sure. Maybe it's too soon to know anything about myself in this new situation. And since I've spent my professional life so far mopping things up into generalisations which sound like some great truth, I think I can only move now in fragments. I don't want to return to the habit of speaking in broad terms about anything, myself included. So how am I today, now?'

I stopped.

'The sun is shining. The breeze is gentle. You're here. And I feel enormous gratitude for your interest, for your concern, and for your having ridden out on the back of my scooter'.

We walked a little more.

'Also', I said, 'you're the first person who asked me that question since I resigned'.

'None of your colleagues in Christ have checked on you?'

'Are you surprised?'

'Yes. I mean no. I shouldn't let myself be surprised'. She frowned.

I laughed. 'Helen, I quit. That causes bewilderment'.

'That's no reason to turn their backs on you! After all, you might be down on your luck, needy, lost'.

I'm fairly sure the cardinal and the others know where I am and that I'm a deliveryman. And therefore that I'm not starving'.

'There's more to life than not starving. So don't start making excuses. What you're saying is that they've dropped you cold'.

I thought about this for a moment.

'Maybe you're right', I said, finally. 'But there's no use brooding on it. Anyhow, let's enjoy the day'.

We walked on. About fifty yards from us the shiny head of a seal rose from the water. Two dark eyes and a set of whiskers turned towards us, measuring us on some deep-rooted scale of danger, and when the creature slid in relaxed fashion back into the current, it was as if we had been given a temporary clearance certificate. I could imagine other circumstances when the bulky brown bodies of its comrades would take fright at our approach and would leap, splashing, into the sea, leaving us small and alone on the empty shore.

'One of the discoveries I've made in this new life of mine is how much I seem to operate on the basis of habit. Of course when I go to work I have to be there at nine o'clock in the morning and there's no choice available in the matter of having to eat and sleep. But try as I do to get away from it, I seem to look at things and respond to things as if I were still a bishop. And that depresses me a bit sometimes. I don't know if I'm making any sense at all'.

She gazed at me in her serious, concentrated way. 'I think I have a glimmering of what you're getting at. But tell me. Please tell me. I'd like to understand'.

I felt a rising helplessness within me.

'I suppose I'm being naïve really. But I think I'd like to get away from the ingrained tendency to make whatever I see shape itself into the condition of being accepted, reshaped or else condemned by a bishop. I'd like to be received by things rather than make them conform to my expectations of them. If I can't do that, then I'm not really open-minded. And that depresses me a bit. No. Not true. It worries me quite a bit'.

I turned to her.

'You're an artist, Helen. I'm sure you must understand what I'm blundering at. I'm sure you must'.

It was an appeal and, of course, she recognised it as such.

'Conor, dear Conor, you can't expect to step out of the only way of life you've known and not feel lost. For a while at least. You're a wounded man, Conor. You have to let life heal you. But not overnight. That's not how it happens. Stay open to things. You're right about wanting that. But let go, if you can. Wait. Just wait'.

She looked at me very sharply. And then I saw a softening in her eyes and a smile of such compassion that I was drawn into it and forgot myself and was taken up by what was there in this moment under a blue sky.

And without thought or calculation I put my arms around her.

'Thank you, Helen'.

For a while nothing more was said. We passed an abandoned house and turned onto a path between stone walls. There were fields on either side of us. A startled wagtail leapt out from behind a bush, and we continued until we reached a grassy bank overlooking the sea. Stones spread below us where the tides had flung them and there were ramparts of seaweed. A tree trunk lay stripped and white. Water gleamed under the sun.

'Are you hungry?' I asked.

'As a matter of fact, yes. All this fresh air, the ride on the scooter, all this ...'

'I know what you mean. Well, let's sit here and open the sandwich packet'.

'Mmm ...!'

We sat side by side with a stone wall at our backs and, in front, a view of low hills and the sea. The sandwiches seemed unusually good, and the white Italian wine, cool but unchilled, had a lingering taste which made me think of rich earth gathering abundance under Mediterranean skies.

For a while we did not say much, but there seemed to be no need of it, and I felt within me a mood which I would have found hard to describe but which seemed very like a wish to say thanks.

Helen sat, hunched slightly, the wind riffling her dark hair. She was watching a far-off ship.

'And you?' I said. 'How is it with you?'

'I'm getting some work done, and that's good. Or, at least, I was. The past ten days or so have been ... Not very peaceful'.

'Oh? What happened?'

'The detectives have been back to me'.

'Why? Are there some developments in the murder hunt?' As I asked this I realised that the killing of Tim McDermott had passed from my mind over the past few weeks.

'Oh, they've gone down so many blind alleys that I think they've been ordered to review the entire case from the beginning. There's a new senior man in charge. They're re-interviewing people. And from the way they act, I'm inclined to think they're still wondering if I hadn't something to do with it'.

'No!'

She smiled at me. 'Is that a shock?'

'Well, what do you think?'

'Thank you, Conor', and she laughed and then frowned. 'I can see their problem. To have that murder unsolved must be a sore embarrassment to them'.

'Maybe so, but ...'

'Oh, I can guess what's in your mind. But the fact is that husbands do arrange for the murder of their wives and vice versa. And besides, they don't greatly like me. It's part of Tim's legacy. When he backed away from me, he made sure to take his family and friends with him. I can well imagine the picture the detectives are getting of me as they carry on their interviews. Tim saw to that. I don't blame the detectives'. There was no rancour in her voice.

'Don't look so upset, Conor! It'll pass. Come on! As you said yourself a while ago, let's enjoy the day'.

But for a while I could not do so. I thought again of what Helen had told me in the aftermath of the murder. I remembered in particular those quiet times when she had spoken of the estrangement between her husband and herself. I had been shocked by the spectacle of her isolation on the day in the cathedral when the family, his family, had remained as far apart from her as the decorum of a funeral permitted.

But then there was that notebook, and the words of it came back and in my mind was the echo of what Tim McDermott had written about her hatred.

'Helen', I said, suddenly. Then I stopped, looked out to the sea with all it's hidden life. 'There's something I have to tell you. I think I may be breaking a confidence in doing so. But I don't want to look at you knowing that I'm putting limits on the amount of truth I speak to you. I may not even be doing you a kindness. I just don't know. But bear with me. I once heard a man say that he loved winter because that was when the trees and bushes were there in all their honesty, with nothing to cover them and nothing to conceal what they truly were. I may not be about to do you a kindness or a favour. But I want honesty to be at the centre of anything we say to each other ...'

My voice trailed off. She drew back a little and stared at me. I told her about the notebook. I am not good at remembering words exactly, but I know how to convey what is essential in the way they are used. So I did not soften or sanitise what Tim McDermott had written. Helen leaned forward slightly as if to ensure that she missed nothing of what I was saying, and when I had finished she seemed for a moment to become rigid before turning abruptly and striding away from me.

I felt sick and began to wonder if I had done something horribly wrong. I saw her left hand fist away some obstacle in the sea air and her footsteps quickened and I followed her and wished for the impossible, for her not to be hurt, for Tim McDermott not to be dead, for me not to be the instrument of anguish.

She whirled around and I halted, awed by her rage.

'What is it about me?' she screamed. 'Why is it that I have to be mauled all my life? What is wrong with me? My mother hated me – told me over and over that the worst disaster of her life was when she was pregnant with me. She never ever cherished me. Not once. I was always in the wrong. There wasn't a thing I could do to please her. She cut me down at every turn, and when she wanted really to hit me she coldly addressed me as Pangalos. Pangalos do this. Pangalos do that. Pangalos, can you ever do anything right? And who was Pangalos? He was a Greek. He was my father and when I was two years old he vanished ... And it was not until I met Tim that I thought a man could be so adorable. I worshipped him and I thought heaven had arrived on earth when I married him. And then he began to push me away. Almost overnight. In fact, after our wedding night. In fact on our wedding night I could see he hated it. And I thought o.k. maybe he has problems here but he loves me and I'm crazy about him and it's not for the sex I'm with him. But he pushed me away. And now you tell me he saw me as hating him, he dreamed of being loved by me. What sort of a twisted mind did he have? God almighty! I was the one who was driven away by him. I was the one who was given the boot. And still you tell me he said it was the other way around. Fuck it, Conor! What plague is on me that I infect people this way? Tell me, tell me'.

And with her two hands she pounded my shoulders yelling into my face, her eyes like those of a maddened bull.

She frightened me. I had never encountered anything to match this eruption of roaring fury. She had turned wild. It was as if I were witnessing a new form of life. I stood in wordless bewilderment, afraid to put my arms around her, afraid to venture consolation while she sobbed and groaned and cursed.

We remained this way for what seemed a long time, until her breath began to slow down and her hands were finally by her side.

'Just think', she said. 'He was turned off on our wedding night and the miserable blind bastard twisted it around so as to decide I hated him. God! No wonder the detectives have the idea I might have had him killed'.

She took a few steps back from me, shook her head and started to walk. I stayed with her. She had crossed her arms and with sloped shoulders she was hugging herself as if against some deadly chill.

'My father would have been able to tune into all this. I saw him once after he had left. I was twenty, and he was dying in a hospital in Athens. He was near the end. His last words to me before he drifted off into a sleep was a question. "How is Medea?" I didn't know what he was talking about. At least not then. It was only afterwards that I came across the story of Medea, of how she avenged herself on Jason by murdering his children. "How is Medea?" Even when he was dying he must still have understood things. I don't know why she hated him but my mother certainly went about the business of killing his child. And she had all the talents for doing it effectively'.

Again she turned from me and started to walk in the direction from which we had come. I tagged along with her like her shadow and when at last we came to where I had parked the scooter she stopped and stood there looking at the broken shells at her feet and saying nothing.

'I suppose we might as well go back to Galway', I murmured. She did not answer. I took a helmet and put it on her, tying the strap under her chin.

'Ready?' She gave a slight shrug. I got on to my saddle and she climbed on to pillion behind me. It took an hour to get back, and I brought her to my apartment because I did not want her to go home alone. I made up the bed for her in my room and threw a blanket on to the sofa for myself. Throughout the evening she sat and gazed out the window and I gazed out the window and I could only guess if she was actually looking at anything. She either shook her head or else did not answer if I spoke to her. The evening passed slowly. When, around eleven, I asked if she would like to rest she stood abruptly, walked into the room and lay on my bed. She did not bother to shut the door. After a few minutes I went in, took my shoes off and put a blanket over her.

'Good-night, Helen. Forgive me if I did the wrong thing in telling you'.

She closed her eyes, and I let her be.

In the early morning when I woke up I found she was gone.

The next few days were the longest I could remember. Several times I approached the phone to call Helen. But I backed off. What was I to say to her?

Over and over I thought back to that outburst on the shoreline. And to that transformation which had so astounded me. I could never have imagined such a change in her. This implied, of course, that subconsciously, I had typecast her and that I had an unacknowledged expectation that she would conform to my view of her. Once I realised this, I could only smile at my own naïve and limited horizons. I had to accept that I had no entitlement to be surprised by what she said or, indeed, by her behaviour. Which, perhaps, was the beginning of letting her be herself.

These thoughts and my images of her played hopscotch in my mind as I continued to make my deliveries around the city. And one afternoon when I was stuck in a traffic jam I heard her voice on my mobile phone.

'Conor'.

'Helen!'

'Is Monday still your day off?'

'Yes it is'.

'Had you any plans?'

'Nothing special'.

'Can I come and see you?'

'I wish you would'.

'Same time as before at the cathedral parking lot?'

'I'll be there'.

And she was smiling when, on Monday, I arrived a few minutes late to collect her. She put on her helmet, climbed up behind me on the scooter and we pointed out of the city in the direction of the Clare hills. It was a sunny day. I had brought a picnic, and we travelled and strolled, enjoying the air and the sights, listening to the birds or to the streams falling among grey rocks. Nothing was said about our previous encounter. Any vague apprehension which I had felt earlier in the morning drained away and I began really to enjoy myself.

Later in the afternoon Helen tapped my shoulder as we were riding along a straight length of road.

'Someone's following us'.

I looked in my rear-view mirror and saw a black Renault. There were two men in front.

'Do you mean they're trying to get by?'

'No. They're following us'.

'Are you sure?'

'Yes'.

The road wound among embankments of hawthorn and elderberry bushes. Sheep and cattle were grazing in some of the nearby fields. The ruins of a medieval monastery came into sight. We passed a house on whose flat roof were sods of grass. Farther ahead was a turnoff into a road barely wide enough for a car. I knew that it climbed steeply up a hill and that on the top of the rise there was a track into which I could turn.

'Hold on', I shouted and began to accelerate. I gave no signal but at the right moment I swerved suddenly off the main road. We were quickly on the hill. At the summit on the right there was a prehistoric tomb. The track lay behind it, and I pulled in and switched off the engine. We could not be seen from the road, and we waited.

A few moments later we heard the car, the black Renault.

'We'll let it pass and then we'll go back down the hill', I said. 'They'll have to continue for at least a quarter of a mile before they can possibly turn'.

With heads ducked we hid behind the ancient tomb and watched through tall grass as the car went by.

'Let's go', I murmured after about half a minute. We returned down the hill and onto the main road, and then picked a lane where we could park the scooter.

'We'll watch for their return', I suggested. 'Since they're faster than we are they'll count on catching up with us. So all we need to do is to see which way they go and then take off in the opposite direction'.

'Good thinking, Conor', she answered, and her tone was that of someone enjoying an unexpected adventure.

Nearly ten minutes passed before the Renault reappeared. It drove away very fast in the direction of Galway.

'There!' I said. 'Now we can go back another way. But what's all that about? Why should anyone want to follow us?'

We speculated for a while and then took off, reaching Galway after about two hours. Helen collected her car and drove home. I returned to my flat and later, much later, woke up in the night to find I had been dreaming of a huge black car which was bearing down and about to run me over. When I went to work in the morning, the manager was waiting for me.

'Come into the office a minute' he instructed, and I followed him. He closed the door. 'There's a pock-marked little bugger nosing around here asking questions about you. Do you know anything about it?'

'No', I answered. 'but that's a coincidence. Yesterday I was out on my scooter in the Clare hills. I had a friend with me. We were followed. Two men. But I managed to shake them off'.

The manager nodded.

'I thought so. Well let me ask you something else. What paper do you read every day?'

'*The Irish Times*'. I answered, growing mystified.

'That figures. Somehow I couldn't see you reading the *Daily Clarion*. That's a family paper, in case you don't know, and it's printed specially for fans of boobs and backsides'.

'I'm sorry. You've lost me'.

'Yes. Right. Well, the *Clarion* has been running a series called 'Where are they now?' Do you remember the politician who had to resign because he was photographed in bed with a prostitute?'

'Yes, I do'.

'And the bank manager who embezzled a million and walked free from court because of a technicality?'

'Yes'.

'And the housewife who used the kitchen knife on her husband's you-know-what?'

'I remember'.

'Well, the *Clarion* has been raking all that up for their series. Last week they showed the housewife. She has a new name. She's in a new neighbourhood. And the poor bitch was out there watering the flowers and thinking it was all over when it wasn't. You can imagine what's in the mind today of the family next door. I'll bet the husband starts thinking of precautionary measures. That's the good old *Clarion* for you. And they're doing the same for the others'.

'So?'

'So, welcome to the club', the manager growled, putting a copy of the *Daily Clarion* on the table. A colour photograph took up most of the front page. It showed Helen and me on the scooter. We were both laughing, and her head seemed to be resting on my shoulder. The caption, black letters against a red background, was 'Bishop and Friend' and in a box underneath there was a short paragraph.

When Bishop Conor Mahon resigned suddenly from his diocese of Dysart, the Catholic Church was rocked. No explanations were given and authorities were close mouthed about the affair. Now the *Daily Clarion* investigating team, your fearless reporters, can reveal the truth. See to-morrow's edition and the next instalment in our series, Where are they now?

A feeling like a sudden loss of appetite began to spread inside me. I sat down near the desk. The phone rang.

'Later!' the manager snapped and hung up. He turned to me. 'Sorry to have hit you with that one. But I had a feeling you'd be only one not to have heard about it, and you know how people in Galway are interested in such things'.

'Thank you. I appreciate that. But. I don't know what to say. I mean. You know. This. And there's ... She shouldn't have to have this done to her. I mean, there's been no affair. That's not why I resigned. Of course, put the word affair beside the word bishop, and you have ... and if you challenge them, they say they didn't mean it that way. And to challenge is to walk into their trap and give them something more to write about. My God, I'll have to think this one over. But ... This is ... I'm sorry, I'm wasting you're time now. It's the shock, I suppose'.

He raised his hand.

'You're not wasting my time. The thing is, what do you want to do?'

'I really don't know ... I suppose I'll have to give up this job'.

'Why?'

'I don't imagine you want this kind of publicity'.

'That's rubbish. I want my groceries delivered, and until you start nicking the salami from Mrs. Kavanagh's box, the job is yours. So forget about that side of things'.

I felt shocked and helpless.

'What should I do?'

The manager picked up the *Daily Clarion* and stuck it in a drawer.

'You really want my advice?'

'I need it'.

'I'm going to leave you here with the phone', he began. 'Call your friend. Tell her what's happening in case she doesn't know about it. See how she takes it and do something for her'.

'And then?'

'And then think over something I'm going to put to you now. That picture is too good for the other papers to miss. They'll want a bit of the action too'.

'What do you mean?'

'Simple. They'll send reporters and photographers along. They'll follow you around, camp outside your flat. They'll bug you with questions. They'll want a better story'. He looked very closely at me. 'Is there a better story?'

For a moment my mind was blank. Then I thought of Helen.

'My friend is the widow of Tim McDermott, the murdered minister'.

'Shit! Oh, beans and shit! Well, that's it. They'll really be interested in you now'.

He put his feet on the desk, took them off again and fiddled jerkily with a paper clip.

'You're going to put something to me', I reminded him.

'Yes, well ... look, as far as I can make out, you're got to decide between one of two things. You can run for it, go into hiding, get yourself bundled on to a plane out of the country. Or ...'. he stopped.

'Or ...?' I prompted him.

'You can tough it out. Stay here. Go about your business. Keep your mouth shut. Don't answer when they yell questions at you. Deny them a story. Any story. Look through them. Bore the pants off them. Stick with that for a few days, no matter what it costs you. And they'll start losing interest. But if you run for it, then you make a so called human interest story and they'll be on your trail for months or even years. Can't you see the headline now?' "*Daily Clarion* locates hiding place of Bishop". No. Stay put. That's my advice'.

His gaze settled upon me and I felt cornered.

'I'll call my friend', I said eventually. 'And my instinct is that your advice is probably the right one. I suppose I have to face those people. Though why I should have ... why she and I should have to be put through this ...'

The manager stood up.

'Use the phone. Call her. Then I'll come back to you'.

He walked out, and for a long time I hesitated before I dialled the number.

'Helen?'

'Conor! What a nice surprise!'

'Thanks. But ...'

'Conor, is something wrong?'

'Yes, I'm afraid so, Helen, and I'm so sorry, sorrier then I can say'.

'So, tell me'.

'We're making news, you and I. There's a picture of us on the scooter under the heading 'Bishop and Friend'. It's in the *Daily Clarion* and to-morrow I'm to be in a series which has included disgraced politicians and embezzlers. And I suppose the picture can only mean that you're going to figure in my story too. I feel sick, Helen. And especially because you're dragged into it. That's just too horrible for words. Of course, once the articles appears to-morrow the likelihood is that a gang of reporters will be in full cry after me. And after you too'.

'Poor Conor'.

'Poor me? What about you?'

But she dismissed my question. 'Never mind that. Have you thought of what you're going to do?'

'Well, the manager has been wonderfully kind to me. In fact, I'm using his phone. And he's put things bluntly.

He says that either I run for it or else face it. That there's no other way'.

'Yes. And ...?'

'And what?'

'You. Have you decided?'

'Well, I've got this news only within the last half hour. Less then that, in fact ... And I think he's right. About the choice, I mean'.

'So?' Her tone was gentle.

'Whatever about the details, I'm not running away'.

She was silent.

'Helen?'

'Yes'.

'What do you think?'

'Does it matter?'

'Very definitely'.

'I think I'm proud of you', she said quickly.

I was startled. Then grateful. More grateful then I had been for years.

'It'll be hell for the next few days', she added.

'I'll keep in constant touch'.

'Do that, Conor. Please'.

I hung up and went to the door. The manager was nearby.

'I'm sticking with it', I said. 'I just hope I have what it takes'.

'Good', he answered. 'Now, for the rest of this week I'm switching you to deliveries in the centre of the city. With the traffic and the parking difficulties anyone trying to follow you around is going to have a rough time. And remember, the word is boring. You're to be as boring as hell for the next week, or at least until the Sunday tabloids have come and gone. That's important. Is your friend okay?'

'Yes, she is'.

'Right. Well, then, to work', and he turned away as if he had anticipated I might wish to thank him.

I went to where the despatcher was making the boxes for the delivery vans. He smiled, and there was encouragement in it. I did not know until later in the day that in the parking lot a car with two reporters in it had been disabled by him. He had let the air out of their four wheels before anyone could stop him.

Next morning on my way to work I bought the *Daily Clarion*.

An image of a bloodied corpse was on the front, and there was an account of a killing during the night.

But I was there on the next page. There were two photographs, one taken a year earlier showing me in a mitre and vestments surrounded by children whom I had just confirmed. Next to it was the shot of Helen and me on the scooter. Strangely, no sub-editor had thought to title them 'Then and Now'. The main article had highlighted paragraphs.

> When the Catholic Church was stunned by the sudden resignation of Dr. Conor Mahon as Bishop of Dysart no explanation were given. The Bishop avoided all efforts to contact him. The Catholic Press Office would only say he had gone for personal reasons. It was well known that Dr. Mahon was being groomed to be the next Archbishop of Dublin. There were no hints that anything was wrong.
>
> Following exhaustive enquiries, the *Daily Clarion* has been able to establish that before the sudden resignation there had been a blazing row between the Bishop and Cardinal Flynn, the primate of All-Ireland. Sources close to the Cardinal were tight-lipped on what had passed between the two men.
>
> Bishop Mahon's last major public appearance was when he presided at the state funeral of the murdered Finance Minister Tim McDermott.

One of the most eloquent members of the hierarchy, the Bishop had on that occasion comforted the bereaved family, especially the widowed Mrs. Helen McDermott.

Since his resignation, the former Bishop has been living in Galway. He is a delivery man for a prominent supermarket and, as our photograph shows, has been seeing Mrs. McDermott. It can be revealed that in the past few days incidents have occurred as part of an effort to prevent our reporters from getting at the truth.

But we will not be stopped. To the question 'Where is he now?' the *Daily Clarion* answers the Bishop Conor Mahon is in Galway and that, as our photograph shows, he has something pleasant to look forward to on his day off.

I read the words again, and a knot of contradictions came to growth within me. I felt rage at the willingness to tramp all over my privacy and over that of Helen. There was anguish too. But there was also a subterranean admiration for the way in which truth as well as untruth had been bypassed. The reporter has led his readers into a valley of insinuations, and who but a very good lawyer could prove that in doing so he had intended to exploit the old tendency in most of us to presume the worst? How could I protest at the declaration that I had resigned for personal reasons? Or that I had argued with the Cardinal? Or that, having tried to comfort Helen, I had put her on the pillion seat of my scooter? Or even that I had something pleasant to look forward to on my day off? How could I protest that these things were not as they had been made to seem when what seems to be the case is, for the majority, what is actually so and when interpretation, like beauty, is in the eyes of the beholder?

I folded my paper and continued on my way to the supermarket. But I pulled over when I saw a phone booth. I parked the scooter and called Helen.

'Have you seen the *Daily Clarion* yet?'

She had not, and she listened when I read the piece to her.

'He's good', she murmured eventually. 'He'll make it to the editor's chair or even to a government job. Yes, the footwork is nice. No court case there, Conor'.

'There's nothing we can do'.

'No, Conor'.

'Helen, I feel I ought to apologise to you. Or something'.

'Why?'

'Because of the way you've been dragged in'.

'Now, Conor, stop wasting time on that. You've an uncomfortable day ahead of you. Maybe many. One never knows with these things. So it is important to keep your eye on the real issue. It'll be tough for you. And you're going to have to live with it. So don't start fretting about me. Please. Keep in touch. Make sure of that. Now if you don't go you're going to be late for work. Call me later'.

I had just started the engine, when I changed my mind and returned to the phone booth and dialled her number.

'Hello', she said.

'Helen'.

'Well! When I said call back later I didn't mean right away! Anyhow, nice to hear you'.

'Helen, I love you'.

The pause was tiny and then she replied.

'Don't do anything on the rebound, Conor. But make sure you call me soon'.

I could tell from her voice that she was pleased. And for the moment that was enough for me. But as I came to a traffic roundabout the realisation of what I had just said nearly made me lose balance. The words had broken through and beyond the mould of habit in which I had been encased for years. They had not been subjected to my usual routines of assessment. Indeed I would have been tempted to define myself in terms of such routines, and yet here were those words. Out of the system. Out of me. And I had meant them. They were true just as it is true that I am over six feet tall, that I have brown eyes, that I wear size nine shoes.

And it was not the love that a Christian one is supposed to have for one's fellow human beings. I was in love. With someone. With Helen.

Amazed and a little uneasy I arrived at the supermarket. The manager was on the watch for me.

'You've seen it?'

'Yes, thanks'.

'Good'.

I went to the desk of the despatcher to get my instructions. About forty minutes later I was on my first round.

Nothing unusual happened throughout the morning or early afternoon. I kept thinking of Helen. I made the deliveries, had a lunch break, took a quick nap in the van. My mind kept on returning to the newspaper article and I wondered how many of those to whose door I came carrying my boxes would recognise me. But, apart from a word of greeting, a quick thanks, a remark about the weather, nothing was said.

Then almost an hour before I was due to finish for the day I emerged from the entrance to a roof apartment where I had left a case of wine and I was coming down to a set of steps when I saw them, a group of reporters and cameramen who were standing around the van. It was too late to turn back. Anyhow, there was no place to hide. And when I was spotted there was a rush in my direction.

'We want to talk to you!'

'Where's Mrs. McDermott?'

'Would you care to make a statement about this morning's article?'

'Have the Church authorities made any efforts to get you out of here?'

'Give us a few minutes of your time'.

'We want to interview you!'

'Dr. Mahon! Bishop Mahon!'

The cameras were active and I knew it was important not to let them see that I was in any way agitated. Above all I wanted no images to suggest I might have a beard and was running away. So when I came near the van I stopped, pulled out a docket, hunted for a pencil and then ticked off a few lines which were actually the titles of some books which had been listed in *The Times Literary Supplement*. I folded the list carefully.

'Bishop Mahon!'

'We want to put a couple of questions. That's all'.

I ignored them, got into the van and turned it into the one way street, which was busy and where drivers, taking their chances on being missed by traffic wardens, had parked outside the cafes, the bookshops and the new doors of long-standing refurbished buildings. There was a spurt of music, a smell of coffee, the slight rise and fall of oncoming promenaders, and for a moment my pursuers were hampered and thwarted.

'They're after me now', I said to the manager when I reached the supermarket.

'And it's only the start', he answered. 'What'll your landlord do when they park on your front step?'

'I hadn't thought of that. But now that you mention it, he's away for a few days'.

'Good. But if he suddenly decides to come back and throws you out, you can stay with me until you find another place'. He pushed aside my emerging thanks. 'Good luck. I'm off'.

I watched him as he hurried out to the parking lot. I realised I had not noticed before now that he was a low-sized man who offset his lack of height by the impression he gave of someone half-crouched for a lethal pounce. The cropped grey hair, with its few reminders of a sandy past, the gruff thudding voice, the hint of barely restrained invective, all this added to the aura of power. He walked like someone hurrying to face down a towering adversary.

I followed him out, collected my scooter and set off. On the way I tried to phone Helen, but her line was engaged, and as I continued in the traffic I began to wonder if I was watched or pointed at. When I reached the apartment the reporters were waiting.

'Dr Mahon!'

'Look, we only want a few minutes. Just a few minutes'.

'Why are you running away from us? Have you something to hide?'

The last two questions were shouted by a man whose tousled curls, blue suit and gold-edged glasses were patterned inside a glow of self-importance. It was a face I had already seen. But I could put no name to it.

'Did your affair with Helen McDermott begin before the murder of her husband?' he asked, very loudly.

He stood in my path, but as I wheeled my scooter at an even pace towards my front door, I made it clear I would run into him if he failed to move. He withdrew the blue-trousered legs at the last moment.

I unlocked the door, then shut it quietly behind me and brought the scooter through the hall and into the shed at the back of the garden. I could hear a few knocks and the ringing of the front bell. But I ignored them.

I was not calm. I sat in my chair, closed my eyes and tried to breathe deeply. But I lacked what I had admired in others, a seeming capacity to withdraw into stillness. There had been times of course when I had felt a spreading quiet within myself, but I suspected that this was something brought on by mood and circumstances rather than by any concentrated effort of my mind and will. Memory could draw up peace, like summer mist on darkening fields. But now, in the room, inside my closed eyelids were the faces and the shouting mouths of those reporters. Their questions, the tone of their demands, broke in on me once again. I could feel the clustering presence beyond the front door. I was sure that one camera at least was poised and alert, ready to pounce if I were to lurk briefly at one of the windows facing the road.

But there was something else. There was anger in me. The habit of many years was trying to smother it, but to no avail. It was seeping through me, an unstoppable sour resentment at being bullied, an exasperation compounded by the sense of finding myself somehow at bay. I wanted to kick out, to smash a camera. I wanted to spit in a face and I was shocked that I could feel this so unmistakeably. It had sunk teeth into me. I stood up to shake it off, like a dog coming out of the sea, but it held on and reached around me and it multiplied and replicated itself as the realisation came that the rage was about Helen too, about the grabbing at her, about the will to tarnish and torment her. Because that reporter in the blue shirt had the nasty glint of a trampler. I had seen the like of him before. I could imagine a guttersnipe giggle or a superior smirk as he moved to skew his prey, and I knew from the look of him that he would not let go until either he had ground his muck into me and Helen or else had been called away to some more promising titbit of scandal. I needed to hear a soothing voice, and so I dialled Helen's number. But her line was engaged, and I wondered if her phone was off the hook or if she were besieged like me. I was beginning to fret. To give myself some coffee. But as I was filling the kettle I heard the phone.

'Yes?'

'Dr. Mahon?'

'Speaking'.

'Father William O'Gorman here'.

I remembered that he had been a secretary to the Cardinal.

'What can I do for you?' I asked.

'His Eminence wished me to get in touch. He was anxious to find out if he could be of assistance to you in the midst of all this ... embarrassing publicity'.

'That was thoughtful of him', I replied, musing that the cardinal if he were so concerned about me might perhaps have been able to lift the phone himself.

'Did the cardinal indicate the sort of assistance he had in mind?' I inquired, guessing already what the answer would be.

'Naturally this scrutiny by the media is very painful. And I'm sure you'll understand that I wouldn't be phoning you if it were possible for me to come freely to see you on His Eminence's behalf. Photographs of a cleric arriving at your house would add a certain piquancy to the situation, as I'm sure you'll agree'.

But I said nothing.

'Dr Mahon, let me try to express as accurately as I can the thoughts of the cardinal on what has been happening. He was very anxious about you. Have no doubt at all on that score'.

'Thank you'.

'But unfortunately in the case of someone of your background there is a public dimension to what should normally be private. I'm not referring now to the photograph in the newspaper ...'

'You've seen it, of course'.

'Oh, yes', he answered, managing a degree of neutrality which I was tempted to applaud.

'Certainly I've seen it, of course'.

'Ah yes. No doubt'.

I was waiting. I could see what was coming, though I could not yet predict the actual words.

'Dr. Mahon', he went on, 'I wonder if I could persuade you to take a moment to consider the situation from a point of view different from your own. Naturally you must be very upset by this publicity. That's only to be expected. And I, and the cardinal, sympathise. It must be quite awful for you'.

'But ...', I prompted.

'Ah yes. But there is another perspective on the matter. Which I would earnestly ask you to consider'.

'Yes?'

'These are difficult days for the Church. I need hardly remind you of that. To put the situation ...'

'Bluntly, I hope'.

'Well, yes. Thank you. The decision and the circumstances of your resignation caused a great deal of hurt. I'm sure you realise that now. The sudden wish to resign, the manner of your departure, the ignoring of the usual procedures in such situations, all of this was very painful. The cardinal was deeply distressed. Still is. And now a wound is being torn open by what is happening. The photographs. The insinuation regarding your involvement with Mrs. McDermott. Surely I don't need to spell it out for you?'

But I continued to be silent.

'Dr. Mahon', he resumed in a patient voice, 'I can't believe that you don't see the harm all this is doing to the Church. Think especially of the scandal to the young. And I'm sure, indeed I'm certain, that just as you can count on the continuing sympathy of the cardinal you, in turn, will wish to relieve the burden of his distress. I know all too well how upset he is. Believe me'.

'That's as may be, but what are you proposing? I'm sure you didn't call simply to tell me about the cardinal's feelings'.

'No. That's true. But it is a factor in the situation'.

'Of course. So?'

'Dr. Mahon, if you were to move ...'

'Where?'

'If you were to leave Galway and point towards another country where your anonymity would be assured, this whole sad affair would fade. And the cardinal would provide whatever financial assistance you might need for your resettlement'.

'In other words, like the parish priest who was after me when I first came here, the cardinal would like me to vanish. Except that he is throwing in a financial sweetner. Is that it?'

'Dr. Mahon, may I say with all respect that the tone of your words is not really called for'.

'Oh? Have I missed something? It is not the case that the cardinal wants me to vanish?'

'Again, with respect, Dr. Mahon, I think that's a rather uncharitable way of looking at this. The cardinal is reaching out a hand to help. He appreciates the distress you must be enduring. He wants to do something for you. His thoughts are for your well-being. That is why he was so anxious for me to get in touch with you. I really wish you would see that this is the case'.

'Father O'Gorman, I imagine I would be more responsive to what you've just said if it hadn't been for some earlier words of yours. Your reference to the manner of my resignation, the bit about tearing open old wounds, the clear wish to put me in the wrong – all this, I'm afraid, pushes me towards a slightly cynical view of our present conversation. Let's be open about this, you and I. The cardinal would like me to disappear. He's even prepared to pay the cost. He knows that his colleagues, such as the Archbishop of Cashel, share his view of me. Of course, because of the sort of man he is, there is a bit of kindness and goodwill to him. But the overriding consideration is that I'm an embarrassment to him. You know it. I know it. An ex-bishop, spoken of once as the next Archbishop of Dublin, working as a delivery man for a supermarket, and now the object of tabloid interest. That's a bit much for him, and so he gets his secretary to call me. He doesn't talk to me himself. In fact until these reporters got after me, I've had not one "hello" or "how-are-you" from the cardinal or from anyone else in the hierarchy since I left. So thank you for your call and please excuse me now if I turn my attention to other matters'.

I hung up.

Almost immediately I called Helen.

'Well', I began, 'Reporters are twittering like the starlings outside my door. The cardinal would like me to emigrate. I'm getting hungry and am going to pull the cork on a wine bottle. How is it in your part of the world?'

'Quiet so far. Actually, I'm cooking my dinner'.

'Oh. In that case I won't delay you. I'll call you later. I just wanted to hear your voice'.

'Don't let them get to you', she said softly.

'No'.

'And you're not emigrating?'

'Definitely not'.

'You told the cardinal?'

'I made my view clear to his secretary'.

She sighed.

'What's the matter?' I asked.

'I can just imagine what you said'.

'I don't think I'm with you'.

'No. I expect not. I'm going to have to take you in hand and teach you some Middle High Arabic words to tell people like the cardinal. You of course wouldn't know about them. They begin with the letter f. Isn't that interesting? My dinner's burning. Talk to you later'.

During the evening I had several more phone calls, a long one from Helen and, after midnight, one from Larry Jordan, the religious affairs correspondent of the national television company.

'Hello, Bish. Just because you've left the parade ground you haven't forgotten me, have you?'

'No, Larry, I remember you well', I laughed.

'Good. One never knows with you unworldly types'.

'Since I'd still like to be a modest man I'll ignore the compliment. What can I do for you?'

'How are you?'

'Surviving so far, in spite of the campers outside my front door'.

'Count your blessings. The weather's nice, so they'll stay'.

'That's a blessing?'

'Better than having them sheltering in a phone kiosk from the rain and making up fake stories about you'.

'I see what you mean'.

'Look, Bish, I'm sorry about all this. But the point is of course that it's happening. So, to repeat myself, how are you really and do you need anything?'

'I'm alright so far, Larry, and thanks for asking'.

'Don't sound so surprised. Some of us are human, you know'.

'Have I said otherwise?'

'No. But the trouble is that because you've said nothing there's plenty of room for people of my type to speculate. It's a professional urge'.

'True. So?'

He paused. I thought he was considering his words until a sound like a kiss, followed by blowing, made me realise he had taken a long puff from a cigarette.

'Have you met Declan Norton?' he asked eventually.

'Who's he?'

'The man from the *Daily Clarion*. The one who wrote the story'.

'I think I may have'.

'Well-dressed man. Curly hair. Gold-rimmed glasses'.

'He was one of the posse outside my house. Could still be there'.

'Right. Well, I don't know what you've decided to do. That is, I don't know if you're thinking of sitting all this out or running for it ...'

'I'm not running', I interrupted grimly.

'No. I didn't think so. Well, Declan Norton's the one you've really got to watch. He's called a dedicated journalist, which in his case means persistent and unscrupulous bastard, but this story is a godsend to him. He's got an agenda and you'd better believe me'.

'Tell me'.

'The *Daily Clarion* is losing money. Fast'.

'Good'.

'Now, Bish, love your enemies and all that'.

'I sit reproved'.

'Right. Anyhow, the point is that the board of directors met last week. They fired Tim Gill the editor, put in a temporary, fellow named Patton, and are meeting at the end of the month to appoint a new chief. They've also decided that sensational, snappy and short is the formula needed to get the *Clarion* around. No more think pieces with words of more than two syllables. Sex, smacko, and gosh. That's how it's going to be'.

'Ah, and Declan Norton is not only throwing his hat into the ring for the editor's job but by the purest of luck he's on to a story with unlimited possibilities for someone with his ambitions'.

'You read me good, Bish'.

XVII

And as if to confirm that this was so I found Declan Norton within ten feet of my doorstep when I appeared next morning. He was wearing the same blue suit, but his curls had been tamed and he had the look of a refreshed man.

'How has Mrs. McDermott reacted to the news?' he asked. It was a good question, well designed to get me talking.

I pushed my scooter onto the side of the road and prepared to leave.

'How is Mrs. McDermott taking it?'

Other reporters had arrived by now and were waiting for my answer to Declan Norton.

I heeled the starter. The engine fired once and then stopped. I tried again, with the same result. It was the first time the scooter had ever given me trouble. I worked the starter, but still to no effect.

I could feel myself getting flustered.

'May I?' It was one of the younger reporters, and before I could see what he had done the scooter hacked and puttered asthmatically until it settled down into its usual buzz.

'Thanks'.

'Tell us about Mrs. McDermott', the voice called behind me.

I was about to drive off, but suddenly changed my mind, and I turned to the man who had helped me.

'I have a lunch-break from twelve-thirty to one-thirty. If you find a room somewhere near the supermarket I'll talk to you. But not now. And not anytime on the side of the road'.

I pointed towards the morning traffic. I did not look back to see if any of the reporters had decided to follow. My mind filled up with a sense of the press conference ahead of me and of my blurted decision to call it. But I knew already that my sudden resolve to talk had emerged from a fear of the hurt which might be done to Helen if the man Declan Norton were not confronted. I dreaded the thought of what he might do to her for the sake of promoting his chances to become editor of the *Daily Clarion*.

But what was I to say to them? My thoughts were empty, and by the time I reached the supermarket I was rimmed by unease. The manager was waiting for me.

'Do you want to go ahead with the deliveries as usual?'

'Yes'.

'Right. Any developments?'

'Oh, they spent the night outside my door. Or at least I think they did. I must admit I didn't get out of bed to check. And I suppose they'll follow me around this morning. I don't know. Anyhow, I said I'd talk to them during my lunch break'.

'Why?' the manager asked sharply.

'To try to protect Helen'.

'How?'

'I don't know yet. I really haven't thought it out'.

He shook his head.

'No offence, but they eat your sort with their cornflakes every day'.

'Thanks a lot!'

He started to walk away, but changed his mind.

'Let me tell you something', he said. 'I have a friend who was surrounded once by such a mob. They were in that special kind of ugly mood that you find in people who are certain they're right. It wouldn't have taken much for them to kill him. He could see that, and was sure he was going to die. So he picked one of them out. He kept looking at him. Looking very hard. In such a way as to send a message. And the message was "If I have to die, so do you". He stared so sharply the other man understood. No mistake about it, and he got scared. Did you ever see a drop of grease fall on water? It snakes across the surface. You can't miss it, and it looks slimy. That's what happened for my friend. He willed the man in the mob to know he'd take him with him. The man knew, and his fear spread into the others near him in the crowd even if they mightn't know the reason. And whatever it did to them they backed off. Snarling. But off'.

'Why are you telling me this?'

'Because in the days before you became a van driver, you were a merchant of parables, weren't you? What's the saying, he had his ears to hear, or something like that'.

He started to leave and, again, stopped.

'Good luck'.

'Thanks'.

I watched him until he had turned into the back of the supermarket in the direction of his office. His words made no sense to me and I soon forgot them as I loaded my van and prepared to set out on my rounds. Most of the boxes carried addresses on the western end of the city. When I came to walk up driveways or knocked at doors, I found myself taking quick sidelong glances to see if I was followed but no cameras were anywhere in sight. Of course that did not mean much. Someone with a zoom lens might be lurking at the side of a distant house. The thought of it made me impose some dignity on the act of brushing a fly from my ear.

There were at least twenty reporters and cameramen in the room when at last I walked in. They stood in groups, and their conversation faded away as soon as I appeared. They had set a table and chair against a blank wall at the top of the room and they shuffled or pushed to their own places when I sat down. No words of greeting came in my direction. I noticed that Declan Norton was directly in front of me.

'You wanted to speak to me. Here I am', I sat back with arms folded. I knew the old trick of zooming in on fidgety fingers.

'Have you any comment to make on the attitude of your colleagues, the bishops towards you?'

'What attitude?' I asked.

'Have they been in touch with you since you resigned?'

'Not directly. No?'

'How do you feel about that?'

'I don't think it matters how I feel'.

'Dr. Mahon, I have it on good authority that some bishops would like to see you out of the country. They think that your continuing presence here is making difficulties for them. For example, they question your judgement in taking up a job as a van driver in a city where everyone can see you. Have you any thoughts on such a point of view?' The questioner had a large beer belly.

'When I resigned as bishop I needed a job', I answered quietly, suppressing a twinge of irritation at hearing the old refrain about the scandal I might be causing. 'My resignation means, among other things, that I was unemployed, and jobs are very hard to find especially for someone like me whose skills are very limited. But I was lucky. I am a delivery man, as, of course, you know, and I am fortunate to be able to carry on without being a burden on anyone. If you are right in saying that this is considered by some to show poor judgement on my part, I can't help that. But I am glad to have work and I am very grateful indeed for the one offer of a place which I received after I left office as a bishop'.

'Does that mean you're bitter because your colleagues didn't find something you might have thought suitable for you?'

'I am not bitter', I replied, 'and the question of suitability does not arise. I am a van driver. I earn a living, and that's simply how it is'.

There was a slight pause and then, from three areas of the room, questions came together.

'Do you intend to settle in Galway?'

'When did your affair with Mrs. McDermott begin?'

'Could you tell us what happened to make you decide to resign?'

The question about Helen was, of course, from Declan Norton. I had not thought much about him while I was on my way to the press conference. My mind had been full of the urge to think of some formula to guide me through what was about to happen. I knew well that I had somehow or other to take control of what went on, and the idea towards which I was edging was to capitalise on the advice given by the supermarket manager, to bore the reporters into indifference. I also recognised that Declan Norton would not be put off quite so easily. He had his own clear objectives, and while I now sat in front of him as he put his question about Helen, I thought suddenly of the other words of my boss at the supermarket. I leaned forward in my chair.

'Taking what you've asked me one at a time, I have no plans to leave Galway', I began. 'And before I deal with the other two matters let me just tell you what my schedule is. For the rest of this week I'll be on my delivery rounds from nine-thirty until about six. My lunch breaks will be at the same time as today. On Sunday after I collect my papers I'll probably take the scooter out to the Silver Strand. I like to walk there if the weather is any way decent. After lunch I intend to settle down with the new study of Pyrrho and the sceptical philosophers of the Hellenistic and Roman world. I'm really looking forward to it. Have any of you had the chance to see it yet? No? It's by a really distinguished Sorbonne scholar. Well, I mustn't linger over it now. The reason I'm telling you this is that if you plan to follow me around and take pictures of me it will be of me lugging grocery boxes. "Bishop gets his exercises". How's that for a headline?'

Nobody was writing anything. I was pleased, and rushed ahead almost breathlessly.

'Oh, and I forgot Monday, didn't I? Yes, well, I'm not sure yet. But I wouldn't be surprised if I'm back to Pyrrho. And then, of course a new week starts on Tuesday, and ...'

'Dr Mahon ...'

'Yes, I know. I'm going to deal with your questions. But I think it's only right to let you in on my plans since you seem so interested. Because ... well, if you want to know my opinion, I don't think I'd like to spend a week following me around. If you get my meaning. And I can tell you that if by Monday afternoon this study of Pyrrho has gone down the road I think it does, wouldn't you be surprised if I opened my door suddenly, looked out and said, "You're all appearance and no substance, there's no assurance that you're even there!" Wouldn't you have something to write about?' I gave a long bray of laughter.

'Dr'.

'Yes. Yes. Why did I resign?'

I sat back, put my fingers together, as if in prayer, gazed at the ceiling, and after a lengthy pause I began to murmur in a voice which was low, intense, and pitched in such a way as not to be easily heard by those in the back of the room.

'I've spent more than thirty years of my life as a priest and bishop. So to answer the question of why I left is not simple, as everybody in this room except one will grasp, though maybe with some disappointment. I did not have a quarrel with my fellow-bishops. Of course, we had our different approaches to issues. But that's normal. I repeat, for the sake of your dim-witted colleague, there was no quarrel. None'.

I could see an exchange of glances here, a bemused expression there. And I rushed on before anyone could speak.

'It's not for nothing that I'm reading this book about Pyrrho', I continued. 'As most of you will know, this was a man who lived in the days of Alexander the Great, and though he never wrote anything he is considered to be the forerunner of the tradition of scepticism in Greek philosophy. And this is nothing very complicated really, though it might be so for the one poor God-help-us creature among us in this room now. For what it has to do with is a sense of the complexity of life and the sloppy ways we have of failing to see that complexity. So we oversimplify. We think and talk in sound bites and slick headlines. No offence, please! One does what's needed in particular circumstances. But the fact is we can literally kill as a result of oversimplifying labels we put on the realities of life. And at the end of the day, that's turned out to be the root of my problem. Probably I'm a slow learner. But you see, by a process too long to speak about here, bishops have been given the status of men – supermen mark you! – who know the score about God, about life and about what everybody must do. And my trouble is that because I understand less and less about more and more I can no longer pretend to have a kind of knowledge which I don't really possess. So it would be wrong for me to continue as the leader of a community of priests and people. Therefore I resigned'.

'Are you saying you don't believe in the Church anymore?' The question was shot in, and I could see that unless I made a fast move there would be some such headline as "Bishop says: I don't believe". It was really time to bore them now.

'I'm saying no such thing. Repeat. No such thing! However, maybe the best way to explain myself would be to take a concrete example. In the creed we say that Christ is one in being with the Father. Part of my job would be to declare what this means. After all, entire congregations recite the words every Sunday. Now, leaving aside the question of whether "one in being" is a proper translation of the Greek original *homoousios*, the fact is that the formula was arrived at in the fourth century after very great controversy. It was a brilliant term proposed to the emperor Constantine as a way of dealing with the Arian crisis. Would you like me to comment in some depth upon this crisis?'

I looked benignly around the room.

'Well, perhaps not now. But I still must make the point that when the council of Nicaea in 325 adopted the *homoousian* formula it was saying in effect that human terms deriving from the human frame of reference were allowable henceforth in any discussion about God. Now I've only recently understood how much that bothers me. It means, among other things, that theologians run the risk of constructing God instead of somehow expressing him. Now that's a shocker. For me anyway, and I can see now that it was the start of the journey which led to my resignation. You'll realise of course that I'm going against my own instincts when I answer your question in this very simple way. But it's the best I can do. Of course if you wish to follow up with more questions, such as my growing problems with the theological apparatus devised to explain the relationship between the human and the divine in the person of Christ I will gladly try to deal with this. That too was an element of the journey which led me eventually to see that I had to resign'.

There was a marked absence of note taking, and when I saw this I recognised that the moment had come to play my last card.

'I've been trying to sketch for you in the barest outline the set of considerations which left me with no alternative but to resign. Given what these were, how could I explain or pretend to the people of my diocese that I could be a leader for them? This is something which all but one of you will understand. It is a great pity that there's one person in this room whose sensitivities are so retarded that there's no point whatever in trying to explain this scene to him. Even in words of one syllable'.

The atmosphere became very still.

'Could you explain this?' The voice came from the third row.

'I've already explained', I answered in a weary voice. 'The man is so stupid that he would have no clue regarding what I've been saying. But at another level he's not a complete dimwit. For, you see, there's blood-letting going on in his newspaper at the moment and a new editor is about to be appointed and he's desperate to get the job. And since sensationalism of the crudest kind is all that comes naturally to him, he has figured that if he can find a story which will sell more copies of his paper he'll have a better chance of being selected for the editor's chair. So he picks on me. And he starts into the heavy breathing act when he sees me on a scooter. It doesn't cross his diminished brain that I can't afford anything else. Then one day he sees I have a friend as pillion passenger. When he finds out that she's the widow of a murdered government minister, his trousers start getting tight around the crotch and he begins to pant. He visualises the headline "The Bishop and the Politician's wife". He has no facts. But naturally that's no problem for him. A few innuendoes here and these will work wonders. So his blood is up. Along with something else. He summons a colleague. The chase is on. They follow my scooter into the Clare hills. And let me tell you that was one of the funniest afternoons I ever spent. You should have seen him. He and his colleague were so incompetent that they even followed the scooter up a mountain road which ended in a bog. I knew this of course, and just nipped behind a prehistoric tomb and waited. Sure enough himself came rushing by with his companions, a bit like something from a Laurel and Hardy movie. He never noticed me. But you should have seen his bulging eyes, and oh Lord were his obscenities ripe and rare! Then I drove the scooter down the hill, pulled in behind a tree and waited. And eventually he came clattering down, went at full speed in the direction he thought I had taken, and I puttered off the other way. I don't mind telling you that my pillion passenger, Mrs. McDermott, laughed so hard that I was really afraid she'd fall off. Then wouldn't you have a story! So, you have it all. One overly ambitious gutter walker, one former bishop photographed on a scooter with his friend, and all of you here now having your time wasted by the ambitions of an idiot. Well, I haven't had my sandwich yet and I have to be back at work in twenty-five minutes. So why don't you put questions to the man who would be King, The King Kong of the *Daily Clarion*. I'm off. I'm famished. God bless you all. Yes, all'.

I stood up and began to walk out.

Declan Norton rose in front of me.

'You fucking bastard!'

'Language, Mr. Newton, Norton or whatever. Language! Or was that a headline?'

XVIII

The media lost interest in me, whether on account of the press conference or because of an unexpected scandal in which a government minister, insider trading, the wife of a tycoon and a corrupt auctioneer provided the ingredients of a long and sleazy drama. To this was added the spectacle of a visiting American senator who had arrived in Dublin airport to conduct diplomatic business and to seek out his Irish ancestry. But when he emerged from the plane he was so obviously affected by large quantities of drink that he had to be lifted eventually off the tarmac, despite his loudly expressed wish to sleep there. The consequent opportunities for speculation, photography and exciting narrative ensured that I quickly ceased to be newsworthy.

So I resumed my ordinary life. Customers continued to greet me, and only rarely was there a half-grin, a question shaped but unasked, a glance of quickening interest.

Within a fortnight of the press conference the events had so far receded that when Helen invited me to pass a weekend at her house I at once said 'yes' and I gave no thought to what former neighbours in my diocese might feel.

I set out from Galway early on Sunday morning. The roads were mostly deserted and the air was cold. I wrapped a heavy scarf around my neck. I wore good gloves and I had put on two sweaters under my jacket. My scooter hummed and I was able to watch the October sunrise spreading a hard light over fields and ditches and along the brown leaves of trees which were beginning the withdrawal into their winter stillness. Cattle and sheep were at rest. Near a river a flock of plovers took off suddenly as I passed nearby. And I heard myself singing.

Soon after nine o'clock I had come in sight of a tall house in a clearing among chestnut and long-lived beech trees. It rose from the side of a hill and its windows seemed barely to thrust out from the guardianship of thick creeper. It faced the morning sun, and for years it had marked for me the boundary into my diocese. Whenever I had glimpsed it in the past I had a sense of being nearly home.

But now I was uprooted, a kind of stateless man without the papers which would proclaim where he belonged. And I felt the irony of it, because over many years I had spoken confidently in public to affirm that there was an assured location for all of us, an unmistakeable arena with its own rules, its conditions of entry, its club decorum, its values, its capacity to comfort and console. My diocese was a visible sign of all this, and whether I thought of myself as the servant of others or accepted without demur the title of Lord Bishop, it was inside frontiers so well marked that I could give a prompt account of myself and could give precise and regularly unasked direction to others. I had been a man of power, the recipient of deference, invited to a front seat on any public occasion, I had been surrounded by strategies designed to keep me calm and agreeable. Politicians quietly checked out my opinions. School managers in the diocese spoke of me as their patron and made sure to keep in line with anything I might have written or announced. A discussion at which I was present could be punctuated by an inquiry as to whether my approval of some suggestion might be taken for granted. I decided where my priests would work. The routines of marriage annulment required my signature. Adult education courses could be stopped if I were thought to be displeased. Even the description of me as open-minded and approachable told its own tale of my power. The system which made me had given me clout, and only death, retirement or bizarre misdeeds could have led to my removal.

But now I was a taxpayer on a buzzing scooter. And in spite of my double band of sweaters I was getting cold. So I parked and decided to give myself a few moments of exercise.

I could feel an enlarged silence around me, and then gradually I began to hear the rasp of dry leaves and the echo of a stream nearby.

I moved towards the sound, and came into a narrow field enclosed by hazel bushes and by tall hawthorns on which clumps of berries, each with a pinpoint of reflected sunlight, hung out against a blue sky. The grass, indented by the hooves of cattle, sloped down towards a holly tree. The stream was behind it, and when I came close to the bubbling clear water I could see a trout, tense against the current.

I watched it, and as I did so a feeling almost like fear came over me. I would have known once how to make words about that fish. And I would have been listened to, not because I was Conor Mahon but because I was the bishop. I would have labelled that fish, slotted it into a context first of flowing water, then between banks of earth, in a corner of a teeming planet, under an open sky, within a universe whose every detail was in place because of a God whose will I was commissioned to declare. As if I knew that will. As if I even knew that fish. As if the application of the name 'trout' gave me an inwardness with its aloneness there on this morning. I could catch it. I could eat it. I could use it to nourish the cells of my body. But its thereness as what it truly was would evade me now or at any time. We were equals, that fish and I, two solitudes at the edge of a wood.

A flutter of wings distracted me for a moment and when I looked back into the stream the fish was gone. I stared at its absence from the patch of gravel over which it had been poised, its fins undulating, its tail feeling the water. I thought of its shimmering colours and deeply wished I had seen it go. Even that much was denied me.

I turned away and went back to the scooter. The feel of its handlebars and the splutter of its engine came as a sort of comfort, an antidote against disorientation. Or perhaps against loneliness. I got onto the main road, continued on my journey, but stopped again after no more than a mile or so. The feelings unloosed in me by that fish were still at work, and I wondered, with a touch of sadness, if I was too old to move beyond the ways of seeing which had become an engulfing habit in me during those long years when I was a clerical student, a priest, a bishop. Would I ever be able to look without the promptings of a transcending eye and heart, without the managing procedures of a programmed mind? Would I be stuck in some kind of no-man's land, unable to make connections with things as I once had, or else bewildered by what was coming at me, in the way I had been startled earlier in the week when I had barely managed to swerve my van clear of a car driver in the wrong direction on a roundabout?

For a moment a cousin or some blood-relation of panic began to claw at me, and to shake free of it. I began to concentrate on the details of what was around me. The sun was at arm's length above the horizon, its light reaching over trees and catching the mane and legs of a sentinel horse. Brown withered ducks rose suddenly, the male in the lead, their flight an erratic oval, their wings a fuss. And then the drake took charge and settled for a landing point near some straggly bushes. There was the touch of a breeze. There was the slanted light. And the patterned sky.

'Helen will teach me how to see again', I murmured. 'I'll be able to learn from her. I must!' I had phoned her several times since the press conference. She had listened in her usual manner to my account of what had happened, but there had been something close to a chuckle in her first comment.

'Well, Conor, I imagine you surprised yourself'.

'In what way?'

'With the tactics you used. And especially in the gutting of the man from the *Daily Clarion*'.

'Are you saying I should have managed it all differently?'

'No, Conor. Don't get defensive! All I'm asking is whether you knew or suspected that you had it in you to do such a thing'.

'Ah'.

I had not answered her. But the point she made had circled around me since then. And it came back to me now on the side of the road. I tried to imagine my former colleague Charles John O'Donnell, the Archbishop of Cashel. How would he have behaved in such a gathering of reporters? Of course it was a silly question, not least because he would never have been photographed on a scooter with a woman holding onto him. Nor would he ever resign for the sort of reasons which had afflicted me. Unless, perhaps, women priests were allowed. But even then I could never imagine him as anything other than he was, insistent on the rightness of his opinion, demanding some form of obeisance, magisterially at home in his self, predictable.

Helen was right. I did surprise myself. I had moved to hurt. To injure massively, if possible, so that Declan Norton would leave me alone. No, not me. Helen. That was it. I had passionately wanted to protect her from the *Daily Clarion*. It had not all been for me. I was sure of that. So perhaps I might be forgiven for not having turned the other cheek. Forgiven? I laughed in the morning air. I had not left everything behind when I had ceased to be a working bishop. At least not yet.

She had heard the scooter and was at the top of the stone steps by the front door when I came to a halt. I looked at her. She had changed her style of hair since our last meeting and its effect was to give her face a youthfulness which I had not seen previously. Or perhaps what I really was looking at was a demeanour, a welcome from the eyes, and the smile of someone glad to see me.

'So you made it on your own', she called.

'Yes. Not a reporter in sight. Unless of course somebody's hidden in one of those big stone pots at the side of the lawn'.

'Well, good luck to him if there is'.

I walked up the steps and she came towards me and we hugged. Continuing to hold my arm she moved back a little.

'Are you alright, Conor?'

'I am'.

'It's been upsetting. For you, I mean. I'm used to being the bad creature in the pack. Thanks to Tim'.

It was quite some time since I had heard a mention of her husband.

She brought me into the hall. I had not really looked at it before. It was like the vast forecourt of a nineteenth-century retreat house for alcoholic priests. It was faintly menacing, stern, and with an abiding atmosphere of winter chill. A fireplace capable of holding long and bulky logs seemed to crouch within a frame of granite slabs. There was a black mantelpiece cut as if to scoop away the heat of any wood or turf or coal. There was a wrought-iron grate and a set of tongs which could speedily batter a recalcitrant man.

The climb up the stairs to the second floor was like a journey out of a pit, and when we reached a double window beyond which were fields and woods I looked back.

'That really is an awful hall'.

She laughed and, continued to link my arm, and she led me towards her studio.

'I never liked it either. Anyhow, it doesn't matter any more. I've put the house up for sale. I was talking to an auctioneer yesterday and he seems to think he can get rid of it for me'.

She led me into her studio, and when I looked at those shapes which she had enticed out of stone and wood I felt as before a diffidence, a sense of being utterly without talent. On her work-table there was a piece of bog-oak on which the profile of a woman's face was emerging, as though out of some night. Her eye was closed, her cheek and mouth and jaw serene. Her self-possession stood against the grain of the wood, the grain of times past.

I turned to Helen. She was smiling at me.

'Thank you', I said.

She laughed softly and brought me to the sofa at the main window. We sat down, her hand still in mine.

'So you like my work?'

'Yes, Helen. I do. Earlier I was thinking I regretted having no talents. But now I'm not so sure. I imagine that since I can be free of the illusion of being gifted I may really come to appreciate and respect what's there. What you have. What you are'.

Her glance moved towards the window.

'Before my husband finally decided not to accept me for what I was, he used to say to people he met that I was his Bohemian girl. It was a put-down, of course. It tapped into those unformulated notions that many people have about artists. That they're not quite respectable. Not to be fully trusted. And probably immoral. Whereas he was the tolerant clean-living man'. She turned to me. 'And do you know, Conor, I was inclined to believe him at first'.

'But that's terrible!' I exclaimed.

She shrugged. 'I was mixed-up in those days. Maybe that was good. It might have been. I don't know. What can I say? But that's how it was. And since my husband's family and his friends bought the picture of me which he was painting, I became more and more isolated. That's one reason why when this house is sold I'll be able to walk out the door without too much nostalgia'.

'I'm so sorry, Helen'.

'No. No need to be sorry. That's all in the past. It's over. I don't brood on it. I'm just explaining something. What matters is now. Let's take advantage of that. Are you hungry? I know it's only just midday. But you've had a long ride in the morning air. How about lunch?'

'Actually, I think I'm starving!'

She laughed. 'Wonderful! Let's be off then. But you're going to have to go back to that hall again if we're to reach the kitchen. Do you think you can stand it?'

'If it gets too much for me, I'll shut my eyes and you can lead me'.

'That's a deal'.

We went downstairs to the kitchen, which was at least three times the size of the living room in my apartment. It had a high ceiling, pinewood cupboards on two walls, an electric cooker, a solid-fuel range and, in the middle of the floor, a table nine or ten feet long.

'I have the starters organised already', she said. 'It'll only take a few moments to set them out. We'll have them, and then I'll get the main course ready'.

'Can I do something to help?'

'Later, maybe'.

'Well, then, I'll sit here out of the way'.

She worked with a quick sure sense of what she wanted to do and as I watched her I began to realise for the first time in my life that food, however simple or elaborate, was entitled to something very much like courtesy. The shopping list for what she put on two dinner plates would have mentioned oysters, Greek olives, crab meat, red and green peppers, dried tomatoes in olive oil, artichoke hearts, capers, black caviar and baguette slices. But no document could have expressed the way she laid them out one by one, placing them so as to enhance each of them within an arrangement which drew my admiring gaze. She glanced at me and smiled as she guessed my thoughts.

'Right. I'll set these on the table inside and if you want to help you can open the wine. It's been about twenty minutes in the fridge and it shouldn't be left there any longer. In fact, why don't you get it out now and go to work. The corkscrew is on the shelf behind you'.

She led the way behind the kitchen into a room where a table was set. From the picture-window beside it there was a view of grass within a broken line of trees and bushes, and at the side there was a turf bed in which three birches rose above clusters of heather.

Through the branches of a sycamore I could see a flight of whooper swans making a journey towards the banks of the river. Thick clouds were spread along the horizon. Fallen leaves stirred occasionally in the grass.

I poured some wine and we began to eat, and a leisurely rhythm descended on us. And our talk moved at its own unhurried pace so that when I asked her why she had turned to sculpture instead of painting or architecture or music, she smiled peacefully.

'I never doubted that's what I wanted', she murmured. But then her expression grew serious. 'But you've asked me why, and that's something I can't really answer. Who can tell? Maybe ... Maybe it had something to do with the fact that I was an only child. Maybe it was on account of my father. He disappeared from my life when I was very young and I never saw him again and I missed him'.

She looked out at the lawn.

'I think he was a compulsive gambler who had to go on the run because of debts. At least that's what I used to think. It was the only explanation which made any sense at all to me. Maybe I was saying to myself that he couldn't help it and that was why he had to abandon me. I don't know. It didn't cross my mind then that he might have wanted to escape from my mother. She refused completely to talk about it. Ever. So I don't know'.

We sat quietly for a while, our dishes empty, the wine tasting faintly of gooseberries and far-off sunshine. We got to talk of travel and books, and politics and of gardening, and most of an hour had passed before she said with a sudden anxiety, 'I think I'm neglecting you!'

I laughed. 'I am very contented, so the word neglect hardly arises'.

'Still, we should think of the next round. I have some brill and fresh vegetables. Come and give me moral support while I get them ready'.

We returned to the kitchen.

'I learned to cook during the time I was in school', she said as she saw me watching her at work. 'It was one of the few outlets I had'.

'How so?'

'I was stuck into a boarding school as soon as I was old enough. I was miserable there, although I tried hard to fit in. But from my first days I was never allowed to think that my best might be good enough. The nuns had a way of conveying to me that they were being very, very patient with me. And without realising what was happening, I slid into accepting the picture of myself which seemed to come increasingly out of the body language used by many of them in my presence. I started to feel guilty, and my guilt grew as I tried to measure up to the standards they were apparently setting for me. It took years to get out of the trap they built for me. In fact, when I said to you a while ago that I half believed my husband when his manner suggested I was at fault –

though what for I couldn't say – that was part of the legacy of being in that school where demons were loaded onto my shoulders. But at least some good things came out of my desperation during those times. The nun in charge of the kitchen let me cook, and I loved it and couldn't learn enough. And in art class I realised I had a talent and that I need only wait and that some day when I escaped from that school my freedom would include being able to mould shapes from wood that had been immersed in life and from stone that had tasted so many centuries as to be almost timeless. Ah well, enough of that! To eat, Conor! The brill is just right and I hope very much that you like it'.

Later over coffee and Cointreau which we drank in her studio she gazed at me for a long moment and then smiled.

'But Conor, dear old Conor, don't get me wrong about one thing. Those demons are mostly gone. I don't feel the need to be intimidated any more. I'm forty-nine and I've come of age. If people don't like me they can leave me alone. As the old song says, "I'll live till I die". Yes, live. Not exist. Live'.

And she laughed.

'Did I ever tell you of the last time I accompanied my husband on an official trip to Paris?'

'No, you didn't'.

'Well he was Foreign Minister then, and as you know, Foreign Ministers have to go all over the place. But there was a particularly important conference in Paris and I was brought along for the ceremonial bits. When the big shots were all at their sessions, I was stuck into a chauffeured limousine with the wife of the Irish Ambassador. At one point we were on an island, at its end, with Notre-Dame behind us. And I was looking down into the Seine, and I began to think of all the free and unfree spirits who had looked into its stream. I even thought of some of the men who in an earlier scene would have been colleagues of yours. I imagined the archbishop who walked in the garden below the cathedral, walked that rectangle in each corner of which was a fountain, and he stopped to take a drink whenever he felt like it. Except it was piped wine and not water. And I remembered another archbishop who used to promenade his girlfriend around that garden and flunkeys used to spread rose petals on the path before them. And as I thought of them all and as I looked into the not-very-clean-river, I too decided that I would greet life, and so I jumped in and swam to the other bank. Well, you can imagine the uproar. But I didn't care and when my husband yelled at me about it later I told him he was damn lucky that at least I had kept my clothes on for the honour and glory of old Ireland!'

I looked at her and I felt tiny, commonplace and very dull.

'Ah Helen! What a Helen! I know – I know there's not much to me, but I am what I am and so I wish, I wish so very much that we'd make love'.

An unmistakeable radiance had come on her and remained with her, and the sage generalities I used to utter in the past about such matters did not rise up to mock me, and there was everything to say and there was nothing to say because nothing could ever ever say it.

XIX

Unexpectedly, I found myself back in her house two evenings later. My brother Tom had phoned me to say he would collect me when I finished my rounds. He added that he wanted to talk to Helen and me together. He gave me no indication of what he had planned, and on the drive to the house he kept our conversation to topics of his choice. I let him be, and bided my time.

He had told Helen he was bringing me to the house, and when we arrived I could see she was as curious as I had been throughout the journey from Galway.

Tom refused her offer of a cup of tea or a drink.

'You have a video recorder in the house?' he enquired.

'Yes, I have'.

'Is it in working order? Because if not, I have one in the back of the car'.

'No, it works'.

'Right'. He followed her into the living room. He had a briefcase with him and when the catch gave him a moment of trouble I heard a low but unmistakable obscenity. Eventually, he managed to extract two tapes. He scrutinised them for an instant, grunted and then fitted the one into the machine.

'There's someone here I want to show you. I think you'll recognise him. It's Adrian Brannigan'.

This was the famous actor, a name and a face familiar to Helen and myself.

'I'm going to show you a bit of film. It's a stupid story for half-wits, but don't mind that. It's Brannigan I would like you to watch out for. By the way, do you know him? Have you met him?'

The question was directed at Helen, who nodded.

'Do you know him well?'

'No. I was introduced to him at a cultural affairs reception when my husband was still the Foreign Minister. Oh, and, now that I think of it he stayed here overnight on one occasion'.

'Did he indeed?' Tom had raised both eyebrows. 'So that was the second time you met him?'

'No. I wasn't here that night. I was in Dublin. But why ...?

'Bear with me for a few minutes, Mrs. McDermott, and then I think you'll see what I'm on about'.

Tom pressed a button and the film clicked into start. It appeared to be a tale set in the days of the Vikings. There were battle scenes, barren landscapes, ships in fjords, weapons clashing and armed men wearing helmets from which cow horns protruded.

Tom pushed the opening segment to fast forward and then he lowered the zapper and I caught my first sight of Adrian Brannigan who was clearly playing the role of a chieftain who was enduring some kind of deadly challenge.

'Watch him now', Tom instructed, and at the end of a sequence he stopped the film, rewound it and played it again for us.

There were many close-up slots of Brannigan, and after a while, I began to understand the reasons for this. He had a deeply scored face, more Scandinavian than Irish, and he was blond with big, slightly bulging eyes. There was a hint of wildness in his gaze, a nuance of lurking manic energy. He seemed always to look past objects and to respond darkly to whatever was in his view. Indeed he had the appearance of someone appalled by what nobody else could see.

At first I thought I was witnessing a character memorably portrayed, but gradually I came to realise that Brannigan was actually playing himself in this Viking adventure. He was like a field of desperate force which was barely kept under restraint. In one battle scene he was not so much a warrior summoning the extra violence necessary for victory as a man flailing to hold himself back from becoming a cataclysmic howl. And when the film reached the closing sequence he was at the edge of the sea trying alone and unsuccessfully to drag a large boat off dry land into the water. It was not the uselessness of the effort which was awesome but the sight of him twisting, turning, falling on to the sand, never letting go of the rope wound along his shoulders flopping and cork screwing like some crazed excrescence from the depths of the tide.

As I looked dumbly I was disconcerted by images in my mind which superimposed themselves on what I was now watching. For there was that other moment at the edge of the sea when the slow rise and fall of Atlantic waters had formed the backdrop to the enraged outburst of Helen as she responded to what I had told her about the notebook. She had seemed like an apparition from a dangerous world of maenads and dervishes. All my words and thoughts had dried up at the spectacle, as they had another day when a woman in her twenties had told me of her plan to have an abortion. I said to her as gently as I could that the Church had taken a definite stand on such a matter, that there was unignorable obligations to be met here. Before I continued she jumped up, leaned over me and with spitting ferocity she roared 'Church? What Church. You mean old men making rules for me. Old men who don't have the remotest idea of what I know. Who don't know how dirty and soiled and filthy you feel after you've been vilely raped as I've been'.

I tried to concentrate on Tom, on the movements of his hands as he extracted the tape from the recorder and replaced it in its container. But I could not push away the thought that the shock of my encounter with seemingly chaotic behaviour might have had its roots in the sheltered days I had passed as a priest and a bishop. Sheltered or just plain stupefying? I wished I knew. But as Tom clicked the starter button for the second tape I wondered then, as I had before, if I could claim to have a self at all, if in fact I was ultimately not much more than a presence lined and packed with the cascades of words supplied by the Church to which I had belonged from childhood.

'Are you ready Conor?' Tom was looking at me.

'Oh, yes'.

'I'm just going to play a small extract from this. It's something shot on location when that Viking film was being made. Somebody seemed to want to keep a diary of what was going on each day'.

At first the sequences appeared to be at random, with the camera going back and forth over groups of technicians and film extras who seemed to be waiting for instructions. Jeans and sweatshirts predominated. There was a lot of puffing on cigarettes. Boredom was in the air and movements were more like nervous tics than anything planned or purposeful.

But suddenly there was a row, and the camera was moved rapidly towards it. The voices came first. 'You're just a piece of shit stuck on the roadway!' The last two words were filmed coming from the lips of Adrian Brannigan. He was roaring at a man who was scratching his head of unkempt hair, smoking, waving, and talking in a continuous calm monotone. The unhurried words seemed to open new seams of fury in Brannigan. Neither listened to the other. Brannigan flung gestures to the air, screamed, spun around like a demented ballet dancer, and was completely ignored by everyone else within the range of the course.

'And this', said Tom, looking to both Helen and me.

It was clearly the same occasion, but the focus was now on an actress who was describing her experiences during the making of an earlier film.

'I'll never forget it. Adrian is one of the most thoughtful and sensitive human beings I've ever met. Really, you couldn't believe it if you hadn't seen it. Like I did. I mean, when I had finished my work for the film I felt empty and ... yes ... sad. It was like some kind of disappointment. I had been looking forward so much to playing the role, and now it was over, and things were moving on. And Adrian understood this. And when I was going back to my hotel for the last time he came along with me and put his arm around me. He was so sweet and gentle'.

The memory of the incident brought out in her the kind of smile which must have passed over her when she was a very young woman.

Another actress described the anguish which had afflicted her when she was playing a small but important part in the same earlier film. Because of her nervousness she muddled her lines, forgot the directions she had been given, and one sequence had to be shot five times.

'You can imagine it. Adrian having to go through this over and over again because of me. And when everybody else was beginning to get very impatient, he kept trying to help, to encourage me, and when at last I got it right you could see he was full of joy for me. For me. He's the kindest man I've ever had the good luck to meet'.

At this point Tom shut off the recorder.

'Right. Enough of that'. He put the two videos back into his pocket.

Then he turned to Helen. 'Mrs. McDermott, was your husband homosexual?'

'No. He wasn't'

'You feel sure of that?'

'Absolutely'.

Tom glanced out the window.

'I'm afraid I'm going to have to disagree with you. I could understand that you'd feel that of all people you should be the one to know, but ...'

'But what?' She was sitting forward now.

'Our investigations have uncovered a number of things which look like coming as a nasty shock to you. The fact is that your husband was an amazingly clever man. And very energetic. And he had a mania for detail, the like of which I've certainly never met'.

'So, what has this to do with what you've said just now? About his being homosexual'.

'Your husband came into politics at a time when to be gay was to draw down great public hostility. It was a period when to be respectable mattered a lot. Of course as we all know there were high profile people among us who fit the bill of being respectable but who were on the take behind the scenes. But that's something else'.

'Are you saying that my husband ...'

'No. Not at all. Your husband was not a corrupt politician. But to get ahead as he did he had to look respectable. And there was one aspect of his life which could have ruined him politically when he was starting his career. That was his homosexuality. He had to hide it. He had to be respectable. That word! Oh, but it mattered. It really did. And that's where you fitted in, Mrs. McDermott.

Her eyes widened.

'What do you mean, I fitted in?'

'He married you, didn't he? The pictures were in all the papers. And there was that exotic memorable touch of your Greek name. You weren't just plain Helen Murphy. It all came together nicely. Oh, and don't misunderstand me. I'm not saying it was completely cynical. You're a very smart formidable woman and in courting days I don't think he could have completely fooled you even if all he wanted was a cover. I'm sure in his own way he had - shall we say - a very high regard for you. But you gave him the shield he needed against prying eyes'.

'Tom, are you sure ...?'

'Yes, Conor. All this has to be said. She has to know. Of course it's horrible and painful, but you're entitled to know. Especially since you were our prime suspect'.

'Were?'

'Yes'. For an instant Tom looked uncomfortable. 'In our experience of murder one starts with the spouse or an immediate member of the family. And you might be surprised to find how often cases are solved in this way. So, yes. You were our prime suspect. And you had enough enemies around you to supply us with the kind of talk that made us want to take a closer look. Your in-laws for instance. I don't have to tell you that you haven't an oversupply of friends there. Can I have a drink?'

'Of course'. Helen started to get up.

'I'll pour one', I said. 'For all of us'.

Tom took a sip of whiskey from the glass I reached over to him. 'It was the detail. He had a genius for detail, that husband of yours. A pure genius. We've found that it wasn't too long after your wedding that the word began to spread that you two weren't getting along. Nothing very world shaking was said. Just enough to give people the sense that they were in the know and could nod and say they'd heard about it. And it was such a pity. Poor man. Not poor you, mind you. Ah no. He was the victim and he should have got a Hollywood Oscar for the way he played it. And of course you got more and more isolated and it was all his doing. A sigh here, a well placed hint there. It was masterly, and it gave him the cover he needed for his ongoing passionate love affair with another man. And that was the way it was supposed to go on, except that he got killed. He had thought of everything else. God knows he did'.

Tom turned to me.

'You remember that notebook I showed you?'

'Yes. And I have to say I've told Helen about it. Maybe you hadn't meant me to ...'

'That's alright, Conor. So you know what was in it?' The question was to Helen.

'Yes'.

'It was all part of the scheming. He kept it on his office desk in Government Buildings. All that was needed was for a snooping secretary to look at it. And, of course, what was in it would get into circulation and add to the picture of the poor man longing to be loved by his wife'.

Tom shook his head.

'In my career I've never come across anything like it. And, you know, Mrs. McDermott, one reason I gave Conor a look at it was because I knew that the two of you were becoming friends and I wanted to warn him against you. That was your husband's doing. The notebook gave us prime evidence to show why you could have wanted him murdered'.

'If that's so, what has changed the picture? Or should I say, what's happened to make you think of me as someone who was set up by my husband?'

'I don't expect there are going to be arrests', Tom said slowly. 'At least, not in the short term. And that's one of the things that makes the life of a detective so very frustrating. Because, you see, we know who pulled the trigger. We know who paid him to do the job. We know why. But we also know that we have nothing by way of solid evidence to make a case in court. And we don't expect anyone to crack, so as to give us what we need'.

He drained his whiskey and shook his head when I offered to get him another.

'I have to repeat, Mrs. McDermott, that your husband was homosexual. And if you still don't believe that's just one more proof of the way your husband invented a public life so as to hide an important part of the real story about himself'.

'Not ...?' I began abruptly.

'Yes', Tom answered. 'Brannigan. It's taken us since the day of the murder to establish the fact. But fact it is. They became lovers when both were at university, and they continued that way through all the years. In fact until only a few months before the murder. Think about it. A famous politician and a famous actor. Constantly in the public eye. And they managed to hide it, even though in its own way Dublin is a small town where word goes around very fast. As I say it's taken us months to be sure that this was how it was. And I think I'd bet my pension that your husband was the master planner of this concealment. Certainly we found out by accident. We have many sources of information, as I'm sure you know, and it was one of them which by chance delivered the vital details. But if your husband was the great strategist, it was Brannigan who was the dominant partner'.

'Why do you say that?' Helen asked.

'We have enough now to be sure your husband was besotted with Brannigan'.

'But you said that this was how it was until a few months ago'.

'Yes, Conor. That's how it was'.

'A few months before the murder?'

'Right'.

'So, what happened? Did they break up after all those years?'

'Is that offer still going of another whiskey?'

'Of course'. This time Helen stood up and poured the drink.

'Yes, they broke up', Tom said. 'Because of the work load, a Minister for Finance is given two private secretaries. And full-time is the word. Because they have to be on call pretty much day and night'. A sardonic expression flitted over his face. 'Yes, indeed. And since this particular minister liked to be at his desk well into the night ...'

'Ah. A secretary'.

'Yes, Conor. He's ambitious. He's young. He's available to the minister. Or rather, he was. Since the minister is no longer in the picture. I didn't think it was just careerism. At least, that's my impression for what it's worth. Anyhow, they became lovers'.

'And Brannigan found out?' This time it was Helen to put the question, in a soft tone. She was beginning to look haggard.

'Yes'.

'And he hired the killers to take revenge?'

'Yes. The deadly insult, as he saw it, was he was being dropped in favour of a younger man'.

'It's beginning to sound like an old story, isn't it?'

'It is Mrs. McDermott'

'Helen'.

'Thanks. Yes, Helen'.

'But you say there won't be an arrest'.

'Doesn't look like it. The killer was Tony Martin. He's done it before. For a good price. All very professional, and leaves no traces. We've questioned him twice. He studied the look of his hands. The only concession, after several hours was that Tony Martin is his name. And he's got witnesses to prove he was miles away from the scene. We can't shake the witnesses. They're professionals too'.

The silence grew deep.

'But Brannigan, what about him?' I asked. 'If he hired this man Martin he has a criminal charge to answer. Doesn't he?'

'According to the statute books, yes. We should be arresting him for murder. But he has left no traces. At least, none we can find'.

'So he walks free?'

'Yes, Conor. For the moment. In fact, I'd say for good'.

'What do you mean?'

'Well, I suppose I'm straying into prophecy now'. Tom said. I suddenly noticed how tired he was. His face was pasty and there were deep lines on his forehead. 'Yes, fortune-telling. Still, I'm willing to risk it. You see, I went to visit him last week. He could tell at once that I knew but that I had not enough evidence. And although I've never seen a cat play with a mouse, I think I have some idea now of what it must be like for the mouse. Brannigan was very confident. And when I put it to him that sooner or later the missing details would appear and we'd get him, he began to smile. And I thought "arrogant bastard". By God you will slip and we'll pounce. He seemed to sense what I was thinking and he started to laugh. It wasn't a laugh really. It was a brag. Until I began to think he was cracking up. Coming apart. As if pieces would fly off him. I never saw anything like it. At first I thought maybe he was putting on an act. But it was for real. It was the energy of it which was the most shocking thing about it. The energy you saw in that film'. He paused. Helen and I had some shared instinct about not interrupting.

'When he quietened down', Tom resumed, 'a very strange look came into his eyes. I'm not sure how to describe it. It was like some kind of authority. As if somewhere inside him he knew where he was and that he was in control and that he couldn't be touched'.

'Is that what you were referring to when you mentioned prophecy just now?' It was Helen who spoke.

'Something like that. You see, I think he's burned out. You noticed that bit in the film when he was trying to haul that boat off the sand. There wasn't a hope it could be done, but you saw the frenzy of him. And that wasn't just a bag of tricks. That was the real thing. And that's what he's like'.

'But the prophecy?'

'Right. I'll stick my neck out. Something massive, a heart attack, a burst blood vessel in the brain, will carry him off. Soon. Long before we can complete a dossier on him. He can't last. He puts too much pressure on his system. There will be a quiet funeral. The speeches will be about his amazing gifts. And very few – just you and I and some others – will know that the minister and the notebook were right. That the unthinkable happened, that Achilles the lover of Patroclus was indeed capable of killing his beloved'.

XX

That was a year ago. And Tom was proved right. Adrian Brannigan was on set for a new film when he was ambushed by a heart attack. He was dead by the time he had completed his sprawl to earth. As for me vast tracts of what I had been taught or else had taken for granted now seemed to slide away without fuss or fanfare. Increasingly, I felt some kind of ease taking root within me, though I could not yet tell whether this was a freedom from something or else the freedom to think and to do what I would never have contemplated in my time as a cleric.

And yet the habits and the mindset of a lifetime could not be banished by a few mere gestures of the will. Even as a delivery man I found myself acting sometimes as if I were a bishop, taking control of situations, or instinctively engaging in moments of power play. This was something I realised one evening while I was bringing groceries to a house near the harbour. After I had knocked on a door painted in vibrant blood red I was confronted by a man who, I guessed, was in his mid-sixties. He had crew cut sandy hair, watery grey eyes, a green jersey above slate-blue trousers. In his right hand he carried a heavy cane, and from the way he began to come out the door to me I could see that he was recovering from a stroke.

'Mr. O'Toole?' I enquired.

'Yes'.

'I have your groceries. They're in the van. I'll get them'.

'No, I'll get them myself', he answered in a firm voice, and he continued towards me. But, meanwhile, I had turned to the van and had lifted out the brown paper bag marked with his name'.

'I'll bring them into the house for you', I said.

'No', he answered.

'But it'll be easier for you if I do', I urged.

'Give it to me', he commanded, reaching out a hand.

'Oh, Mr. O'Toole, I'm sure it would be better for you if I brought them in'.

'Are you sure now? Isn't it a fine thing to be so very sure?' He grabbed the bag.

I watched his slow walk, the drag on his foot, the grocery bag embraced by his left arm, the shoulders salvaging a morsel of his remembered independence. And I felt a great pang of embarrassment and shame at my own unthinking instinct to make decisions for him.

Indeed the incident left me really downhearted during what remained of that day, and as soon as I got back to my apartment I settled into my chair and made ready to phone Helen. We talked every evening. I spent the weekends with her, and just as a compass needle tilts unfailingly to the north, so throughout my hours alone in Galway my mind branched off to her in that bunker of a house. As I drove my delivery van I knew where to turn my face so as to be looking in her direction. I imagined her at work in her studio. I could visualise her clothes. I could almost see the intent look in those increasingly beloved eyes, the relaxed lips, the hands moving surely over stone or wood. Apart from the clink of chisel on rock the silence would grow dense in that studio, and if there was any beckoning sound at all it could come only from outside, the song of a bird, the push of wind in the old beech trees, the faint echo of a barking dog.

I was about to pick up the receiver but stopped. I thought again of Mr. O'Toole, of my own lapse of sensitivity towards him. I began to wonder about habits in me, known or, worse still, unknown, which I might be too old or too careless to dislodge. The burden of it swelled in me and I was prodded again by shame now. But there was an escape route. I knew when I talked to Helen my spirits would lift as I entered into the sound of her words, into the tones which emerged as a response to me, into that special sense of her when, miles away, she would tell me the details of what she was doing and would share in the anticipation of our coming weekend. Remembering Mr. O'Toole, I could count on that revised buoyancy of heart and mind which, as I realised now, only she knew how to call up in me.

Recognising her power to transform me, I marvelled at my good fortune, for I am inclined to be a moody man. I think I even have a capacity for despair which, fortunately, I have so far managed to keep mostly at arm's length. Of course I have had to work hard sometimes to remain ahead of those forces which would pull me into bleakness, and I am certain that I was helped for a long time by the fact of being a bishop. To have been chosen for the job, the awareness of my status, the knowledge that I could directly help people, all this carried me along, gave me a sort of skin to be placed over my own. But as I drove around Galway with my boxes of groceries I began to understand that more and more I had come to depend on that skin. Certainly this was so during my last year in office. But the flimsiness of it had become clear to me in several ways. There was that morning, for example, when remembering my parents, I had suddenly thought of the potential brothers and sisters of my own who had not come into being. On the other hand a series of chances had co-operated to let me through into life. But it need not have been so, and earth would not have missed me, that earth described from the moon by an astronaut as a blue dot which he could wipe from view simply by raising his thumb to eye level.

However, despite the moments of doubting self-regard my career as bishop had continued to be filled by patterns of authoritative gesture. I was constantly faced by the spectacle of people who agreed with whatever I said, yielded to anything I proposed, pushed aside their point of view in favour of mine and, for all I knew, looked on meekly as private hopes and cherished projects withered in the face of my indifference, my assertiveness or my inability to understand.

Now my encounter with Mr. O'Toole raised the question of whether anything but the context of my activities had really changed. I was plain Conor Mahon, deliveryman. I was no longer possessed of authority. But had the mentality of power remained? I did not know. Yet this small episode involving a bag of groceries and a partly crippled man left me uneasy. Of course I might be blowing the matter out of all proportion, and in any case the chance of being able to act like a bishop during my work for the supermarket did not appear too great. On the other hand, life did not cease when I clocked out of the job at the end of the day. And the problem to be faced now was whether, without my realisation of it, I was still talking and acting as if I were a Lord Bishop. Again, this might seem a not very important topic were it not for one fact which, day and night, stood sentinel over my mind. I had asked Helen to marry me. It had seemed the obvious thing to do. More importantly, it seemed right and appropriate that I should make the proposal. She had smiled, hugged me, looked deeply into my eyes and returned an unambiguous 'No'.

We had spent Sunday and Monday together in what, each week, had become an experience filled for me with delight. Those times with her had been so important to me, so layered in joy that when nightfall was delayed more and more in early spring it became easier to spend extra time with her by setting off on Saturday evenings and making the journey to her house. On one weekend we travelled to west Kerry, stayed at bed and breakfast houses, ate in the fish restaurants of Dingle, held hands as we moved through bracken and heather, laughed like children who have been let out unexpectedly from school. Still, when I asked her to marry me she refused.

I was deeply upset, and also puzzled. As I delivered groceries during the following week I kept wondering what I had done that was wrong. She had offered me no explanation and yet she appeared to be surprised and even distressed when I had wondered aloud if her refusal meant that I would have to stop seeing her. Before my words were fully out she had rushed her fingers to block my lips. And yet the more I thought about it the greater my bafflement. Could it be that there was some rite which, in my ignorance, I had neglected to follow? Should I have gone on my knees to her when I proposed marriage? I had not thought of first buying a diamond ring, and I wondered if I should have done so. Had I transgressed against some protocol obvious to everyone except to me? Yet I had no sooner returned to my apartment on the day of her refusal that she had phoned to make sure that I had arrived safely, and there was such love in her last words to me that, as in the previous days and months, I was overwhelmed by amazement and gratitude.

A few days later I tried again. We had been walking by the river near her home. It was evening, and the sky was getting ready to make way for stars. The trees were silent. Helen had an arm around my waist. At a lull in the conversation I turned to her.

'Helen?'

'I think I can guess ...?' She smiled slightly.

'Well, anyway, don't you really think we should get married?'

'That's a bishoply way of putting it', she commented. 'Conor, dearest, darling Conor. No'.

'But'.

'No', and that was it.

When she managed at last to sell her house I spent every possible hour with her during the days before she had to move out. Although most of her furniture was taken quickly by interested buyers, there was still a lot of packing to be done, and I helped her as much as I could. My boss allowed me to borrow a delivery van one evening and I used it to make two round trips between her place and Galway. I stored boxes in my apartment and I was especially pleased to be able to give a temporary home to her sculpture. It was after one o'clock in the morning when I set off with my second load to Galway, yet an awareness of being tired was pushed aside not only by the satisfaction of having eased matters for her but by the way she had been around me. At one moment when I was on a ladder and was lifting a box down to her I caught a look on her face and the mingling there of contentment and love reduced me to a heart-turning stillness.

'And just think', she remarked, 'I'll be able to see you more often once I move to Galway'.

She had been offered the use of a bed-sitter attached to a studio in the city, and until it became vacant Helen was to stay at my apartment.

On her last full day in the house I phoned her during my lunch break.

'No unexpected jobs, I hope'.

'I don't think so', she answered.

'And what are you doing?'

'Not much. Mostly just walking around the place and in the garden. It's nice and sunny'.

'I'm glad to hear it'.

'Is everything alright for you, Conor?'

'Oh yes. Busy. Remember the woman I told you about who likes to invite delivery men into her house and then takes off her clothes?'

'You don't mean to tell me ...'

'Yes, Helen. I brought her three boxes this morning. Three! And they were heavy. One of them had wine bottles and it's a good thing I've been training for this sort of lifting and ...'

'Conor! What happened?'

'Well, the box with the bottles ...'

'Conor! Detestable, hateful, nasty man!'

'You could be right about that. Because nothing happened. She didn't even take off her about-time-you-finally-arrived look. I was crushed. I must be getting old'.

'Of course, dear. Anything you say, dear'.

'Oh well. I'd better be off, my love. Talk to you later'.

'Yes', She paused. 'Conor'.

'Yes?'

'Not one of my former in-laws called to wish me luck or to tell me to go to hell. I don't think I'm looking forward to spending my last night here alone'.

'Want me to come up? It would be late and you'd have to kick me out at the crack of dawn. If you don't mind that, then I'll come'.

'Would you?'

'Silly question'.

'Bless you, Conor'.

'You too. See you'.

We spent the night – or rather, what was left of it – on a mattress beside the fireplace in her studio. Once or twice when I woke up suddenly I found her, eyes open, lying very close to me. I held her in my arms, drifted off into busy dreams and then went under so deeply that Helen had to shake me out when the time came for me to set off again to Galway.

I felt badly about the fact that I could not be with her when she finally closed the door on her house that day, and I thought of her constantly as I went about my work. By five o'clock I was impatient and I hurried to finish my rounds. But I was delayed at two houses, and on my journey back to the supermarket I was trapped in a melee of cars and trucks which had to be cleared from the main road. When I finally got back to base the despatcher was waiting for me, his face pale with shock. A message had arrived to announce that his wife had been taken seriously ill. He had been unable to start his car and he needed urgently to get to the hospital. So it was an hour later than usual when I got back to my apartment.

There was a light in my bedroom and I was about to call her name when I glimpsed her. She was asleep, stretched out on top of the blankets, her head highlighted by the whiteness of the sheet. There was a shoe near the bed. The other was half off her foot. With my back against one side of the door frame I slid to the floor. And I sat there and I watched her and time seemed to slip away out from under any reckoning and quietly her chest lifted and lay down and I became very still. I thought of our times together, but mostly I looked at her as she was now, for me grace at rest, a marvellous creature whose presence changed every colour and tone and nuance of a landscape. What she was remained unshaped, unconstrained, undirected by me or by anything I might have wished. I had nothing whatever to do with the way she was, and yet the tide had brought her into my life and I could only pause and watch with an astonished heart.

Then a strange mixture of thoughts came into me as I sat on the floor gazing at her. I remembered Mr. O'Toole and the habit of command which had led me to decide what was good for him. And I wondered if any connection could exist between the persistence of old ways and the refusal of Helen to marry me. At first the idea seemed uncalled for, even silly. But if there really was such a connection could it be that Helen, in her own loving manner, had put me in the position of having to discover it myself? I had still so much to learn. I had become sadly aware of how far behind the most ordinary people I could be. The housewives to whom I brought groceries seemed often to be life-wise in ways completely out of my reach. When I had asked Helen to marry me it had appeared to be the evidently right thing to do. The decision that it was right was mine. Or so it appeared on the surface. But sitting on the floor I realised that as a response to a situation my proposal of marriage was the gesture programmed in me by the decision of men like me, bishops, who had laid claim to knowing what has to be done or avoided in every set of circumstances. Could it be, therefore, that when I asked Helen to marry me I had reached first for a principle and not Helen? It seemed like a strange notion. But if it actually were so then, being much wiser than I, Helen would have instinctively understood the case.

There was one way to find out. I got up, crept across to the bed so as not to startle her, and kissed her awake.

'There's something I need to find out', I said.

'What?' she asked sleepily.

'Will you just live with me? Please? Please?'

Her eyes widened. Then she sat up, looked at me for a few seconds, took my face in her warm hands.

'I was beginning to be afraid you might never ask', she replied.